BEFORE THE BALANCE

-THE HALLOWED STAR SERIES-

Book Two

First Paperback Edition 2025

Cover Illustration by Elizabeth Jenney

Edited by: Lucy Connery

Paperback ISBN:

To the LGBTQIA+ community.

A LONG TIME AGO

(66 million years, give or take)

It was a day like any other day as far as the inhabitants of Earth could tell. Simultaneously across the globe, they were fighting, eating, napping, or roaming. In certain regions, the sun was high in the bright sky, and in others dark storm clouds moved across the lands, whipping winds into a frenzy as rain pounded the earth into the shapes we still see today.

They had no idea that in a few seconds, a 6.5-mile-wide rock from the farthest depths of space would hurtle into their atmosphere at 45,000 miles per hour. There would be no time to look up and inspect the object, even if they had the desire to do so.

Maybe a few creatures caught a quarter second glimpse, and if they did it might have caused them to experience awe, however brief.

Amidst the bland brown and grays, twisting through the icy exterior of the giant space rock were stunning stones of emerald green, ruby red, sapphire blue, and several other colors more vibrant than anything seen before on Earth.

As it crossed the path of the sun for just a fraction of a second before impact, it looked as though it was glowing. Not from heat, but from the stones embedded into the rocks and minerals.

It crashed into the Yucatán Peninsula, in what was for a long time known as Mexico, and the hole it created was 120 miles wide. But the point of impact wasn't the only thing it left behind. The comet was blown to pieces as dust and dirt were flung into the atmosphere. So too, were 5 stones of differing shapes and sizes.

Reaching thousands of feet in the air, these stones were launched to the farthest corners of the world. Maybe coincidentally, maybe not, one of the stones landed in Toronto, where it would stay for the next 66 million years.

A (MUCH LESS) LONG TIME AGO

(250ish Years Ago)

A couple hundred years before Finley was born, on December 18th, 1867 around 3pm, one of the worst train disasters in history occurred in the small town of Angola, NY. The New York Express was traveling from Cleveland to New York City and derailed in Angola.

In those days, trains only traveled around 15 mph, so the journey took a while. As it crossed a bridge over Big Sister Creek, the last train car derailed, eventually taking a second and third car with it before it crossed the bridge.

Almost 50 people died, and of the cars that slid down the steep, rocky, 50-foot embankment and into the icy river below, only two people survived. More of the train cars derailed above, and many passengers were hurt.

Several hours after the disaster, a stranger appeared at the derailment site and asked to see any survivors. As they had already been transported to a local hospital, she asked where that would be located. The police, as usual, were much more interested in writing her a ticket than they were in giving out any information.

Her offense? Wearing pants in public.

She also had on some old, brown, beat-up boots and a dark green cloak wrapped around her shoulders, mostly covering a thin tan jacket. A curious outfit for the middle of December, and especially one this frigid. Her eyes were green, but not like anything a young Alice Finch had ever seen before. They weren't just green, they *glowed* green.

Alice had heard stories before of the "Woman Who Could Heal." Her mother told her many tales, and Alice was certain it was her. No one she had seen in her 11 brief but difficult years on this planet had ever looked anything like that. It was strange to Alice that so many adults the woman passed by didn't even notice her eyes.

The stranger stood by the edge of the embankment, looking at a large, creased map. The other passengers who survived the crash were still milling about, alternating between staying warm and talking to the police. The train company representatives were busy trying to find accommodations for the passengers, and the shock of the situation was still written on the faces of everyone around. Everyone except the woman in the green cloak.

Alice walked up to her, careful not to scare her, lest she fall off the edge herself.

"Excuse me, miss," she said, standing five or six feet away.

The woman turned to her, a piece of fabric covering the lower half of her face, glowing eyes staring at her intently.

"My mother, she…" Alice trails off.

The stranger partially folds up the map and lowers herself down onto one knee.

"Did she die in the crash?" The woman asks in a low, steady voice, a practical if not sympathetic question.

"No. We're alright. But we are on our way to New York City, just me, my little brother, n' her. My momma's been real sick, and we're trying to see a doctor. No one in Dunkirk could figure out what was wrong with her, so we got on the train at the last stop before the crash," said Alice.

"That's rough, sweetie," The woman replied, her voice still steady and unwavering.

"I was wonderin', if you had a second, if you could come over and heal my momma. It won't take much time, I'm sure. She's just a hundred feet or so that way. Just a quick second. Then you can be on your way," Alice said, her voice starting to plead halfway through.

The woman's eyes grew big, and she quickly rose to a standing position. She looks around to see if anyone else heard the girl's words, and no one seems to have.

"What are you talking about, healing your mom?" She finally asks Alice, in a short, concerned voice.

"Well, I mean, you're The Woman Who Heals, right?" Alice asks.

"What on Earth would make you think that?" The woman responds.

"Your eyes, they glow green, like the stories I've been told," Alice replies.

The woman bends down onto one knee again and motions Alice to come closer. She stares into her eyes for a moment, and says,

"Did anyone ever tell you that you have a small bit of glowing green around your eyes as well?"

"No," Alice says, "no one has ever told me that."

"It's little, but it's there. You have a bit of a gift yourself," the woman says.

She then lowers her eyes to the ground, in the way that adults always do before they're about to deliver bad news. Alice had seen this hundreds of times in her life.

"I'm really sorry, kid. I am. But I have to get to the hospital and help some people. I just don't have time to help your momma. But I'm sure she'll be okay. Maybe you can try and heal her yourself. You might have a little bit of that magic in you," the woman says.

With that, she folds up the rest of her map, places it in her pocket, and pats Alice on her shoulder. She then pulls her hood farther over her head, stands up, and walks quickly away. After a minute or two, she disappears from sight, gone as quickly as she came.

Alice tears up as she begins to walk back towards her mom and brother.

The next few days she stays close to her family. She doesn't know how to heal someone. Is it words? Does she have to make a certain motion? Even when they nervously get on another train the next day to head to NYC, she tries to figure out how to help her mom. How to save her family.

By all accounts, how to save herself.

As they pull into New York City, Alice tries to wake her mother up from a deep slumber. As passengers file out and the train empties, Alice and her brother stay waiting, next to their mother's seat, as a train rep finally comes to their section.

Their mother never did wake up again, and Alice Finch and her brother Henry were placed into custody of the state.

She never did forgive herself for not being able to heal her mom, but even more so, she never forgave The Woman Who Heals for not doing the one thing she's meant to do.

A (MUCH, MUCH) LESS LONG TIME AGO

(Last Night)

Excitedly, we sprinted towards Toronto. Time stopped entirely for the first couple hundred yards, but as my lungs began to burn, and my ankle began to throb, I realized I wouldn't be sprinting all the way there in this moment. Once completely out of breath, we stopped, gasped for air, and hugged each other. Tears welled up in my eyes.

It was dark out, but the nearly full moon illuminated the world enough for me to see Garven gently crying. While catching our breath, we talked amongst ourselves.

"Should we get to Toronto tonight?"

"Do you think it's really Auryn's ship?"

"Do any of us have the strength to actually make it tonight?"

"Is Kian still back there in one of the tents?"

After talking, I'm reminded of something Auryn told me before leaving.

"When we come back to Earth, we're going to have to wait on the ship for a half day or so. Something about a quarantine spray we'll have to have," she said.

As I tell Esha and Garven, we decide to walk back to camp and try to get some sleep. For the first time in a long while, Kian isn't the first person I want to share news with.

In fact, he might be the last.

CHAPTER 1: A FEELING

I am woken up, like many mornings, by the warmth of the hot sun beating down on my faded tent. Sweat is already trickling down the side of my face. I use the back of my hand to wipe it away and as I do, dirt smears across my temple. Much to my surprise, light is already filtering through the rips and tears of the nylon fabric.

When I laid down last night, I didn't think I'd sleep a wink. Now, I listen to see if I hear any noise outside, but all is quiet. It must still be early. I reach over and unzip the tent, and as I slowly crawl out, my bones pop loudly back into alignment.

As my eyes adjust to the sunlight aimed directly at them, I see Kian is the only one awake. I smile at him and notice he has a small fire going, with the pot for mushroom coffee hanging above it. I take a few steps over and sit right next to him on the log we dragged over last night. It creaks loudly as I do.

He gives me a quick glance then looks back towards the metal pot, making sure he isn't burning the coffee.

"Hey, Kian," I say while touching his right arm lightly. "I have some news."

He turns to look at me and chuckles.

"Well, that's quite a serious face you have going on there. Am I making the coffee wrong? I swear I've paid so much attention to when you all make it," he says.

I smile again and clear my throat. For a brief second, I look towards the ground to gather my thoughts. This is both an exciting conversation, and a nervous one.

"Last night, after you fell asleep, the three of us were up watching the sky, and something miraculous happened," I pause to give him time to respond. He doesn't.

Instead, he looks at me with a raised eyebrow and tilted head, his brown hair falling gently on his face. It's getting long. I can hear the water boiling over the fire. I take a deep breath in, and everything slows down. I can feel the warm breeze and see rays of sunshine peeking through the trees, illuminating Kian's face.

"So, as we were looking up at the stars," I started, "we saw a comet shoot across the sky. At least, we thought it was a comet. At one point, it slowed down and started heading straight for us."

I take a long pause as the slow realization starts to creep across Kian's face.

"Kian, a shuttle has come back to Earth. A ship has come back for us," I say.

"Wow," Kian says, followed by a long pause.

That might be the understatement of the year. As much as I had always hoped a shuttle would be coming back for us, all the times I put on a brave face for Garven, I'm not sure I ever actually believed it. As my thoughts continue, Kian finally talks again.

"Fin, what are you going to do if it's not Auryn's ship?" He asks while looking towards the ground nervously.

This question stops me dead in my tracks. All night I had just sort of assumed that it was going to be Auryn's ship. That we were going to be united, and that we would head back to the planet they've found. Hugging with Garven and Esha, jumping up and down and high fiving after we chased the path of the ship a few hundred yards away from camp. Even one of the dreams I had last night was about seeing her. That and a weird one about dinosaurs. But what if it was meant for a future moment, and not here in the present?

"I honestly don't know what I want to do if it's not her ship," I finally reply.

Kian's about to say something back when we hear a noise coming from Garven's tent. Unlike his normal slow, stumbling self, he has some energy in his steps this morning.

"So, you tell Kian the good news yet?" He asks.

"I did, but he's wonderin' if the ship that came back might not be Auryn's," I respond.

I thought the statement would shake him to his core. That's his sister we're hoping is back, assuming is back, and if we get there and it's the rich people ship? That would be devastating.

"Oh, I'm not worried about that, I know it's her ship," he says while smiling calmly at me.

"Wait, you could tell which ship it was way up in the sky?" I ask.

"No, but I just know," he says back.

"How?" I ask.

"Well, a couple reasons. First, the rich people ship is never coming back for us. They could have had the easiest journey possible and found the most wonderful planet in the known universe, and no matter what they're not coming back for us. Secondly, the third ship that took off hasn't been gone long enough. There's no way they could have made it to their home and back already," he replies.

"What if they had issues and turned around to come back?" I ask, still wondering how he can be so calm at a time like this.

"Well, if that's the case, which is very doubtful, that means that they'll be back here living on Earth, and we don't have to make any sort of decision about leaving anyways."

As he finishes, I can't help but think how right he is. I hate admitting it, but everything he says makes so much sense.

"What if it's the right ship, but the wrong people?" Kian suddenly asks out of the blue.

"What if Auryn, or anyone in your family, isn't on the ship?" He says.

"They are," Garven says, "Well, Auryn is, I can feel it."

CHAPTER 2: THE RETURN (15 MONTHS AGO)

Everyone on the colony came to the launch. It was more crowded than Auryn had seen since the ship landed. The 1,600 people making the round trip back to Earth received a hero's goodbye. Families being split, people hugging each other for the last time in at least a few years. While walking towards the ramp leading to the ship, Auryn spotted her mom, dad, and younger brother in the crowd, pressed right against the makeshift divider.

She walked over to them, and although they had already said their goodbyes that morning, she gave her mom, Alia, another hug. It'll be the last time she sees them for a few years. Forbin, her younger brother, will be 16 by the time they get back. As he looks at her, tears begin to well up in the corners of his eyes. Clouded and nearly closed, they begin to look up at Auryn, and she feels a pang of guilt about leaving for the first time.

"You keep making friends here, alright? And if anyone picks on you while I'm gone, write their name down and I'll beat 'em up when I get back," Auryn says.

Both Forbin and Auryn's dad, Arthur, laugh at this, while their mom rolls her eyes and sighs. Auryn gives her brother and dad each another hug, then takes a few steps back to look at all three of them.

She's had a nagging thought the last few days that she can't seem to shake:

What if this is the last time I ever see them?

Maybe something happens to the ship, and they don't make it. Maybe she gets back to Earth and Garven and Finley haven't made it to the launch in time. Would she fly all the way back? Would she wait for them, stranded on Earth without knowing if they're even alive?

Standing there in her gray, colony issued flight suit, she tries to break her chain of thoughts by briefly thinking of how much she likes the color gray on her. Random thoughts like this are always jumping into and out of Auryn's head, and right now she's thinking about how the cold gray of the suit makes the warmness of her dark skin really pop.

I look pretty good in this, she thinks to herself.

It's not a conceited thought, it's true, but she laughs to herself about how ridiculous it is that it's what she's thinking about at this moment.

She refocuses and concentrates on her family once more. She can tell her parents are proud of her, if not a little sad that both her and Garven are now gone from their lives for a while. After a few seconds, she smiles, nods, and turns to walk towards the ship.

One thing that has helped Auryn remain confident through everything, is that setting up the colony and running it has gone so smoothly. *Surprisingly smooth*, she often thinks to herself. People are still adjusting to longer days, but otherwise everyone, for the most part, is thrilled with how everything has gone.

Soon after the ship leaves, they'll be holding elections for people to serve on the Colony Council, and the work of moving to phase three will truly begin.

Auryn won't be there to see it, but she knows it's all in good hands.

Before boarding, she pauses and takes one last look at the outside of the ship. It has a little more wear and tear on it than it did before it left Earth. From down here on the ground, she can't see all that much of it. The loading door they're all walking through, the silver panels that adorn the entire outside, one of the rear liftoff engines jutting out the side and resting no more than 40 or 50 feet above the ground – all the same things she has seen the last 6 months when looking outside the Central Park Dome.

Yesterday while packing her room was the first time back on the ship in almost a month. It was a nice break, especially with how long she'll be on it back to Earth. This time she at least gets bigger living quarters and more room to roam. There's a giant u-shaped couch in the middle of the main living area with a circular table nestled into it. The small kitchenette has a microwave and a built-in coffee maker. All she has to do to get a coffee in the morning is press a single button, a luxury not afforded to her on Earth or the colony.

Her sleeping quarters are through a doorway off the main living area. She feels fortunate that on this trip she has a queen-sized bed, unlike the trip to B.52.C where she had a single, which she almost rolled off of every night.

She takes a few more steps towards the ship and an overwhelming feeling of anxiety hits her. Not nearly as severe as Finley described their panic attacks, but enough to get her heart racing and her palms a little sweaty inside her gloves.

Will Garven and Finley be there? If they're not, what does that mean? What if no one is left on Earth, and there is nowhere for the ship to land? While working on the ship, she's had several talks with Mina about the fear and apprehension she feels about no one being left on Earth. She often mentions Garven, but has rarely, if ever, mentioned Finley to her.

Mina calls it survivor's guilt. "Since so many people left behind were poor and sick, it's natural to feel guilty about it," she said.

"Plus, you were put in an impossible situation because you had to leave family behind. That's a lot of stress and guilt for a, what, 15-year-old?" Mina said once.

Speaking of Mina, as Auryn looks up, she is standing there waiting for her at the bottom of the long metal ramp. They smile at each other and begin to walk towards the ship arm-in-arm. They step in unison, boots hitting the metal of the ramp at the same time. Once inside, they turn to each other and share a hug.

"You ready?" Mina asks.

"Not sure I have much choice at this point," says Auryn while chuckling, an unsure smile spreading across her face.

"If you made a run for the door, I wouldn't stop you," Mina replies.

"Maybe you wouldn't, but he would," Auryn says, pointing at the large man standing at the entryway to the ship.

He's one of the few security officers that are making the journey. They've mentioned several times that if you change your mind about the journey back, they're "open to having a conversation," but putting guards with dart guns and batons at the entrance to the ship makes Auryn think they might not be so open to it now.

Mina smirks, grabs Auryn's hand, and swings her arm back and forth, as if they were skipping, but without the footwork. Auryn appreciates Mina's positive energy, she's going to need it to survive the next year in space.

Once inside, everyone heads to their quarters. Unlike the trip to B.52.C, if you don't want to share a room, you don't have to. As Auryn and Mina hop into the elevator, Auryn presses the button for deck 24. She looks at Mina and asks,

"Which floor you heading to?"

"Oh, I'm on deck 24 also," Mina responds, and gives Auryn a wink.

Auryn smiles, thinking the odds of each of them being on the same deck improbable, but maybe it has the best rooms for lower-level crew. Once the elevator reaches deck 24, both hop out. Auryn mentions that she's in room 13.

"There used to be an old superstition on Earth about room 13," she says to Mina. "Apparently it was bad luck."

"Actually, that was about floor 13. You'll be fine in room 13," Mina responds.

"Oh!" Auryn says, and then thinks to herself, *I'm going to have to look that up later.*

She hates being wrong about things.

As Auryn stops at room 13, she says her goodbyes to Mina. Mina waves, walks 20 more feet, and stops at room 15. She waves her badge across the sensor, and the door opens.

"I'm sure we'll be seeing a lot of each other around. Don't be a stranger," Mina says.

With that, she walks into her room and Auryn pieces it together. They're on the same floor not by some random occurrence, but because Mina requested it.

They have rooms next to each other not by accident, but because Mina wanted it that way.

"This should be an interesting trip," Auryn says quietly to herself.

With that, she swipes her badge over the sensor and enters her new living quarters for the next 15 months.

CHAPTER 3: THE BEGINNING

As we pack up our gear and head towards Toronto, towards the ship, and towards Auryn, we're all quiet. Finally, Kian breaks the silence.

"I had the strangest dream last night," he starts. "I could see a group of people in an old church, they were 25 feet away. They're all wearing green robes with hoods covering most of their faces. As I stood in the doorway, they didn't seem to notice me at first. They chanted together in rhythmic uniform, and as they separated to make the circle bigger, I gasped in surprise."

The three of us, myself, Garven and Esha, stop what we're doing and start paying closer attention.

"Standing there in the middle of the circle, touching a glowing object, unaware of their surroundings, was you, Finley, and you were in a trance of some sort. I wanted to rush in and see what's going on, but before I could move, someone from behind me grabbed my shirt and pulled me backwards, down to the ground. I then hit the cold marble floor hard, and while staring forward I tried yelling to get your attention."

I place my hand on his upper arm and stroke it once, before lowering it and locking eyes with him.

"Before I could get your attention, the huge wooden ornamental doors slammed shut. I tried making out what the intricate carvings meant, but I didn't recognize any of it. I turned around while on the ground to see my attacker, and as I did, a fist hurtled towards my face. Right before impact, I woke up and sat up immediately, totally out of breath. It was still dark in my tent, and everything was quiet except the breeze coming off the lake."

"Well, if we come into a situation like that, we'll have to make sure and be extra careful, alright?" I say, trying to sound sincere and upbeat.

"Yeah, I guess," Kian says, unconvinced.

"I guess it's one more thing I have to worry about today," I say with a bit of exhaustion in my voice.

"One more thing?" Garven asks.

"Yeah, I also had a dream last night."

I think about what parts of the dream I want to share with everyone, but especially with Kian. In it, I saw Auryn. Her gorgeous, wide smile, her beautiful hair, her perfect skin. She is older now, grown. She is stepping off a ship, laughing and smiling with someone, arm in arm with this stranger I do not recognize.

We make eye contact and freeze for a moment. I want to run up to her and hug her, but something is holding me back. I realize Kian is next to me, and he and the stranger next to Auryn are wearing the same expression on their faces.

"Well," I start.

I proceed to give everyone a watered-down version of my dream, where I say I have a nervousness about Auryn's traveling partner. I hate myself for doing it, because honestly, I'm just jealous, but I can't say that to Kian, right? This is a problem for future Finley though. Right now, there's only one thing that keeps running through my mind:

For the first time in years, this world is more exciting than the one in my dreams.

CHAPTER 4: A DISCOVERY (14 MONTHS AGO)

After four weeks on the ship, Auryn has run out of things to say during her video messages to her family. Most days have been pretty similar to each other, and a little lonelier than the initial trip. With only 1,600 people filling the place meant for 80,000, you can wander down entire hallways without seeing another person.

On some days, when she is getting too far inside her own head, Auryn heads to the halo-recreation room. Here, anything you program can become real, or at least real enough. The one rule, both posted in the room and built into the coding, is that you cannot make a person you already know, so Auryn cannot hang out with Finley, or Garven.

Instead, she has perused the selections of pre-built vacation destinations. Her favorite so far is "Early 2000's Caribbean Beach Vacation." She has easily spent 10 hours in this simulation over the first month on the ship. She always sits in a beach chair and pushes her toes through the sand and listens to the sounds of the waves crashing.

Then, after a bit, she grabs a fruit flavored non-alcoholic cocktail, a "mocktail" the menu calls it, and heads to a beach club that plays pop music from the same time period.

She tries to not pay too close attention though, because when she does, she notices the patterns.

The same people walk in the same directions, and have the same pretend conversation, every 30 minutes, unless interrupted in some way by Auryn. Last time she was in this simulation she tried talking, or high-fiving, or somehow interacting with every pretend person, to see how it would impact the program.

It didn't do much, and after 10 minutes, everything was right back on track again.

None of this was helpful in what to say to her parents though, and right now she sits in front of the camera and monitor, trying to think of anything noteworthy. After staring blankly at her own reflection in the monitor, she presses the record button. As soon as she's about to talk, there's a loud and frantic banging noise on the doors to her quarters. Auryn tells the virtual assistant to open them, and Mina appears in the door, hunched over and out of breath.

"I need your help; I know you're good with these things!" She says in between big gulps of air.

"I think I figured out a way to take almost 2 months off the trip back to Earth," she continues.

Auryn, with a full look of surprise on her face, turns back to the camera and stops the recording. She tries to press "Delete," but instead hits send. Apparently, her parents are going to be some of the first people to hear about this.

"What do you mean, you think you can cut two months off the trip?" Auryn asks.

"Well," she starts, still a little out of breath, "with the propulsion system, we still have it calculated for carrying an entire ship full of people, since we're hoping to pick up a lot of people back on Earth. But what that means for just 1,600 people, is if we boost the performance of the engine from the solar sails, we could save about 12% of the time it takes to get there. 78,400 people combined is like 11 million pounds! Even at reduced gravity, that's not nothing."

Auryn thinks it over for a second. How did no one in the colony account for this? That seems like such a major oversight.

"How was that not factored into the return trip?" She asks.

"I'm not sure. We still have so many supplies on board – food, medical, all of that — for the new group of people returning, maybe they just didn't want to reprogram it for just this one way? Or maybe they didn't want to push the Solar Sails to below 60% capacity for some reason," Mina replies.

"Well, okay, let's take a look," says Auryn, excited at the possibility of getting off this ship sooner.

They leave the room and head to the elevator. As the doors slide shut, Mina presses level 7. The secondary bridge is accessed right outside the engine room, a design flaw that bothers Auryn to this very day. If anything were to catch fire, or explode in the engine room, the secondary bridge could be taken out as well.

Here, the crew could control the ship if anything were to happen to the main bridge near the front of the ship. As they walk in, it's empty. There is nothing but the occasional lights blinking from the consoles and the low hum from the engine next door. As they enter, Mina says "Lights," and low-level lighting turns on in the room.

"Brightness level 6.5, warm light," she then says, and all the lights in the room adjust accordingly.

"It's so weird how quiet it is in here," Auryn says, "On the way to the colony, it was always so busy and filled with the second bridge crew. Feels weird with it being just the two of us in here."

"I know, right?" Mina says, "It's been just me in here for a few days trying to figure this out and test run the programs, but I wanted an extra hand now. I know you worked with your mom on a lot of this stuff, so I figured you were the extra hands I wanted in here with me."

For the next several hours, they test and retest Mina's hypothesis and, over and over again, it cuts significant time off the rest of the journey. Auryn helps add in some scenarios which Mina didn't originally account for, like solar flares or the solar sails partially failing. After the 5th successful simulation, they both yell excitedly and hug.

Then, caught up in the moment, Mina looks directly into Auryn's eyes. As they stood there for no more than a second or two, it felt to Auryn like the universe had stopped expanding. The stars, the planets, all of it had briefly paused their never-ending march into darkness in order to make this singular moment last a hundred lifetimes.

As Auryn stands alternating between no thoughts and every thought in the universe swirling around, she looks at Mina's lips. It's not like she hadn't noticed them before, but now, in this never-ending moment, her radiant, full lips could talk her into the impossible.

Without saying a word, they do. As Auryn's heart rate reaches what must be a thousand beats a minute, Mina slowly closes her eyes and leans in.

It was a short kiss, that much Auryn can remember. No more than a few seconds long. She could feel the blood rushing to her cheeks, and the sweat start forming in her palms. She remembers how soft Mina's lips were, how gently they pressed against hers. Then, lifetimes before she wanted it to be, it was over.

After, Mina stepped back and walked towards the doors.

"Let's go tell the captain the great news!" She said.

With that, she leaves the room, and the doors slide closed behind her.

Why would we tell the captain about our kiss? Auryn thinks to herself.

Then, almost immediately, she realizes that's not what Mina was referring to.

Still a little stunned, she takes a moment to remember how to breathe. She's smiling, and her face feels hot. She had thought that Mina had been flirting with her the past few months, but she had been so wrapped up in worrying about Finley, worrying about Garven, and worrying about the trip back, that she never really gave it the time.

A wave of guilt now rushes over her. She brings her hand up and rubs her forehead.

Finley, she thinks to herself. *I'm literally on a ship, traveling back to Earth, to rescue my brother and Finley, and now is the time that this happens? Oh Auryn, what are you doing?*

The doors make a *whoosh* sound while sliding open, and Mina pops her head back in.

"You coming or what? I don't want all the praise heaped on me after we tell them, but I'm willing to take it!"

She laughs and then waves for Auryn to follow. Auryn starts to head towards the doors, her legs remembering the motion of walking a little more each step, and they make their way to the bridge to share the news.

"How sure are you about this?" The captain asks, his face stern, jaw clenched, and lips pursed when done asking.

His medium-length brown hair, usually slicked back, falls slightly over his forehead, barely reaching his eyebrows.

"I'd love to sit here and say 100%, sir, but that's mathematically improbable, so I'll say I'm as close to 100% as I can possibly be," responded Mina.

"We ran the simulation five full times, the lowest amount of days it would cut off was 51, and in one simulation it took off as high as 57. We're very confident, sir," Auryn chimes in.

He rubs his chin and raises his eyebrows, then lets out a deep sigh. He hasn't stopped staring at the desktop hologram of the projections. They remain in silence for another 20 seconds before he looks up and says,

"Mina, I obviously know you very well. Auryn, on the other hand, I'm not sure we've really talked before. I'm Captain Rossi."

Captain Rossi was the second in command on the voyage to The Gray. At just 38 years old, many people had questions about his ability to command a ship if something were to happen to the First Captain. By the end of the trip, there were no longer questions.

About six months into the original journey, the ship's captain, Frances L. Stanz, came down with a rare illness, and had to be placed into medical bay for almost 11 days. Once cured, she retook the command, but during that time, through a lot of uncertainty, Captain Rossi did a commendable job at the helm.

"It's a pleasure to officially meet you, Captain. My mother Alia and my father Arthur have always spoken very highly of you." Auryn says.

"You're Alia and Aurthur's daughter!" Captain Rossi says, his face lighting up, "Two of the people who are truly the reason we made it to The Gray. Next time you talk to them, please tell them I'm a big fan of theirs."

Auryn smiles and thinks to herself that she knows what she's going to say in the next video message home to them.

After some more back and forth with the captain, explaining the situation more thoroughly, he calls to the bridge the remainder of the engineering team and a few other key senior personnel.

"I want you to know, it's not because I don't trust your numbers, Mina. I just have to double and triple check before making such a huge decision," Captain Rossi says.

"Of course, sir, I completely understand," Mina replies.

Once the rest of the personnel reach the bridge, Mina and Auryn go over all the details. They explain that the solar sails are capturing more than enough extra energy to increase the power in the engines. They run the first simulation over the course of the next 40 minutes, and it comes back taking off 53 days from the journey, right in the expected outcome range.

A new energy takes over the room. Faces have smiles on them, and the crew seems genuinely excited for the first time in a while.

"Alright you two, we're going to run this another half dozen times. It seems you've both been at this for a while, so why don't you relax for a bit. We'll call you back up to the bridge before any final decision is made," says the captain.

With that, Mina and Auryn head back in the direction of their quarters. Once inside the lift, Mina turns to Auryn, leans in, and kisses her again. After a few seconds, Auryn backs up and says,

"Wait, wait. Hold on."

"I'm sorry, am I not a good kisser? I've been told I'm a great kisser," Mina replies with a confidence that startles Auryn.

"No, no, I mean, yes. I mean," a flustered Auryn takes a deep breath to collect her thoughts.

"You are a good kisser. A great kisser. But there's some things you should know."

The lift doors open and the overhead voice says, "Deck 24." They both step out.

"So, you know that part of the reason I'm heading back to Earth is for my brother, Garven," she says.

"Yeah, of course, you've talked about him a lot," Mina says.

"Well, Garven isn't the only reason I'm heading back to Earth. There's something else there. Well, there's someone else there."

Mina looks at Auryn for a moment and smiles.

"Okay," she says, a smile still stretched wide across her face, eyebrows raised high.

Auryn looks confused for a moment, starts to speak, and fumbles her words. She then looks down at the floor, unsure of how to continue the conversation.

"Look, Auryn. Obviously, I like you. You're smart, funny, beautiful, and just the right amount of awkward," Mina says, "I'm not looking for us to settle down and get married on this trip. I just thought, since we're spending so many months together, maybe we can just, I don't know, have a good time together."

Auryn laughs nervously. She's never had the ability to just "have a good time." First there was the end of the world, then the second ever manned human spaceflight to colonize another planet, followed, of course, by setting up an entirely new civilization for humans.

"You know, that sounds really nice," Auryn says.

"I've got a couple other ideas that might sound really nice," Mina says, leaning in closer to Auryn as she says it.

With that, Auryn starts to blush.

"You think you're pretty smooth, huh?" Auryn asks.

"I know I am. Now if you want, we can go kiss some more in my quarters, and afterwards you can tell me about this mystery person. Or not, up to you."

With that, Mina walks to her door, scans her badge, and the door slides open.

"If you're coming, don't wait too long, alright?"

With that, she disappears into her quarters.

Wait, did she mean that the talking afterwards was optional, or the whole thing was optional? Auryn thinks to herself. She takes one step towards Mina's door and then pauses.

"It's fine. I'm allowed to have some fun. I'm allowed to enjoy myself. It's totally fine," she says to herself.

With that, Auryn walks towards the door, and it slides open. Mina turns around and smiles.

"Glad you didn't take too long," she says, while taking off her shirt and walking into the bedroom.

Auryn follows. She doesn't want to be rude.

...

Brzzt brzzt.

Brzzt brzzt.

Auryn is rudely woken up by the sound of her communicator buzzing over and over.

Brzzt brzzt.

Brzzt brzzt.

She wipes the sleep from her eyes before realizing that on the other side of the bed, Mina's communicator is also going off. Getting up to one elbow, she grabs for hers and presses the small button on the side to turn the screen on.

"10 Missed Pings - Captain Rossi," it says.

"Mina, MINA, wake up! Captain Rossi needed us at the bridge," she looks at her communicator again, "an HOUR ago!"

She springs out of bed as she's yelling, and as Mina wakes up, confusion spreads across her face.

"Wait, what?" Mina asks.

"They've been pinging us to come to the bridge for an HOUR!" Auryn yells back in response.

"Oh crap!" Mina says and shoots out of bed, "We gotta go now!"

With that, they pull their casual uniforms back on, a gray t-shirt and black pants, tie up the laces to their boots, and rush out of the room, sprinting towards the lift. These uniforms are different from the ones they wore the day of the launch. Captain Rossi spoke to the crew on that first day and said there was no reason that anyone needed to be uncomfortable on this trip, so everyone was allowed to wear the backup uniforms, which are made of softer fabrics, and are considerably more comfortable.

Mina presses a button Auryn's never even noticed before, and a beeping sound comes through the speakers.

"Bridge. No Stops. Code 081084," Mina calmly says.

"Granted," the generated voice says.

With that, the lift heads towards the bridge, and doesn't stop at any other floor. Mina looks at Auryn and smiles.

"Being a part of the engineering crew has its advantages," she says.

As the lift gains speed, Auryn looks at Mina, raises her hand, and gently flattens the hair on the back of her head.

"Good catch," Mina says, laughing.

They reach the bridge in record time, at least for Auryn, and quickly walk towards the rest of the group.

"Captain Rossi," Mina says.

The captain turns around and looks at the both of them. Each a little disheveled, they stand at attention.

"At ease you two, no need for such formality," Rossi says. "What took so long?"

"Apologies captain. We both passed out. Thankfully Auryn woke up and then came to my door and woke me up. Apologies, it won't happen again," Mina replies, knowing full well they could check the card swipe logs and see if this was a lie, if they really wanted.

Captain Rossi seems satisfied enough with that answer, if maybe a little annoyed. He tells the two of them that after a half dozen simulations, they were getting similar results.

"The only thing Lieutenant Rawland noticed was a chance for one of the engine components to overheat, so we're going to need to keep a constant eye on it. We're actually thinking of putting you two on the team that watches over the engine while we increase power to it. We know you have the skillset for it, Mina, and if you've spent even five minutes with your parents onboard, Auryn, we're pretty sure you're more than capable to help fix any problem."

"She absolutely is, sir," Mina says, "We worked hand in hand often while preparing the ship for this trip, and I have the utmost confidence in her."

"Alright, just make sure that both your wake-up alarms are working at all times moving forward," Captain Rossi smiles as he says this.

"You're dismissed from the bridge. Excellent work, you two."

Mina blushes a little, and they head back to the lift. Before they leave, Captain Rossi says,

"I want you both to know that you'll be properly recognized for this discovery. I, and everyone on the bridge, appreciate the work you've done. Mina, I wouldn't be surprised to see a promotion in your very near future, and Auryn, we'd be happy to have you as a full part of the crew moving forward, if you're interested."

Mina and Auryn both nod and exit onto the lift. Auryn presses the button for Deck 24, and the lift begins, this time much more slowly. They both let out a deep sigh and slump their shoulders in relief.

"So, I woke up first and came over and knocked on your door? That's what we're going with?" Auryn says, while starting to laugh.

"I know, but it was the easiest way to not have any follow up questions asked. I don't know how they feel about people in relationships working on the same projects together," Mina replies.

"In a relationship, huh?" Auryn says.

"Well, I mean, yeah," Mina pauses, "Right?"

"Deck 24," the overhead voice says.

Auryn walks quickly out of the lift and says,

"Yeah, we'll see I guess," a smile quickly creeping across her face, and then a laugh.

"What do you mean 'We'll see?'" Mina asks.

Auryn swipes her badge at her door. They open and she takes one step in before turning around. She looks at Mina and says,

"If you're lucky," and then winks.

The door closes with Auryn inside. The energy from her blushing could power the ship all by itself. A few seconds later, there is a knock on her door. Auryn opens it and standing there is, of course, Mina.

"You think you're pretty funny, huh?" Mina says.

"I mean, you said so yourself a few hours ago," Auryn grins while saying this.

"I knew I never should have given you compliments!" Mina replies, while walking into Auryn's room.

She heads right to the large couch and throws herself onto the cushions.

"So, you never told me about the someone you're going to see on Earth again, I'd love to hear about them." Mina says.

This is already the strangest relationship I've ever been in, thinks Auryn, *although there's only been two of them.*

Auryn talks about Finley for the first time in a long while. It feels really good to remember them. As she's talking about their past together, she mentions that Finley had a dream about Auryn meeting someone on the trip. Specifically, Fin said, someone with chin-length dark brown hair, a slender but strong body, and brown eyes. At the time, Finley had no idea who the person was, just "someone really smart on the ship."

Looking at Mina, she realizes this is exactly what she looks like.

"Wait, so they had a dream that you'd meet someone that," she pauses, "pretty much describes me?" Mina says.

"Yeah, yeah, I guess so. Sometimes they had dreams that eventually came true, but it wasn't all that often. We figured it was just a coincidence." says Auryn.

Mina gets quiet for a couple seconds. She takes a few deep breaths and rubs her left temple. Her face tightens up and she looks like she wants to say something. Auryn decides not to push it.

"So, I've never actually told anyone this outside of one person, but sometimes my dreams would come true after I had them as well. But it stopped once I left Earth," Mina finally says.

For a moment, Auryn stands there in disbelief. What are the odds the only two people she's ever been with could both see the future in dreams? She then walks over to the couch and sits down close to Mina.

"How often did this happen?" Asks Auryn.

"Well, when I was younger, not very often, but as I got older it started happening more, or at least I started remembering them better. I didn't really have anyone to tell, so I always kept it to myself. Honestly, I sort of pushed it out of my memory, until I met you. I dreamed about meeting you a few weeks before we left, and then we ran into each other a couple times on the ship."

She continued,

"At first, I thought we had met before. I couldn't shake the feeling that I knew you somehow, but then it finally hit me. You were, literally, the girl in my dreams."

"How come you didn't say anything?" Auryn asks.

"Because it would have sounded insane. 'Hey, I know we just met, but I dreamed about you before we ever left the Earth and now, you're here!'" Mina replied.

"It wouldn't have been any crazier than me starting with 'Hey, you're the girl from my partner's dreams!'" Auryn says while chuckling.

They both laugh together at the absurdity of both statements. Auryn then reaches out and places her hand gently on Mina's leg.

"So, I asked Finley this once and they didn't really have an answer, but what do you think it means?" Auryn asks.

"I don't know. I try not to think about it, honestly. Especially since it doesn't happen anymore. I'm a little scarred from it," answers Mina.

"Why scarred?" replies Auryn.

"When I was really young, I lived with my Great Aunt Aoi and Great Uncle Makoto. They were the only family I had left. My Auntie had a habit of asking what my dreams were every morning, so on that day I told her. Like I said, I didn't dream often, so I figured I would share it with her because she was always asking. It was something about meeting a man at the front door of their apartment. He was dressed in all black. He removed his hat and looked very sad."

Mina takes another long pause, and her eyes start to well up.

Auryn moves her arm and puts it around Mina's shoulders. She gently plays with her hair, and Mina lays her head onto Auryn's shoulder.

"About a half an hour later, a man came to the door, dressed in all black. I remember standing next to my Auntie as he removed his hat and lowered his head. The next thing I remember is her nails digging into my shoulder, and her stumbling a little bit. The man had come to tell her that her husband, my great uncle, had died unexpectedly that morning."

"After that, she would barely speak to me. Honestly, for the longest time I thought it was my fault. Imagine that kind of stress on an eight-year-old. The only time she ever talked to me about it again was a few months later. She told me that my mother had this same curse. That she could cause terrible things to happen with her dreams. It wasn't until I was a teenager that I realized I didn't cause these things, but I also couldn't seem to stop them."

Mina raised her head up and looked Auryn directly in the eyes.

"My auntie told me a story about a group of people, zealots she said, who controlled a stone that gave people the ability to see and control the future in their dreams. The Green Cloaks, she called them. They had thin, nearly glowing green bands around their eyes. She said the stone empowered people with different curses, but that was the one my mother had, and what I have." Mina said.

"Different curses like what?" Auryn asked.

"She said some of them could make the future happen in their dreams, some people could tell when others were lying and use it to manipulate people into believing anything they said about others. She even said that back in the day, those with the greatest power could use it to heal people's sickness." Mina responded.

The conversation paused for a moment while they both collected their thoughts. Auryn, still gently running her fingers through Mina's hair, then said,

"That doesn't make sense though, why would these abilities start getting stronger all of a sudden?"

"She said it was because the Earth was in trouble, and the stones are there to protect the Earth, but these groups, they take the stones for themselves and use it not for good, but for evil. For control."

"Do you think she was telling the truth?" Auryn asked.

"Honestly? No idea, but she was willing to strain her relationship with her only living relative over it, so she definitely believed it," Mina said.

"What," Auryn says, "if it's not a curse, but a gift?"

"What kind of gift allows you to see death and destruction, but not be able to do anything about it? What kind of gift even is that?" Mina asks.

"A powerful one." Auryn responds.

CHAPTER 5: ENTERING OZ

As we start walking the final few miles into Toronto, all the aches and pains I normally feel each day have evaporated. It's amazing what excitement and anticipation can do for a body. Even after a quick sprint last night, my ankle feels better than it has in days.

As we hop on the highway, I see large green signs with a thin layer of rust above that indicate our current road, the Queen Elizabeth Way, will eventually turn into something called the Gardiner Expressway. The road is decaying in multiple areas along the way, and I feel a certain unease while walking it.

After thirty minutes of carefully avoiding crumbling spots on the road, I spot another group of people ahead. Three of them, walking up the ramp on the other side of the median. They're maybe 150 feet ahead of us, but one of them looks vaguely familiar from this distance.

"Let's be careful, there's some people up ahead," I mention to the group.

Our pace is quicker than theirs is, and over the next ten minutes, we catch up.

During that time, they hadn't turned around once to see us, which is surprising for its lack of survival instincts. We're impossible to miss, just like they were. Now, being no more than 30 feet in front of us, but across several wide, barren traffic lanes, they spin around and see us. At first, they freeze from panic. The three of them each grab each other's arms and whisper to each other.

The tension of just existing in this world is overwhelming, add in not having any idea who is friend and who is foe? It's exhausting. Both groups want to size each other up. Both groups are no doubt taking stock of how much energy they have left to fight or flee. It's an exhausting existence, and I would be halfway to a breakdown already if it wasn't for last night, and the excitement of the day.

Then, before anyone makes a move or a sound, it hits me. The familiar feeling I experienced during the last ten minutes was right all along.

"Hey Llama, what's up?" I yell at the top of my lungs.

"What the h—" Garven starts to say, before being cut off by Esha's sudden burst of laughter.

"Fin, do you know that person?" Kian asks.

As he does, I keep watching the other group. They're talking amongst themselves. After a few seconds, a I hear a voice yell back,

"How's the leg holding up?"

A smile spreads across my face, and I chuckle lightly. Quickly, I remember that she was with The Raiders, and I don't know who she's currently walking with. I feel safer with there being four of us and only three of them, and the fact that none of them have their sleeve ripped off.

"She's the reason I'm alive. She's the one who saved me in the woods from The Raiders. You know, after I stabbed that guy?" I say.

"Do you recognize who she's with? Are they Raiders too?" Garven says, while unbuckling the strap over his machete.

"I can't tell, but I don't think so. They're not dressed like Raiders," I say back.

"Well yeah, if they're trying to get into the city they wouldn't be," Esha says.

After our brief conversation, Llama starts walking towards us, with the two other people about ten feet behind her. The two women behind her struggle with each step, and as we get close you can see the exhaustion on their faces. We both reach our side of the median before stopping.

"Looks like the leg healed up alright, barely even a limp," she says.

"All thanks to you, honestly. I wouldn't even be alive if it weren't for you. I still can't thank you enough," I reply.

"Don't even worry about it, I'm sure you'd do the same for me, given the circumstances," Llama replies.

"Speaking of your circumstance," I say, while looking at the two women who were still standing ten feet behind her. They could be twins; they look so much alike.

"How did yours change?" I ask.

"Well, long story short; these two weren't nearly as lucky as you. That terrible group I was with found and captured them. Who knows the unspeakable things they would do to some young girls. So, the first night I offered to guard them, and we all escaped. We've been on the run ever since," she says.

"That's horrible," I respond.

"Yeah, it got even worse after you left. We ran into a couple of people hiking, called themselves Green Cloaks and explained they were part of an organization that would repay us tenfold if we helped get them to Toronto. Tell you what, if the way they torture people is any indication of the organization they work for, I want nothing to do with it," she says back.

I look at the two girls and yell out,

"She saved my life, too. You're in good hands."

They smile weakly, and I ask Llama if they've had anything to eat since they escaped.

"Some small vegetation I managed to find, but not much, no," she says.

I flip my backpack off my back, open the dusty top, and grab my three remaining food rations and a silver hydration pack. A sip for each of them should help immensely. I hand them over to Llama and she nearly tears up.

"I don't even know how to thank you. We were just hoping to make it to the city today, but we were fading fast," she says.

"It's the least I can do," I say back.

While talking, the two women approach her nervously and she hands them the food. She also explains the water pack, and that they need to each only take a single sip, and that'll be enough fluids for the day.

The first girl takes a big sip and takes down half the pack. Her eyes looked terrified after taking too much and nearly breaks down into tears. A sure sign of someone who's had a past filled with traumatic experiences. Before I can say anything, Kian takes a couple steps forward and says,

"No worries, we have more where that came from."

While he says it, he hands Llama two more hydration packs.

"You saved my favorite person on the planet. The least I can do is give you some water," Kian then says.

The girl who took a large sip smiles at Kian. She then sits down on the concrete and begins to devour her food ration. The second girl carefully opens a hydration pack and takes a sip of her own. She then says, in a dry, scratchy voice,

"She told us about you, you know. We weren't sure if we should trust her or not, and she told us the story of how you two met. I'm glad we trusted her, and that we get to put a face to the story," she said.

I smile knowing I played some small part of them being here right now.

"I didn't catch your names?" I then ask.

"I'm Etta, that's my sister Evrim. She doesn't talk much."

"It's so nice to meet the both of you. Your companion here, the one who saved me, told me her name is Llama Llama," I chuckle as I say it.

They look over at her, each with an eyebrow raised, and then start laughing, the kind of laugh that grows louder and louder in between deep breaths. Evrim is doubled over on the ground, still holding half the remaining food ration.

"I had to think of something on the spot!" exclaims Llama.

"My real name is Lyra Lilium, LL for short," she says.

"Ah, LL, like Llama Llama." I respond.

A smile creeps across her face.

"I knew you were a smart one," she says.

We chat for another 30 seconds or so before I make formal introductions between everyone. We ask if they'd like to walk with us to the entrance, and they happily agree.

"Sorry if we have to take it a little slow, we're just so exhausted from walking through the night. We were afraid of them catching up to us," Lyra says.

Before she's done finishing her sentence, something in the distance catches my attention. A half mile down the road, away from Toronto, I see another group of travelers coming up an onramp and onto the highway. The expression on my face must have changed dramatically, because immediately Lyra asks what's wrong.

As everyone starts to turn towards where I'm looking, Kian says the words that send an immediate shiver down my spine.

"I think that's Luna and Harlian with a bunch of other people," he says.

"We traveled with them for a day or two. I would recognize that hair anywhere," a shocked and terrified sounding Lyra chimes in with.

"How?" Esha says.

"They must have found each other and teamed up," I say as Etta and Evrim get up on their feet.

"We have to go, NOW," Garven yells.

We all turn and start jogging towards the city. LL, Etta, and Evrim are moving slowly, Etta with a pronounced limp.

I try to offer some words of encouragement.

"This will be the last time you have to run for a while, maybe ever, as long as we get to Toronto!" I blurt out.

I'd guess we have a mile before we reach the city proper area, and I'm hoping with our head start we can make it. 75 feet ahead there's a break in the concrete median and when we reach it, the three of them come over to our side of the road and continue running.

About the same time, the ankle I was convinced was healed lets me know that I was wrong. Every time my foot hits the ground a shooting pain engulfs my lower leg. I can't help but slow down slightly, even as it means the group slowly pulls away. Everyone but Lyra, that is. I turn my head to the left to see her smiling. She keeps pace with me when I know she could be going faster. She can no doubt sense I'm wondering why.

"Don't worry, Fin, everything's going to be okay," she says.

For a brief moment, I believe her. I once again look forward, and in the near distance I can see the density of the buildings increase. The gigantic green overhead signs above are moving at a snail's pace, my pace, and seem to be mocking how slow I'm running.

I look behind me for a second and Luna, Harlian, and their new group of six Raiders are in pursuit. It looks like she's screaming in our direction, and they're gaining ground on the two of us. I turn back forward and concentrate on where I'm stepping. There are rusted out cars and debris littering the road everywhere. To the left and right are crumbling concrete barriers with sharp metal rebar sticking out, like dangerous metal spikes waiting to impale anyone not paying enough attention.

Just like the highways back home near Cleveland. It seems like no matter where we are in this world, something will always remind you of home.

A hundred feet later, the rest of the group notices just how far behind we've fallen. Garven yells for Etta and Evrim to keep going at the pace they are, which is surprisingly quick for someone who nearly passed out on the road a few minutes ago.

Esha, Garven and Kian slow down enough for us to catch up and reform a group run. Garven in the very front, Esha in the back, and Lyra, Kian and I in a bunch in between. At this pace, it's only a matter of time before they catch up, but the real question is can we make it to the entrance of Toronto before they do.

I do my best to keep looking ahead. I push a little harder no matter how stiff and painful my ankle is. I'm grimacing with each step, but I know if we can reach the city, I'll have plenty more time to rest.

As I keep looking forward, I see Garven a few feet ahead, his backpack bouncing with every step, his head turning from left to right and back again. His machete being flung wildly back and forth, sweat dripping down his arms. He's like a machine right now, no doubt fueled by the idea of seeing his sister for the first time in years.

We run for another five minutes, and Luna and her group are only a hundred feet behind us, when suddenly we hear a man yell,

"HALT WHERE YOU ARE RIGHT NOW!"

Out from behind an overturned semi-truck, a group of eight people spring out. Four of them aiming bows at us, two with swords, and two with guns. We stop immediately. I notice up ahead a few dozen feet, Etta and Evrim are stopped by a smaller group of two people. They start being walked back to us.

"Everyone put your hands in the air immediately," the man yells.

He's tall, really tall, and even more muscular than Garven is. He has a blue bandana wrapped around his forehead, which his ear length hair falls over top of, and he's dressed in a blue jean vest with green cargo pants. There's no uniform amongst the 10 of them. It's hard to tell if they're a part of the Toronto group, or a random gang.

"We're being chased by the people behind us, they want to kill us!" LL shouts at them.

The man looks at another member of his group, she's about 5 '8 with brown hair up in a bun, a green jacket with both sleeves cut off, and a pair of brown shorts that probably used to be pants. She takes five others and circles behind us, putting a space between us and Luna's group.

"We'll get all your stories in just a moment. For now, we wanna know what you're doing here," the woman says.

Luna's group approaches the rest of us cautiously. They've been spotted so they probably feel it's too late to turn around without looking suspicious. Instead, they walk up and Luna yells,

"Those thieves took everything from us! Check their bags, they have our stuff!"

"LIAR," I scream, without having given it even a thought.

"Alright, alright. Everyone calm down. We'll get this all sorted."

CHAPTER 6: A RACE (13.75 MONTHS AGO)

It's been two days since Captain Rossi agreed to Mina's plan. Over the last two days, teams have been assigned, limits have been agreed upon for how hard they're willing to push the system, and an exit strategy in case things go wrong has been talked about.

Auryn, Mina, and two others, Sakito and Orion, are in the engine room. Mina and Orion on controls, Auryn and Sakito physically close to the main engine components to spot any physical issues that might happen. They're also standing right next to the emergency shut off valve, which would be a last-ditch attempt to vent the room and cool the engine back down, if it needs it.

The highest point of danger for this entire operation is the first hour. The ship has been cruising steadily along for over a month now, so pushing it harder than it ever has been, even if it's within its limits, is stressful. Captain Rossi comes over the intercom system.

"All teams check in, engine room ready?"

"Engine room ready, Captain," Mina replies.

"Solar Sail team ready?"

"Solar Sail team ready, Captain."

"Bridge, ready?"

"Bridge is ready," with that he chuckles, Captain Rossi both asked, and answered the last question, and cracked himself up in doing so. The entire ship could hear him laughing at his own joke.

Auryn looks through a protected control room window, back towards Mina, and Mina rolls her eyes at the captain's joke. Auryn turns back towards the engine and chats with Sakito for a few moments.

After another minute, Captain Rossi comes over the intercom again.

"Alright crew, all systems are go. Prepare for increase."

"Alright, here goes nothing," Auryn says to no one in particular.

With that, she and Sakito can feel the power of the engine expand. The constant humming it makes grows louder. The room vibrates at a slightly lower frequency. Maybe it's just a trick her brain is playing on her, but Auryn swears she feels the ship physically moving faster.

She turns once again to look towards the control room with Mina and Orion in it. She tries to give Mina a thumbs up that everything looks good in the engine room, but Mina is looking down at the control panel.

Through her helmet shield, which they normally wouldn't wear but put on in case this goes south quick, Mina looks worried. Over the past two days while the crew has been preparing, she's felt a lot of extra stress and pressure.

"I feel like if it all goes wrong, it'll be my fault. What if people die, Auryn?" She said last night while lying in bed together. Auryn could make out the contours of her face from the low LED lights hidden under the shelving panels in the bedroom. She looked worried.

"It wouldn't be your fault, Mina. The captain and all the senior level crew members all signed off on this. The final decision was theirs, not yours," Auryn responded.

"Sure, I guess. But the original idea was mine," Mina replied.

"Trust, me Mina, you're just not that important," Auryn said, as a joke to lighten the mood.

It didn't work.

"If people die, I'm never going to let myself live it down."

As Auryn is trying to get Mina's attention once more in the control room, the voice of Sakito comes into her helmet.

"Does it feel warmer to you?" He says.

Now that he mentions it, it does seem like it's heating up quickly in here. Auryn turns and takes a few steps towards the engine and sees parts of it glowing red hot. Several of the huge gears, 15 feet in diameter, start glowing a dark orange color. She tries turning on her in-helmet intercom system, but no one can hear her. The ship has had constant problems with the intercom system in some of the suits. She turns around and runs towards the wall with the ship-wide intercom button.

She rips her helmet off and presses the button down.

"Some of the gears are overheating and it's getting VERY hot in here, really quickly. Nothing else seems to be wrong on our end, but I can't stress enough how much it's heating up."

She places her helmet back on just in time to hear Mina come over the intercom in everyone's helmets and say,

"I'm seeing the same on my readings, Captain. If they get much hotter, we'll have to shut the entire thing down and let the ship coast for who knows how long. It might cost us a few days, or even a week, in time."

"How much time do we have to figure it out, people?" The captain shouts into the intercom.

"An hour, maybe two," responds Orion.

"Well then, people, let's get this figured out, and quick," the captain replies.

As the sweat starts to bead on her forehead, Auryn searches the engine area with Sakito for any sign of what could be wrong. Pulling panels and checking intake and vent systems, Sakito notices there doesn't seem to be a proper airflow throughout the engine room. After 20 more minutes of investigating, he spots the issue.

"Captain," he says into the intercom system, "an exterior vent didn't open properly. The engine room is heating because there's nowhere for the excess hot air to go. I've spotted it through a long tube from the inside here, but the vent is stuck on the outside of the ship."

"What's the fix?" The captain responds.

"Don't know yet, sir, might have to manually open the vent," Sakito says back.

"Alright, and how do we go about that?" Says Captain Rossi.

"I'll have an answer on that ASAP, sir."

Both Auryn and Sakito investigate further what's wrong with the air vent. It appears as though one of the hinges is bent, which never would have come up in a regular safety check because these vents are almost never opened. The only way to get it fixed is to straighten it out entirely, which can only be done if the vent is open.

The only way to open it now? From the outside.

Sakito looks over at Auryn with a knowing look. They mark the vent on the ship's system and then head for the door into a more protected side room and take off their helmets to talk. Sakito looks at Auryn with his light brown eyes, both of them are sweating profusely, and gulping at the cooler air while breathing.

"Looks like we're doing a spacewalk today," he says.

There have only been three outside spacewalks in total on the ship, all of them on the way to B.52.C. All three times the ship was able to slow itself before anyone went outside.

The first time was to clear some space debris and dust off a sensor. The second was to recoat a few windows where the outer layer had been cracked slightly, and the third time was to fix a small fold in the solar sail. All of them done at a slower speed, all of them with days of planning.

This was the first time Auryn or Sakito would have to go out, and the first time anyone did it on such quick notice.

"You wanna tell the captain, or should I?" Sakito says.

"I'll do it. He might actually let me," Auryn says with a chuckle.

She walks over to the intercom button and says,

"Captain, I have some good news, and I have some bad news."

"Let's hear it, Auryn."

"The good news is that Sakito and I can fix it if you give us 45 minutes, maybe an hour."

"That's great news. So, what's the bad news?

"We can only fix it by going out for a spacewalk," Auryn says.

There's silence over the intercom for a few moments.

"There has to be another way. That could be really dangerous at our current speed," a voice cuts in to say. It was Mina's.

"Is there any other option? It's spacewalk or back to the original time schedule?" The captain asks.

"Considering the limited amount of time we have to fix the issue, I believe so, Captain. Not only that, if this thing overheats, we might lose some days off our original schedule," Auryn responds.

"Alright, give us a few minutes up here on the bridge to consider it. Until then, ready your spacewalk suits in case you get the go ahead," the captain responds.

"Will do, Captain," Auryn responds.

Her heart rate is increasing, and she and Sakito look at each other, sharing the same nervous apprehension.

"What did we just get ourselves into?" He says.

"Something we can brag about for ages, if we make it," Auryn responds.

As Auryn reaches for the door to leave the side room, it swings open. Standing there is Mina. Before Auryn can say anything, Mina says,

"Sakito, can you give us 60 seconds alone real quick?"

"Um, sure. I guess," he says, "Auryn, I'll be in the change room next to the second bridge getting my suit on, if you wanna meet me there in a minute."

"Sounds perfect, see you there," Auryn says.

With that, he leaves the room and shuts the large heavy metal door behind him. Mina, helmet held under her arm, walks up to Auryn and gives her a big hug.

"Look, I know I can't stop you from doing this, but it's so dangerous, Auryn. It's so dangerous and it might not even work. Wouldn't you rather just slow back down and wait the extra two months to get back to Earth?"

"And kill our legacy? Your legacy? You'll forever be the person who saves the crew two extra months of madness on this ship." Auryn says, with a little bit of a chuckle.

"Oh, who gives a crap about legacy? You can't be serious," Mina says.

"I know. I don't really care about that. I just think it would be really, really cool to do this, and help everyone at the same time. Like, how often do people get to do a spacewalk on a ship that's hurtling through the galaxy? It's an adventure."

"I think I liked the Auryn that just wanted to eat snacks and hang out in the Halo programs all day better than this adrenaline junkie version," Mina says, a smile creeping across her face.

"But seriously, think of how cool the stories will be. You, figuring out how to make the trip significantly quicker. Me, spacewalking under insane conditions? It'll be awesome," Auryn says.

"It'll be something, alright," Mina responds.

With that, they embrace once more, and then Auryn opens the door, and walks towards the engine room. She gets to the side room with the spacewalk suits as the captain comes over the intercom again.

"Alright, team. We have an outer access port right off the secondary engine room down there. From where you marked the damage, you'll only need to go about 80 feet to reach the damaged vent. There are four grappling lines, so you're going to have to each connect to two of them. Gear up and be ready in ten minutes."

"Alright, Sakito, are you ready to spacewalk at the speed of light?" Auryn says.

"Not even a little bit," he says back, shaking his head as he laughs to himself.

THE SEVENTH DREAM

It flashes in front of my eyes for a brief second, but it lasts the length of an entire dream. I am awake, but in the amount of time it takes to blink, a new vision appears.

A fireball shoots across the daylight sky, brighter than the sun. For a moment I shield my eyes from it, before once again focusing on its direction. It came from west of the city, and its trajectory is from the ground, heading towards the sky. It is of this Earth, and it's fast, screaming through the sky quicker than any vehicle I've seen.

Where it's heading, I do not know, but in its path lies destruction, for that much I'm sure.

As quickly as I blinked, I am back in Toronto, disoriented, and people are arguing all around me. No one else wiser to what just happened.

CHAPTER 7: THE SPACEWALK

Auryn and Sakito both ready themselves to pull the hatch handle. They've placed two lines each onto one another, which, in the event of an emergency, should keep them tethered to the ship.

"Alright you two," Captain Rossi begins over the intercom system, "If anything feels off, if anything goes wrong, your direct orders are to come right back to the hatch."

"Yes, Captain," Sakito says.

"Yes, Captain," Auryn says. She's picked up a new helmet with a working comm system.

"Commence when ready, and good luck," the captain says.

The two of them look at each other and are about to pull the latch when Mina comes in over Auryn's comm.

"Hey, Auryn. It's Mina, I'm on a solo line to just you right now. I just wanted to say: be safe, and I'll be here when you get back."

Auryn can feel the warmth in her voice.

"I'll be back before you know it," she responds.

With that, Auryn and Sakito place their hands on the hatch and lift up. The door pops outward, and then manually slides open, along tracks on the outside of the ship.

The opening is small, only three feet in diameter, and Auryn goes out feet first. She has to contort her body so it's parallel to the outside of the ship, with her back facing it. Once halfway out she turns on the magnetic component of her boots, bends her legs, and her feet then yank hard towards the ship.

It shoots Auryn upright with more force than she could have possibly imagined. It felt like, for a brief moment, she was about to go flying into the abyss.

As she stands there waiting for Sakito to exit the hatch, she can't help but stare off into space. There is something about looking into the void. It calls to her. The vast emptiness of space. If she were to float off the ship, by the time the crew noticed, even if it were short, they would be tens of thousands of miles away from her already.

She would never float away on purpose, of course, but there's something inside her pulling her towards it. The world's tiniest voice, buried deep in the recesses of her mind, saying,

Go ahead. Unlatch. Float forever.

It scares her, and she shakes her head back and forth quickly to try to get the thought out of her head.

She also feels the strange sensation of moving thousands of miles per hour, yet the landscape barely changes.

She can see distant stars moving ever so slightly, but they're so far away she still feels like she's barely moving at all.

As it's happening, she doesn't notice that Sakito is halfway out, and needs to occupy the same space she's currently in. As he flips his magnetic switch, his boots zap towards the ship's metal, except Auryn is in the way. She feels a sudden sharp pain in her ankles and would be knocked forward towards the ship if she was able.

What saves Auryn, her boots, endangers Sakito. With his boots not reaching the metal, the force rotates his body so his shoulder lands hard onto the side of the ship and he bounces off. His tethers wrap around Auryn, one on each side, tightly. So tight it feels like her ribs are about to break.

Through the blinding pain and suddenness of it all, she looks up to see Sakito floating 5, then 10, then 15 feet from the ship. The tethers are long, over 100 feet, and with her wrapped between them, if he reaches that distance away from the ship, it could crush her or maybe even split her in two.

"Auryn, little help here," he says over the intercom.

A shockingly calm statement considering the circumstances.

"Everything okay out there? Our external camera can't see Sakito," Mina says.

"Everything will be alright in just a second," Auryn struggles to say, barely any breath left in her lungs.

She looks up and sees Sakito slowly floating farther away from the ship.

"What do you mean, in a second?" Mina asks.

The vast darkness surrounds him, and he gets smaller in her vision.

"Any time now, Auryn," says Sakito.

The tethers pull further and further away from the ship. They tighten harder around her ribs and chest.

"What's going on out there?" Captain Rossi cuts in.

Auryn's breathing is so labored she's getting tunnel vision. She opens her eyes as wide as she can, but it's no use.

"Is everything alright?" Mina says, sounding frantic.

She is surrounded by the void. Her eyes are losing focus.

She hears multiple voices over the intercom system, with varying degrees of panic.

"GIVE ME A FREAKING SECOND!" Auryn finally yells, the frantic sound of her voice surprising even herself.

She rotates herself so the straps are now on the sides of her body instead of across her chest and back and takes a deep breath. Her chest screams in fiery agony.

That's at least three, maybe four broken ribs, she thinks to herself.

Auryn then grabs one tether with both hands and pulls hard. She looks up and Sakito whips to a stop, his body bending backwards in a near crescent moon shape. She has no way to move her feet, since walking on the ship requires you to turn off the magnetic powered boots one at a time via switches in their gloves, so she starts pulling as hard as she can.

Through the pain, she pulls, one arm at a time on the strap, bringing Sakito closer to her, a foot at a time. At his farthest, he was floating almost 40 feet from the ship, so she's going to have to pull 40 times, at least. If she wasn't between the tethers herself, she could have gone back in the hatch and activated the automatic pulley system to bring him back.

Against the backdrop of the vast darkness of space, Auryn uses every ounce of adrenaline her body will give her. Screaming through the agony. Yelling over the shouts of Mina, Captain Rossi, and Orion. She can't even respond to their inquiries. She can hear the panic setting in from the internal crew, but all she can do is scream through the pain and pull. And keep pulling, because a life literally depends on her.

Through the yelling, Sakito finally breaks through and says,

"Everything is fine, Auryn is hurt but we'll be okay."

Why he says this with 15 feet of pulling left, Auryn doesn't know, but she appreciates the few moments of silence that follow.

Five more pulls: she can feel new bruises forming on her sides.

Four more pulls: her left arm is starting to go dead.

Three more pulls: Sakito is almost at arm's length.

Two more pulls: he is nearly parallel with the ship.

Suddenly, the tension releases and Auryn gasps.

The next half second feels like a thousand years as her eyes try to focus.

The deep breath she attempts to take feels like the fires of hell burning in her chest and lungs.

She looks towards the never-ending skies and sees the tether, realizing that Sakito hasn't floated off again. He activated the magnetic function of the boots and is now safely on the outside of the ship.

As safe as the insanity of this is, at least.

They lock eyes through the clear visors in their helmets, and Auryn starts to cry, and then begins to laugh. The laughing, however, is short lived, because the pain it causes her ribs is immense.

Sakito makes a motion to change comm channels, to just the two of them, so Auryn reaches up to her helmet and switches over.

"So, thanks for saving me," he says.

"Well, it was my fault you flew away in the first place, so it's the least I could do," Auryn replied, between labored breaths.

"Nah, could have happened at any point. That being said, I saw what happened with the tethers and your ribs. Think you can still spacewalk with me or you wanna head back in?" Sakito asks.

"It's a two-person job, and we don't have much time, so I'm coming with," she says.

"You really don't have to do this, Auryn. We can figure something else out," he replies.

She shakes her head and makes the motion to switch back to bridge comms. Reluctantly he does the same.

"Sorry all, small hiccup there, but everything's fine, we're starting our spacewalk now. We'll keep you updated," Auryn says.

"Is everything alright, team? Are we sure you're gonna be okay?" Captain Rossi says.

"We're good, Captain," Sakito replies.

Through the immense amount of pain, the rest of the spacewalk goes surprisingly smooth. They make it to the broken vent and manage to open it. The only real issue is that it's opened permanently now, so upon entering Earth's orbit, they'll need to install an additional heat panel from the inside.

After 45 minutes, they make it back inside. Once inside the hatch, Mina comes running up and gives Auryn a giant bearhug.

"Oh my god, please no," Auryn yelps, surprising both Mina and herself.

"I'm, I'm sorry," Mina says, as she backs away, obviously hurt at Auryn's response to physical affection.

"No, no, I'm sorry. I injured my ribs out there. I have to get to medbay." Auryn grunts out between labored breaths.

After being placed in a medical cryo sleep for 2 weeks, Auryn wakes up feeling as good as ever. She also gets the good news from the bridge: After venting the engine room, the process worked, and they'll be arriving on Earth nearly two months ahead of schedule.

CHAPTER 8: NEW ARRANGEMENTS

It took an hour to get everything figured out at the entrance to Toronto. We explained our side of the story, and Luna lied about theirs. I could point out every lie they were telling, even the ones I wasn't there for somehow. But no matter how much I pleaded, they refused to believe me.

At one point, I saw Luna talk to one of the main guards privately. She said something, motioned over towards me, and they both looked at me for a moment. As they did, the hair on the back of my neck stood up and I had an uneasy feeling sweep across my body. Staring back at him, he had an ever so slight sliver of green in his otherwise dark brown eyes.

Shortly after, another group of four from the Toronto security team met us all on the highway. They split our group off first, with me, Kian, Esha, Garven, Lyra, Etta, and Evrim following them onto an offramp and into the city. Several hundred feet behind us, Luna, Harlian, and one other member were following in the same direction. I could no longer see the rest of their group.

One of the new people, Nix, seemingly the one in charge, was leading the way.

"Look, I'm sorry to have to quarantine you all separately for a little while, but when two hostile groups try to enter, we have to be as safe as possible," he says.

He's wearing a blue short sleeved shirt with the top two buttons undone. He's a large man, at least 6 '3, and muscles that look like they're about to rip the sleeves of the shirt. Along with his tan shorts, he wears a belt with a large knife on one side and a pistol on the other. The gun looks in much better shape than any I've seen over the last few months.

His left arm is covered in tattoos of, frankly, poor quality, and he talks like he was trained in the military before it disbanded. I'd guess he's head of security here.

"Where are you taking us?" I ask.

"There's an old office building where we'll be putting each of you into separate rooms and asking some questions. As long as everything gets answered in a satisfactory manner, you'll be out in no time," he answers.

"So, jail?" Garven responds.

"If you wanna call it that, go for it. I don't care. My job here is to make people safe," he says.

"You don't understand, my sister is on that ship that landed last night, I have to see her!" Garven raises his voice while saying this.

Nix and the rest of our escorts stop and turn to face us. Their patience has worn thin.

"The only things you have to see are the things we're going to allow you to see for the next few days, understand?"

I can tell by the tensing muscles in his neck, and eyebrows scrunching towards the middle, that Garven is angry.

"Yeah, I understand," he mutters under his breath, in an unexpected show of restraint.

As we continue walking, Nix tells us the building is a mile and a half away from where we were. As we walk through the streets, there's even more people here than there were in Buffalo. It's an entirely different vibe though, with massive buildings 30-40 stories high surrounding us. Some in great shape, and some looking like they might topple over, taking out an entire city block with them. It's hard to see more than two or three blocks in any direction at one time because of how large the buildings are.

That makes turning onto the next street all the more surprising. As we round the corner, a few blocks down I see it:

The Amelia Erhardt. The same ship that left us years ago is there, right in front of us, nestled into the cityscape like another building. It's a little rougher looking than when it left, but aren't we all?

I stop in my tracks and compose myself enough to look to my left, over at Garven. He is standing motionless, staring at the giant ship, his mouth partially open, eyes wide. He turns to look at me and I see them welling up with tears, same as mine.

He then smiles the biggest, most heartfelt smile I've ever seen from him, and we take a couple steps towards each other and hug. He wraps me in his arms, and we sway back and forth crying tears of joy.

"Hey, cut it out, we got places to be," Nix's voice cuts through. Garven and I keep embracing for a few more seconds before facing back in the direction we were walking.

"Geez man, give 'em a minute," Esha then says.

He ignores her, and we start walking towards the ship again. I look to my right and Kian is there, eyes straight ahead, walking while staring at the ship. I know it's hard for him. Here I am, celebrating the return of my first love while he has to stand by and watch.

So many thoughts are swirling through my head as we walk down the center of the road. We're on a road called Yonge, and an old, broken sign says "Winter Garden" a few stories off the ground. I try to imagine what it must have been like when this was a thriving metropolis, but all I can really think about is that giant, beautiful ship straight ahead.

As we get closer and closer, I notice the large opening in the city around the launch pad. The ship, still so enormous in size, takes up several city blocks. Nix tells us we're going to walk right by it on the way to Bloor Street, which sounds made up, where the building is.

We walk the final block before the ship, and I can't help but feel this all looks so familiar. The shape of the buildings, the way the sky looks, the smell of the air, crisper than normal with a breeze off the lake.

Then it hits me, and my heart begins to race. This was in a dream of mine; if I keep walking straight ahead, I'm going to see her, Auryn, and the mystery person she's with. I don't know if I want to see them, I don't know if I want this to happen. Can I change it if I want to?

"Hey Nix," I start, "Any way we can take a detour around the ship? Looks like a big crowd ahead?"

Out of the corner of my eye, I see Garven snap his head in my direction. I can feel him burning a hole through me with his eyes. To the right I see Kian also looking at me. I turn slightly towards him, and I see a puzzled look on his face. No one seems to know what I'm getting at, and why would they?

"Absolutely not. Crowd or no crowd, my job is to get you there as quickly as possible, he pauses for a moment before saying "Besides, I thought you were excited to see the ship?"

I'm desperately searching my mind for a reason, any reason, why we would need to go around the next block and I can't. It's as if my own brain is against me and is making sure the future it dreamed of comes true before my very eyes. Is the future so set in stone that once I dream it, it will become reality no matter what? Do my dreams overwrite free will?

My pulse starts to quicken, and I feel my anxiety spiking. Free will. Auryn. Toronto. Jail. It's all too much.

What if Auryn isn't on the ship, or worse, she isn't even in love with me anymore?

What if I'm stuck in this Toronto jail forever and I never get to see her?

What if one of these buildings comes crashing down onto us, and everything we fought for ends in the blink of an eye?

What if Auryn doesn't love me anymore.

What if she doesn't love me anymore.

My vision begins to blur, my stomach starts to turn, my walking becomes unstable. I turn towards Esha to warn her.

"Nix, NIX!" Esha yells. "Fin's gonna collapse, we gotta get their medicine out of their bag."

"You gotta be kidding me." he replies, exasperation flooding his tone.

"Fine. Do it quick."

With that, I go down to one knee, place a hand on the hot asphalt, and steady myself as I sit on the ground. I slowly try to take off my backpack, but my arms don't quite do what I want them to, and my depth perception is off. Esha kneels next to me and grabs the pack. I can barely see her going through it until I hear the shake of my pill bottle. Not many left from the ones Dr. Rai gave to me in Buffalo.

I'm relieved the guards who searched our bag let me keep them, if not still annoyed they tried taking them in the first place. It took some explaining during the kerfuffle on the highway, but when I talked about how much I needed them, I think they could see the desperation in my eyes.

Esha hands me half of a pill, and I take it with a swig of water. It won't really start working for 15 minutes, but knowing I took it sometimes helps in bringing my heart rate down.

"Alright, you good? We gotta go," Nix says impatiently.

"I mean, not really, no. Can I hang onto someone as I walk?" I ask.

"Fine, whatever," he replies.

I stand up, and as I'm about to lean on Esha, Kian walks up.

"I'd really like to help, Fin, if you'll let me," he says.

I turn to him and smile.

"Of course."

I use my right hand and wrap it under and around his left arm. I don't need much for stability, but it helps calm me down as well.

We walk slowly towards the shuttle, and towards our jail cells. My ankle hurts from running and my brain hurts from a chemical imbalance. As we approach the intersection where the ship begins, I wonder to myself if stopping back there changed what was going to happen now. By delaying our timing to reach here, would I no longer see Auryn? Would I just miss her, and therefore everything else about the situation would change?

I don't have to wonder long, because I can see the crew walking down the platform of the ship. It's right on our corner, like I had dreamed, and as people come into focus, it happens.

The delay didn't cause things to change, it made sure they stayed the same.

I look at the ramp, and the world around me freezes. I see Auryn in her space gear, helmet off. She is older now, grown. She is stepping off a ship, laughing and smiling with someone, arm in arm with this stranger I recognize only from my dreams. Auryn's cheekbones reflecting the sunshine, her eyes sparkling in the light. I am instantly in love again.

But who is the woman she's walking with? Is she the woman I dreamed about before Auryn left?

She is short, with shoulder length straight black hair. She's pretty, so very pretty. They walk together in a comfortable closeness that makes my insides churn and my heart sink, before I remember that Kian not only exists, but has been helping to hold me upright for the last several minutes.

Without thinking, I move away from him a few inches.

"I'm okay, I got it now," I say to him.

He looks a little confused by my sudden ability to do this myself, until he notices me staring at the ramp from the ship. He also notices Garven staring as well.

"Fin!" Garven says excitedly.

"I see," I respond, sheepishly.

We both look at each other for a second, and decide to try and run towards Auryn. In the heat of the moment this felt like the natural thing to do. It's been years since I've seen her, and not once in the thousands of times this scenario ran through my head did I imagine I would be on my way to jail.

We take two or three running steps before suddenly I am pulled back hard. One of the guards caught us running immediately and tugged on my backpack, stopping me in my tracks. My foot slips out from under me and with all my weight I hit the ground. I scramble to get up and try again, but I'm being controlled by the heavy hand on my backpack. I am a tornado of arms and words, both pleading and demanding to be let go.

We're no more than 40 feet away from them now. There's a small crowd of people in between us, cheering for all the people exiting the ship.

I try to yell for Auryn, but she doesn't seem to hear. Garven then yells at decibel levels I didn't know were possible; a desperate cry to see his sister, his family, for the first time in years. These past few years he never allowed himself to believe they made it, to believe they're still alive, and here she is returning to Earth with a hero's welcome, just out of reach.

After a few seconds of screaming, Nix tells Garven to shut up, but it's already worked. I see Auryn narrow her eyes, put a hand up to shade her eyes, and starts to scan the crowd. After a few seconds, she spots us. First Garven, then me, standing once again. We lock eyes for the first time, and the tears break through like a breached dam.

She was walking arm against arm with the other girl before this moment, but much like myself with Kian, she quickly puts a few inches of distance between them. My heart sinks because I know what it means, but it soars because she is back. Auryn is back.

I am struggling to keep walking towards her as the guards continue to hold Garven and I back. Garven is pleading that he sees his sister, please let him say hello and give her a hug. The guard's refuse. Auryn takes notice that we're not allowed to approach the low metal fencing that meets in the middle of our two groups. She notices that I'm being held back, and her face turns from exuberance to worry.

I need to see her, to hug her, to tell her I love her. My eyes are filled with tears as I struggle against the guards. She mouths the words,

"It's okay, I'll find you," to me, and I nod.

I mouth back "I love you," to her, and she smiles.

"I…"

As she begins to respond, she enters a part of the ramp too low for me to see her any longer. After all these years, I have to wait even longer to see her say the words we used to so casually say to each other every day.

As I strain to find her through all the people cheering and raising their arms in the air, I lose her entirely. Who I can see out of the corner of my eye is Kian, and what Kian just saw must be heartbreaking for him.

"Kian, I'm sorry," I say.

He stares straight ahead, eyes glistening in the sunlight.

"Kian, please," I plead.

He keeps staring straight ahead, and a tear rolls down his left cheek.

"Kian, I…"

I trail off, not knowing where to even begin. I feel trapped between frantically trying to catch a glimpse of Auryn through the crowd and trying to get Kian to look at me.

I've messed up, that much I know, but I also never expected to be in this situation either.

The mood is uncomfortable for the rest of the walk. It's hard to feel hopeful and defeated, exuberant yet crushed, all within a few feet of each other. After a few more blocks of silent walking, we reach the building where we'll be held captive for a few days.

We enter the lobby, and new security guards come out to greet and process us.

"The next group is going to be held here as well, but they aren't allowed to be close to each other, alright?" Nix says to the security guard at the front desk. He nods that he understands, and Nix and his crew leave the building the same way we came in.

The lobby of this place is beautiful, not quite as intricate as City Hall in Buffalo, but really well maintained. It stretches in several different directions, with a long hallway down one side. The hallway has a series of rooms and a line of people formed outside. One of the new guards sees me looking and says,

"That's the line that gives you housing if you get to leave this place."

"If?" I ask.

He doesn't answer and swiftly looks away.

I share a look with Garven and Esha, this doesn't feel like a warm welcome. Esha moves closer to me and says,

"We'll be out of here in no time, don't you worry."

"I've waited three years for Auryn to come back, what's a few more days, I guess," I respond, trying desperately to keep my cool.

Once we're through processing, they bring me up, by myself, to my new room for the foreseeable future. A converted office with a bed and a singular chair is inside. It's actually not too bad, in the grand scheme of things.

Although I've only been awake a few hours, the anxiety that has come in waves over and over again has exhausted me. Not to mention how tired the medication makes me. I lay down on the hard bed and drift off to sleep once more.

THE EIGHTH DREAM

We are searching in an unfamiliar area. Esha, myself, and the others. I watch Mina as she picks up large stones and moves them out of the way. All around us, people are speaking in a mix of English and Spanish. I've picked up some Spanish over the years from Esha, so I can catch snippets and phrases I recognize.

"¿Podría ser? No, no hay manera."

While trying to focus on the hushed tones, Esha moves quickly towards something in the rubble. She starts tossing rocks and bricks all around, frantic with desperation. After a moment, she turns around, looks in our direction, and takes her pack off her back, removing some towels. As she bends down to grab whatever it is she's trying to grab, there is a voice that awakens me.

CHAPTER 9: ANOTHER REUNION

"I came as soon as I found out where they were keeping you. It took two days until anyone would tell me."

The voice hits me like the collapsing wall of a derelict factory. A voice I haven't heard in years, and even though it's a bit different now, my heart races hearing it.

I open my eyes and look towards the opening of my cell. I use the term loosely, since it's actually a decent office with a locked metal gate where a door would usually be. I'm sitting on a soft, comfortable, brown plush chair, the only one in the smallish 10'x12' room. There's a window where I can look out over a small part of Toronto. I'm only on the 4th or 5th floor, so I can't see much beyond the tall buildings that surround me.

Once the initial shock wears off, I stand up from the chair and run to the gate. Standing there, like she never left, is Auryn.

It's been close to three years since the last time I saw her. She's a little taller than before, a little more muscular too, and more beautiful than ever.

I try to say something, anything, to her but instead I just begin crying. I can't believe that the first time I am with her again, I'm trapped behind these bars. As I begin to feel like I'm collapsing in on myself, I see her hand reach through the bars. I grab it with mine and squeeze it tight, making sure that this isn't a dream, that this isn't in the future.

She smiles and brings her face right up against the bars, which are 4 or 5 inches apart. I let go of her hand and reach my hands out through the bars on each side of her head and hold her face for a moment. Then I lean in and kiss her. Even though it should have been difficult, kissing between the bars on a cell door was the easiest, lightest thing I've done in years.

My heart races, and I feel the tears well up again. Her lips as familiar as ever, the rhythm of our kiss as natural and easy as I remember. She stops kissing my lips and starts kissing the tears running down my cheeks. She makes an exaggerated "smooch" sound, which makes me laugh. Then she takes a step back and says,

"It's been awhile, hasn't it?"

I smile, look her directly in the eyes, and say,

"Just a minute or two."

After a few minutes of talking, she eventually sits on the floor outside my room, and I do the same inside the bars. It's like no time has passed at all. We talk about the colony and the trip, and I listen completely enthralled. She could always paint the brightest pictures with her words. I can vividly imagine the dome at Central Park, the gray hallways, and the night sky of a distant planet.

She's so confident while regaling me with all these tales of adventure. I could listen to her talk forever, watch as her eyes beam with excitement, see her lips alternating between moving rapidly, and not at all. As she continues though, I can't help but feel a pang of jealousy.

The last two and a half years here on planet Earth haven't been filled with exciting space adventures. They've been filled with betrayal, survival, and a steady dose of depression and anxiety. While I'm happy for her, and truly I am, it does feel unfair that because her parents were in a higher tax bracket than mine, she had adventures while I had near death experiences.

She must have noticed me in my own thoughts, because she stops talking. She raises an eyebrow and looks me in the eyes.

"Is something wrong, babe? Am I talking too much?" She asks.

"No, I love listening to you talk. I'm sorry, it's nothing," I say back to her.

"Come on, you can't do that. We haven't talked in almost three years and you're going to shut down on me?" Auryn says.

In the past, this was the point where I would tell her not to worry about it. It's just a me problem, and it's something I would sort out on my own, but just like she isn't the same Auryn anymore, I am not the same Finley, either.

"Look, I am genuinely so happy for you. Your experience sounds amazing, and I don't know a single person in the world who deserves it more than you," I start.

"But the last few years for me have been hell. Worse than hell. I have looked death in the eyes and blinked second. I've seen sadness and heartbreak so intense I didn't know it was possible. I've seen the hope of people rebuilding, and the soul crushing defeat of those closest to us literally ditching me on the side of the road, leaving me to the scavengers. There have been very few moments that I would consider good, let alone happy."

I pause, collecting my thoughts.

"I am not mad at you, or your stories, but I am mad at the circumstances this world has given me."

"Finley, I'm so sorry. I didn't mean to…"

I know she's sorry, I can feel it in my bones. Ever since I came to this place, I can tell when someone is lying or telling the truth just by listening to their voice and closing my eyes. Before she could continue, I cut her off.

"I'm not asking for, nor deserving of, your apologies, Auryn. We were kids, neither of us had a choice. I just need you to know that I'm different now, and I know you're different too, and within that difference, some days are going to be hard for us."

She looks at me for a moment. I tense up because I know the old Auryn, the only Auryn I've ever known, would get defensive over this. She would tell me how hard it was to be on the ship. She would tell me about the stresses of trying to save humanity. That any second, the most minor thing going wrong could have meant the end for her and tens of thousands of other people.

She would be right, of course, but I could still feel an anger bubbling up just thinking about it.

"I'm sorry that I've been here, visiting you for a while, and didn't even ask you what you've been through. That was selfish of me, and that's something I've been trying to work on. What you've been through sounds horrible, and whenever you're ready to talk about it, I want to be there for you," she says.

Not that she would lie to me, but I somehow know, deep inside me, that she means it.

I once again reach my arm through the bar and grab her hand. I lace my fingers through hers and give a gentle squeeze. Slowly I lower my forehead towards the bars and rest it gently on them, as Auryn does the same from the other side. Our skin barely touches as we sit there, in silence, for a few moments.

Afterwards, Auryn gently lifts her head away and says,

"We're only allowed a few minutes for visitation, but I'll be back as soon as they allow me. Do you have anyone here that I could talk to, to maybe find out more about what's going on?"

"I think everyone I came with is also in one of these rooms somewhere. It's Garven and Esha, of course, but also Kian, Lyra, Etta and Evrim. I don't know the last three all that well except Lyra saved my life after I stabbed a guy," I respond.

I know I didn't have to put the stabbing in the description, but I got such a kick out of how the rest of the group reacted, I wanted to feel that rush again.

Auryn's eyes widened after I said it, and she says,

"You really *have* changed."

She pushes her face up against the bars one more time, and we kiss briefly. My heart flutters like I'm 15 all over again.

I walk back over to the chair and slump down, somehow both more hopeful than ever, and simultaneously more depressed than I've been in months.

As Auryn walks down the hallway and back towards the stairwell, she hears a voice from a few doors past the stairs.

"So, you're the one Finley was trying to meet here, huh?" The voice says.

Auryn looks towards the direction the voice is coming from.

"Are you Lyra?" Auryn asks back.

"Ha. That lucky loser? No, I am not Lyra. My name is Luna. They didn't happen to mention me, huh?" Luna says.

Auryn hesitates for a moment, then walks over towards Luna's door. She peers in and immediately notices the brightest, most white-blonde hair she's ever seen. Otherwise,

Luna looks a little rough around the edges. Her face smeared with dirt, her clothes ripped and tattered.

"I wonder what else they aren't telling you," Luna says while grinning directly at Auryn.

"What's that supposed to mean? You could be anyone, or a total nobody," Auryn responds.

"First off, I'm definitely a somebody," Luna says, looking agitated while standing up from her chair. A chair which looks very similar to the one Finley had in their room as well.

"And secondly, I know Finley, maybe even better than you."

It's now Auryn's turn to be agitated. Luna continues,

"I'm guessing Finley didn't tell you about the dreams, and how they come true?"

"You are a nobody," Auryn snaps back, "that's old news."

"Well, the new news is that Finley is the Stonekeeper. Did they happen to mention that?" Luna replies.

Auryn stares at Luna for a moment. Mina used that same term when they were talking about her ability to dream the future on Earth.

"Ah, so they don't tell you everything. Funny," Luna says, a smile slowly creeping across her face.

As Auryn is thinking of something to say, she hears footsteps from the stairwell. She turns around to look and one of the guards is here to patrol the floor.

"Hey," he says, "that's not the person you're supposed to be here to see."

"Sorry, my mistake, I was just trying to find my brother, Garven. Do you know where he is?" Auryn says back.

"I think you've been here long enough. Your time is up, so head on out," the guard responds.

She thinks about arguing, but she's not sure how long either of them are going to be in here and doesn't want to lose her visiting privileges. Instead, she quickly brushes by him and walks down the five flights of stairs and out the building, her mind bouncing back and forth between missing her brother and wondering what Luna meant.

As she exits, waiting outside for her is Mina. They walk through the streets and back to their apartment building in mostly silence, passing by skyscrapers is varying degrees of decay, and occasionally missing roads they were probably supposed to take. After several blocks of walking, Mina says to Auryn,

"So, how was the kiss?"

Auryn freezes in place, as if she were caught in the act itself. She stumbles over her words for a moment before finally blurting out an especially loud,

"What?"

Auryn is rarely, if ever, speechless, and her face turns a deep shade of red.

"I mean, after a couple years apart, it had to have been pretty dang good, right? The stuff of romance novels probably," Mina says, shrugging her shoulders.

"How do you even know we kissed?" Auryn says, panicking.

"Oh come ON, Auryn. Young love, torn away from each other, lost for years? I'm surprised you had all your clothes on correctly when you came back out!" Mina says, laughing as she does.

"There were bars on her door! We didn't… or couldn't have… or," she's stuttering as she talks.

Mina is nearly doubled over in laughter. Tears start streaming down her cheeks as she gasps for air a little.

"Are you enjoying this?" Auryn then asks, incredulous.

"Yeah, obviously," Mina says between breaths.

"I told you on the ship, I'm not expecting us to get married and live together with just each other until the end of our days. Sure, I still wanna be with you, but I also hope that you experienced a hell of a kiss back there. Those two things don't have to be mutually exclusive," Mina says.

"I," Auryn pauses, "I always thought they did."

"Well now you know. So, get to it," Mina replies.

"Get to what?" Auryn asks.

"Telling me how the kiss was!" Mina says.

Auryn stares at her for a moment, trying to study her face, understand what this all means, before responding with,

"Absolutely not."

They walk back to their apartment in silence, Auryn feeling overwhelmed, and Mina feeling completely and utterly amused.

CHAPTER 10: A DAUGHTER

The next day, I get another visitor to my cell. As they approach, they knock on the bars to get my attention. It takes a moment to register because I'm looking out the window at the small slice of Toronto I can see. It's been three days inside here, and I'm growing ever more frustrated.

"Finley, right?" the voice says.

I sigh, assuming they're here to take me to the bathroom or give me lunch.

"Yeah?" I respond.

"It's nice to meet you. My name is Archie, and I'm here to take you to a meeting downstairs," she tells me.

Archie. That name sounds so familiar, where have I heard that before?

"A couple of people here would like to talk to you. If it makes you feel any better, this is usually the last thing you have to do before they assign you an apartment and you're free to go," she says, with a helpful smile on her face.

"Well, that's good news, I guess. Are any of the other people I came with going to be at this meeting?" I ask.

"I'm not really allowed to talk about anyone else who's in here. They really frown upon it," she says.

She takes a key and unlocks the door. It swings inward towards the room. As she walks in and I can get a better look at her, she looks so familiar.

"Have we met before?" I ask.

"I… I don't believe so. I've been in Toronto for a few years now, and you just got here," she responds.

The feeling I know her keeps nagging at me as we walk out of the room, make a right, and head down the hallway towards the stairs. It's midday, and the light from the windows floods into the hallways, making them bright, if not a little drab.

"So, what made you come to Toronto?" I ask, attempting to make small talk on the way.

"Well, my ma and I were living in a little shack outside Hamilton, and it was just so lonely, I decided I wanted to come to Toronto. Heard most people were headin' this way anyways," she says.

It clicks. I cannot believe it. By all accounts, the population of Toronto has grown over the past few years since the ships took off. The best estimates I've heard is that it's gone from about 80,000 people to around 100,000 people. What are the odds that I run into her here?

"You said your name was Archie, right?" I ask, still not believing that's what I heard a few moments ago.

She looks at me with one eyebrow higher than the other, head tilted slightly, and answers,

"Yeah."

"Is your mom Lorena?" I ask.

She stops immediately and turns directly at me. We're on a landing between the second and third floor, and blood has disappeared from her cheeks. I could swear she's seen a ghost.

"How…" She pauses.

"How do you know that?" she says in utter disbelief.

"It's a long story, but I met her on the way here. Even stayed the night. She practically made me," I smile as I share the memory with her.

"That can't be possible. She was living in the middle of nowhere. I didn't think anyone would find her, unless it was someone you didn't want to run into. For the last year I've told myself there is no way she made it. With all the Raiders and other horrible people making their way up here, there was no way…" She trails off as she says it.

Staring off into the middle distance, she stops talking for 15 seconds. I stand there quietly, giving her the time to process with this new information.

"How did you meet her? Like, how did you find her? She was building this defense system thing for the cabin we were living in as I was leaving. Seemed like she definitely wouldn't have talked to a stranger wandering by," Archie asks.

"Of course. Well, I had just hurt my ankle being chased and nearly killed by Raiders, and I just so happened to stumble upon her cabin while trying to stay far off the roads. When I saw it, I was desperate and hungry, and I ended up watching her through the window of her cabin. I'll admit, it was weird, what I was doing. I was just hoping she was going to throw out her food scraps and I could take them. But after a while she invited me in, and she fed me some veggie and potato soup."

"She just let you in? Seems like she's getting soft in her older age." Archie says.

"Well, she pointed a bow and arrow at me first," I blurt out.

Archie chuckles and says,

"That sounds like Ma. I can't believe it. I really just can't believe it," Archie says.

"Is her soup still as good as it used to be?" She then asks me.

"Might be the best food I've ever tasted, if I'm being honest," I reply.

We start taking the stairs again and keep talking about her mom on the way, before we exit the first-floor staircase, she turns and hugs me tight. The exact kind of hug I had hoped to give Auryn when I had first seen her.

"It's okay if you still don't want to tell me," I say, "but are the other people I came with getting out?"

She looks around the stairwell and listens to see if anyone else is walking down before responding.

"Yeah, actually. Well, one of them. Kian, the tall guy you came in with is in the meeting room right now. He asked that the two of you get seen and let out together," Archie replies.

I was about to ask her about Esha and Garven as well, but she opened the door into the lobby and quickly walked through. As we pass by the front desk that I had just seen a few days prior, one of the security guard's glares at me. After I pass him, I turn back to look, and he's still staring, this time making a small note in his notebook as I get further away.

Archie then leads me to a room with a large old conference table in the middle.

"We're here. Please head on in and see the council. Thank you again for everything," Archie says to me.

I smile and tell her it was no problem at all.

I was about to take another step away and she quietly says,

"Wait,"

So, I do.

"Please be careful of the man with the dark black hair in there. I'm… I'm not supposed to say anything, but he belongs to a dangerous organization and—"

"The Green Cloaks?" I respond.

"So, you do know of them. Yes, the Green Cloaks. There are rumblings that they're looking for someone who looks a lot like you. I just have to tell you, you shouldn't trust them," she whispers, and quickly turns and walks away.

First the Raiders, now the Green Cloaks? Can't we all just live peacefully for a bit? I think to myself.

As I step into the room, I see Kian looking up at me. The last time we were together, I had mouthed the words "I love you" to Auryn, and he was, understandably, shaken up by that, so I didn't know how he would react to seeing me again.

I shouldn't have worried, as his beautiful dark brown eyes stared straight at me, and a smile spread across his face.

"Hey, uh, thanks. Also, I'm sorry about—" I say as he cuts me off.

"No worries. Let's get out of here and we can figure it all out," he says.

On the other side from where we are sitting, across the big table, are three stern looking people. The woman on the left is mid-50s, graying shoulder length hair, with a worn blue blazer on. Next to her, sitting in the middle, is a younger woman, probably in her late 20s or early 30s, blond hair back in a ponytail, and wearing a simple button up shirt, gray in color.

To their right, a stern looking man, mid 40s, with short black hair, looking impatient.

"Kian, Finley, we're going to be asking you some questions, and we're going to need you to tell us the truth," the man says. I can tell by the tone of their voices how serious this is.

After 45 minutes of intense questioning about how we got here, who we came with, why we're here, who are Garven and Esha to us, and who is Luna, they left the room to talk for a few minutes.

"You think we're going to get out of here?" Kian asks.

"Your guess is as good as mine," I say back.

"I'm really glad to see you again," Kian says after a few seconds of silence.

"I'm really, really glad to see you too," I say, meaning every word.

As we smile at each other, the door swings open and the man with jet black hair and a permanently annoyed face enters back in.

"You two are both free to go," he says.

"We'll have Kian leave the room first, I just have a few things I'd like to ask you, Finley," he says in a way that feels like there's little room for argument.

Kian looks towards me with some apprehension, but I nod, letting him know it's fine. He stands up from his seat and walks out the same door I entered through a while ago. Behind him, the door closes, echoing loudly as it does.

"So, one of our sisters mentioned to me that you might have some… special abilities," he says, staring daggers at me.

I sit there in silence. What sister? How could he have known?

"I'm not sure what you're talking about," I finally say.

"Thats not what Luna told us when she arrived. She actually thinks you might be pretty powerful," he replies.

Luna. Am I cursed with her trying to ruin my life at every turn?

"I think your friend Luna is actually something of a *lunatic*, so maybe don't believe everything she has to say," I snap back.

"She said you'd say that. But even here, across this table, the angrier you get the more the green ring around your eye glows. I think she may be right about you," he says.

I stare back at him, and firmly say,

"If there's nothing else, I'd like to leave now."

"Yes, that's fine, but don't expect this to be the last time you see me," he replies.

I place both hands on the table and shove myself upwards and out of the seat, glaring at him as I turn my head away. I stomp towards the door and shove it open, only for it to nearly hit Kian as it swings out.

"Whoa, what happened in there?" He asks.

"I'm never going to be able to escape Luna and her merry band of cultists," I reply as I keep my hurried pace.

Kian jogs to catch up as we once again walk through the lobby of this giant building, making a beeline towards the front doors.

"Wait, we have to get our housing accommodations," Kian yells towards me, and I stop in my tracks.

As much as I hate crying in public, the tears begin to flow, and my heart rate quickens. I begin rubbing my hands on the sides of my hips, partially to take the sweat off of them, partially to feel any kind of tactile stimulation.

Kian comes up from behind me, places an arm around the middle of my back, and steers me towards a hallway with considerably less people in it.

"Here, sit. The cold floor should help," he says.

My legs begin trembling underneath me as I try to lower myself to the ground. He grabs my upper arm and helps support me on my way down. Once I reach the floor, I place both hands flat on it, and its cool temperature feels much better against my skin. It is not lost on me that this also happened the first time we met.

"I know things feel overwhelming, but they're going to get better," Kian says.

"I've been saying that every day of my life since Auryn left. Since then, my parents have died, I've almost died, and I have someone out to kill me at this very moment. What if it doesn't ever get better, Kian? What if it just keeps getting worse until we give up or give in?" I say.

"Do you really believe that?" He asks.

"I don't know what I believe," I snap back.

I know I shouldn't snap at him; he's only trying to be helpful. The guilt rushes over me, now in a tug-of-war with my panic. If I really am this powerful being they talk about, then they're screwed because I'm going to be the worst one ever.

Kian lowers himself to the floor to sit next to me, but instead of continuing to try to make me feel better, he places a hand on my thigh, leans back against the wall, and sits with me.

I try to do my breathing exercises, and they help a little. I then look over to Kian, still not looking at me, and say,

"I'm a difficult person to exist with, and I understand if you don't want to stick around. I don't mean to snap at you and be rude to you, but sometimes it's just the way I am. That's no excuse, and I'm sorry."

He looks me directly in the eyes and says,

"It's true, you can be very difficult. It's also true you shouldn't snap at me," with a level of frankness I am not used to.

"But you're also a million other things I love and appreciate."

"Love?" I ask.

"There are things about you that I absolutely love, yes, but I'm not telling you I love you yet, you weirdo. I've known you like, a month," he says, smiling.

"I don't know, it doesn't seem that unfathomable that one of us could love the other," I say, trailing off towards the end.

The silence was only a second or two, probably, but it might as well have been years. My mind has never raced faster. He needs to say something, or do something, immediately, otherwise I'm going to melt into this floor and disappear entirely off this plane of existence.

Why am I freaking out? I didn't tell him I love him; I just said it wouldn't be so crazy if I did.

He removes his hand from my thigh. Great, I've scared him away. The yelling and snapping didn't do it, but this did? Is he so afraid of his feelings he can't handle the possibility that we might love each other someday? Well fine, good, I'm glad he's going to walk away. I don't want to be with someone like that anyways.

As I'm spiraling, I feel his hand on my shoulder, then it smoothly moves across my back so it's on the other shoulder, and his arm is wrapped around me. He pulls me in close to him, side by side, and says,

"No, Fin, it wouldn't be so crazy that we would love each other," he pauses, "someday."

CHAPTER 11: CELLMATES CHAT

"You think Fin and Kian got out yet?" Esha says while sitting next to the barred door to her office cell.

"Who freakin' knows, Fin always seems to have a good luck charm on 'em somewhere," responds Garven from the door right next to Esha's.

"Always? Not sure they had it on them when they were left for dead on the side of the road," Esha reminds Garven.

"Sure, but they made it out alright, didn't they?" Replies Garven.

They sit in silence for a minute before Esha says,

"Man, I gotta get outta here, I feel like I'm gonna lose it soon."

"Yup," replies Garven.

Silence resumes once again, with Esha daydreaming about a crazy dream she had last night.

CHAPTER 12: TWO PATHS

Eventually, we got off the floor, headed to the housing department, and received our accommodations. After checking with some superiors, they allowed us to be on the same floor as Auryn and her friend Mina. We also checked to see if Esha and Garven had been let go, but they wouldn't tell us. Kian and I decided that we'll take tonight to settle in, then go visit them tomorrow afternoon.

As we step out of the building, I hear the voice again. I turn to see Auryn, this time with no bars between us. Standing there in the golden sunshine, smiling from ear to ear. For a moment she's all I see in the world. A wide grin creeps across my face, and I feel tears beginning to well up in my eyes. I run up to her and as I do, I become aware that her travel companion is standing right behind her, but for a brief moment I do not care.

Auryn, myself, Kian, and Mina are all here, on a sidewalk in an unfamiliar city, meeting for the first time. It feels like my emotions change each second I stand here. One second gratitude, the next jealousy. One second hope, the next dread.

I hug Auryn with both arms, squeezing her across the back, my mouth close to her ear, I whisper,

"I've missed you more than words can describe."

She hugs me tighter and says,

"I know, little penguin. I know."

We embrace for 20 full seconds before remembering that yes, other people are around. As we step back, our hands gently run across each other. I want to grab hers but instead let them fall to our sides.

"Oh, um, Auryn, this is Kian. Kian, this is Auryn," I say.

Kian takes several steps forward and reaches out his hand. Auryn grabs it to shake.

"It's great to finally meet you, I've heard so much about you," he says.

"Oh, have you now?" Auryn says, eyebrows raised.

Kian lets out an awkward chuckle.

"Finley, Kian, this is Mina. Mina, this is Fin and Kian," Auryn says.

"I've also heard a lot about you, Finley," Mina says while smiling.

She better have, I think to myself before trying to fix my thoughts.

"It's really nice to meet you, Mina," I lie and reach my hand out to shake hers.

I can't help but feel a little annoyed that my first meeting with Auryn had bars between us, and the second has this person I don't know here. As the jealousy infiltrates my brain, I remember that I, too, brought someone new to the party, and I should keep reminding myself of that.

"So," Auryn says, "this is even more awkward than I thought it was going to be. If you want, we can show you both the way to the apartment building."

"I think that's a great idea," says Kian, with a forced cheerfulness in his voice.

We walk the streets of Toronto for the first time as free people, Kian and me. All four of us leave plenty of space between each other, and as we do it means taking up almost the entire double width sidewalk. I make it pretty obvious that I'm not from here, or at least haven't lived here long, by constantly looking up and around at all the giant buildings.

Cleveland was a pretty tall city, buildings wise, while Buffalo didn't have the height, but had a lot of beautiful old buildings. Neither were like this though. There are dozens, and maybe hundreds, of giant buildings as we walk. Looking down different streets, it feels endless. How did so many people live in a single city like this?

"I can't even imagine all these buildings being filled with people, and shops, and things," Mina says.

Stay out of my brain, lady, I think to myself.

"It's crazy. They say millions of people used to live here," I instead reply.

"I believe it, there must be hundreds of apartments in each and every one of these huge buildings," says Kian.

"I wish I could have seen it all at its peak. Clubs and restaurants and sports and stuff," Auryn says, "my parents said the old videos of it were pretty spectacular."

I nod along with everyone else, and silence begins to take over the group again. It really must have been something. Would I want to experience it, though? I don't know, considering how overwhelmed I get when there's nine or ten people around. Being in a place this big, filled with so many people, feels a little terrifying.

Mina breaks the silence.

"So, how was getting into Toronto, was the security tight?" She asks.

"Yeah, super tight. Plus I'm apparently being stalked by a group called The Green Cloaks, so that's an added bonus," I respond.

As I do, Auryn whips her head around to look at Mina. Afterwards, she turns to me.

"Did you say Green Cloaks?" She asks.

"Yeah, one of the leaders of Buffalo who tried to kill me on the way up here is apparently one of them. Why?"

"My family told me about them a long time ago. Said they were zealots, and very dangerous," Mina replies.

"Well, I think your family is right," I say back.

Silence overtakes the group again. For me it's the exhaustion of it all.

We turn left once, and then right a block or two down. It's hard to tell how far we've gone since each block is so gigantic. When we finally reach our building, I begin feeling anxious.

Are Auryn and I going to talk separately? Will Kian want to talk about everything that happened? Is Mina going to be here all the freaking time?

I then realize I'm thinking on much too small a scale.

Is Garven or Auryn going to go back on the ships to the colony? Am I? What about Kian? What's Esha going to do? Are we all going to split up?

I don't want to split up. I want to be where all of my people are. I just finally got everyone back, and in like, 6 months, we might have to separate.

Nothing about this is fair. One step forward and what feels like a thousand steps back. I already had a panic attack like an hour ago, but my body feels ready for another one.

Let go or be dragged.

Let go or be dragged.

I close my eyes for a moment, and I say the words over and over again. Suddenly, I feel my left hand being grabbed. They squeeze rhythmically, but gently. It's Auryn. Even after all this time she can recognize the early signs.

As I'm about to open my eyes and smile at her, a hand is placed firmly on my right shoulder. It rubs my shoulder and upper arm gently for a moment. It's Kian. I open my eyes and look quickly back and forth between the two of them before staring straight ahead and blushing. In my peripheral vision, I see them suddenly look at each other, then Kian yanks his hand away as Auryn does the same.

I stand there, blushing, looking straight ahead, and unsure of what to say or do. From the awkward silence, Mina starts laughing. First as a chuckle, then as a hearty laugh.

"Woo, boy, looks like you all have some stuff to figure out," she then says.

She's right, of course, but that doesn't make me any less annoyed by it.

We enter the building and to the left is the staircase. We take it slowly, and I count, like I always do, each step as I go up. It's not something I do consciously most of the time, although the first few times up and down I tend to think about it more often.

After many minutes of boring gray concrete walls, metal doors to floors we don't live on, and an occasional dead electrical wire hanging haphazardly from the ceiling, we reach our floor. Dusty windows at the end of the hallway barely allow the rays of sunshine to filter in.

"Mina's right, we should all have a sit down and talk about, well, all this," Auryn says. She swirls her finger around a few times as she says it.

"Yea, that's probably right," I say solemnly.

"It's been a long day, though. Maybe we all head back to our rooms and recoup in the late morning. Maybe take a trip down to the food disbursement area and talk," Auryn says.

"That sounds nice," I reply.

With that, I lean into her and give her a kiss on the cheek. She turns, along with Mina, and walks down the hallway. Out of the corner of my eye I look to see if they enter the same apartment, and much to my delight, they don't.

I grab the key to unlock the door.

"So,"

I'm startled before realizing that Kian is still standing there. I jump slightly but compose myself quickly.

"Did you just forget I was here?" he asks.

"Of course not," I lie.

He looks sad for a moment, so I lean in and give him a kiss on the cheek.

"So, no spending the night together I guess?" He asks.

"Not tonight, no. I'll see you in the morning, though," I say while smiling at him.

He nods, smiles at me, and walks to his own apartment. He slides his key into the handle, opens the door, and smiles at me again before walking in and closing it behind him.

I stand in the now empty, dimly lit hallway of the apartment building and briefly look in each direction. Two paths have merged and where they will split off again, I have no idea.

THE NINTH DREAM

I am startled off the couch by the sound of knocking at my door. It takes me a moment to realize I am inside a dream, and once I do, I look around the room to notice how identical it is to the room in real life.

One couple inches-wide, nearly round hole in the wall next to the door. The couch with a small tear on the cushion to the left. I look behind me and see the kitchenette with an old metal countertop, sheen diminished and scratched a long time ago.

The knock happens again, and I finally walk towards the door. Once I get there, I peek through the eye hole. I see three people standing there, all of them wearing green robes and hoods, so it's impossible to see their faces.

I go to open the door, and instead darkness engulfs the opening. Wind begins to whip into the room, and I can't keep my eyes open. I hold onto the door handle as I'm being shoved backwards by the wind. Through the noise, I hear a voice, or more accurately, hundreds of voices, all saying one thing in unison.

"This is only the beginning, Finley. I am waiting for you."

The desire to follow the voices is undeniable. In the dream, it's my singular focus. I yearn for the voices, lust for the voices. I cannot describe the pull I have toward them. I don't know what they are, but I know I need to meet them.

CHAPTER 13: A MEETING

I am startled off the couch by the sound of knocking at my door. It takes me a moment to realize I am outside a dream, and once I do, I look around the room to notice how identical it is to the room in dream life.

A couple inch, nearly round hole in the wall next to the door. The couch with a small tear on the cushion to the left. I look behind me and see the kitchenette, with an old metal countertop, sheen diminished a long time ago.

The knock happens again, and I finally walk towards the door. Once I get there, I peek through the eye hole. I see three people standing there, all of them wearing green robes and hoods, so it's impossible to see their faces.

Wait, do all the Green Cloaks literally wear green cloaks? They can't really be that obvious, right? I think to myself.

After chaining the door so no one could barge in, I open it the eight or nine inches that the chain allowed and peek out. One of the three cloaked people, the one closest to the door, looks up at me. I can now see her face.

She has blue eyes so light they're almost white, with a green ring around the center, and blonde hair down to her chin.

She's no more than five feet tall, and underneath the large, flowing fabric of the cloak, you can tell she's small. It seems purposeful that they've sent her to talk to me, so that I don't feel intimidated.

"Hello Finley, my name is Colere. We've heard so much about you," she says, smiling excitedly. She continues,

"We're sorry if this is a bad time, but we were hoping you would come with us, we'd like to ask you some questions, but I'm sure you knew that already."

For a moment, I say nothing. I continue to look at Colere, and then both of the two still cloaked figures.

"I would consider it, on three conditions," I finally say.

"Of course, what are the conditions?" Colere asks.

"First, that I can bring someone with me, for safety."

"Of course," she responds while smiling warmly.

"Secondly, I will not go anywhere that sociopath Luna is," I say.

"From what I know, sister Luna is still in the holding cells. But no matter, she won't be anywhere near where we're heading," she replies.

"Good. Thirdly, I want to see the faces of the two people behind you," I ask.

She stops looking at me and looks down at the floor. Her lips purse and it looks like she's concentrating hard. She looks back up at me and speaks.

"We would really rather not. Most of our members' identities are hidden, and we're not sure you are who others say you are. Until that time, we would prefer not to reveal any more of our members than necessary."

"Well then, I wish you the best of luck. It was nice to meet you," I respond back and close the door.

Once the door clicked shut, I could feel the adrenaline rush through my body. I don't particularly like confrontation, and after that unsettling argument with the guy at the jail building, I don't know who among the Green Cloaks to trust, if any of them.

As I take a step away from the now closed door, there is a light tap on it once again. I turn around, take a deep breath in, and make sure the chain is still attached. I open the door again to find a second cloaked individual has taken their hood off.

He's older, probably in his 50s. His short brown hair is almost entirely gray on the sides, He's a little taller than Colere, around 5'6, with broad shoulders and a wide chin. Strong, for sure.

"As you can see, we're more than willing to compromise, Finley. We're not trying to alarm you or scare you off. It's just that, much like you like to keep some of your secrets, we like to keep some of ours as well. I hope that by having Zev show you his face as well, you can begin to trust us a little more?" Colere says.

"'Zev,'" I respond, "that name means 'Wolf.' Was that your birth-given name, or something that the Green Cloaks decided to give you?"

At the mention of Green Cloaks, Zev shoots a concerned look at Colere. I've struck a nerve. It wasn't intentional, but it is interesting.

"We prefer not to use the term 'Green Cloaks,' Finley. People use it in such a spiteful way. Those of us who willingly use the term tend to be zealots. Unfortunately, every group has them. Also no, Zev was not his birth name, he chose it for himself. We believe in choice," Colere says again.

"Does Zev get the opportunity to speak, or do only you get to talk about the multitude of choices Zev is allowed?" I ask loudly, issuing what is, essentially, an immediate challenge.

She turns around partially to face him, and nods.

"Everard was my birth name," he starts, "but when I came to Toronto and was saved by the Followers of the Five Stones, they allowed me to begin again, which allowed me to also choose a new name for myself."

I nod at him, and he pulls his emerald green hood back over his face. I look back towards Colere and stare at her for a minute.

"One more question," I say. "What was the deal with the guy at the jail yesterday? He was confrontational and aggressive. Really soured me on you all."

She nods, solemnly.

"Like I said before, every organization has some loose cannons. He's actually no longer a member of The Followers, after several previous incidents. He and a couple of other rage-filled knuckleheads have formed their own group, and we don't like to associate with them. I do hope you accept my apology," she explains.

I stand there, only a thin sliver of my head and body visible to them. What she said seemed reasonable enough, and a tough story to come up with on the spot if she was looking to lie. Plus, my gut tells me very strongly when I think someone is lying.

When I blink, my eyes stay shut a half second longer than normal, and in that time, I hear them again; the voices.

"This is your opportunity, Finley. Seize it," they say.

I open my eyes.

"Okay, I'll come along. I have to be back in a few hours though, so it can't take too long," I say.

"That will be no problem at all," she replies.

"I'd prefer if you meet me downstairs, in the lobby of the building. I want to get changed, and grab a friend before I come down," I tell Colere.

"That'll also be no problem. We are in a bit of a hurry though, so please don't take too long," she replies.

With that, she places her hood back over her face, and the three of them turn towards the direction of the stairs. I turn around and walk into my bedroom to grab a pair of pants that can conceal my small knife. I have vowed that I'll never walk into an unfamiliar situation without protection again.

After changing, I leave my apartment and lock the door behind me. Normally in this circumstance I would ask Esha to join me, but she and Garven aren't out of jail yet, which I'm hoping to help take care of today.

I would also normally ask Auryn, but I'm not really sure what's going on with us right now. Would she want to invite Mina? I'm only allowed to bring one person, and the thought of having to explain that annoys me greatly. I decide to knock on Kian's door. He's been through the fire with me, and I trust him without a doubt.

I rap my knuckles on the door several times, and after a few seconds, I can hear a groggy,

"Coming!" From behind the door.

I hear him at the door, and then some silence. I assume he's looking through the peephole. Another second later, I hear him fumbling for the handle, and the click of the door unlocking.

He opens it with one hand while wiping the sleep out of his eyes with the other. They're glazed over, and he's got a goofy smile on his face. I missed him the past few days. I've been so used to walking and holding hands, talking and laughing, that him not being a part of my life feels weird.

"Hey, so, I had a dream last night where the Green Cloaks knocked on my door and invited me to come with them," I say.

"Ew. No thanks," Kian replies, making a disgusted face while saying it.

"Yeah, normally I'd agree, but as I opened the door to my place, everything became dark, and voices were whispering to me," I respond.

"Wait, in real life or in the dream?" Kian asks.

I stare at him for a moment, tilting my head slightly as if to say,

Seriously, dude?

"Dream, yes, got it. Sorry. Continue," he says.

"The voice, or voices I guess I could say, said that it was only the beginning for me," I say.

"Weird. Is it the type of dream you think is going to come true soon?" He asks.

"It already did. I was woken up by them a few minutes ago," I respond,

"So, the hallway DID open up into a big, swirling blackhole?" He says with an extreme level of unearned confidence.

"What? No, just... can you please shut up for a second?" I ask, trying to use the friendliest tone I can muster.

"Normally I wouldn't even think about going. Especially after what happened yesterday as we were leaving the jail. But those voices. They were calling to me in a way that makes me think I have to follow. So, I was wondering if you would come with me, maybe as a little bit of protection or, I don't know, strength in numbers or whatever."

"Oh. Yeah of course. I'm always here for you Fin. Did you, um, already ask Auryn or anything?"

"No, I came to you first, Kian," I respond.

A smile creeps across his face until he is beaming. The tiredness is now fully gone, replaced with energy and excitement.

"Yeah, of course! Let me just grab a few things and we can head out. Wanna come in for a sec?" He asks.

"No, that's okay, they seem to be in a rush. Just make sure one of those things you grab is a knife, alright?" I say.

"You're acting like this is my first time going into an unknown and weird situation, Fin," he says while smiling.

Kian then closes the door, and I wait in the hallway for him. While this is a much nicer building than the one we were living in while in Cleveland, the longer I'm here the more things wrong I notice with it. This hallway, for example, has soft spots in the floor that are going to eventually cave in.

It's also very dark. Since the entire building is powered by solar panels and small wind turbines, and there are a couple hundred people living here, they only have light bulbs every 30 feet in the hallways. If your room is near a working light, like mine is, it feels considerably safer. But here, outside Kian's room, it feels like things are moving in the shadows, even as the sun illuminates the day.

The door swings open and startles me. Kian walks out wearing a knife in its sheath strapped directly to the waistband of his pants.

"What good is that going to do if they confiscate it at the doors?" I ask.

"You should know me better than that! It's my decoy knife. This cheap thing will break in two the minute it gets struck by anything halfway durable. I found it a long time ago while living in Buffalo and it's just for show. Don't worry, my real knife is hidden," he answers.

"Don't worry," he says to me. I'm about to walk into what is, as far as I know, a strange cult, and he's telling me not to worry.

We walk down the hallway and reach the stairs entrance. The 15 flights of stairs will make sure that I stay in good shape while I'm here. As we take a slow pace, Kian asks me what I think they want with me.

"Well," I say, "obviously they know about my dreaming, but they mentioned that they are the Followers of the Five Stones. I've never heard the name before, have you??

Kian thinks for a moment.

"Hmm, it sounds familiar. I think I might have heard Luna mention it to someone else. I can't be sure though," he responds.

Even just hearing her name sends shivers down my spine. I hope she's still locked up somewhere.

"Well, whatever it is they want with you, I'll be there to protect you. You know I'm always here for you, right?" Kian asks.

For a moment, I don't respond. I noticed that on the tenth floor, the amount of steps is one less than all the other floors. All the other floors have 22 steps between them. Between floor 11 and floor 10 there are only 21 steps. Did I miscount? Should I turn around and recount? Is it a permanent change? I don't think so, when I counted yesterday, I thought I remembered all of them being 22.

Finally, my brain registers what Kian has asked me.

"Thanks again for coming with me. I know we haven't been able to talk much since all the commotion happened when we arrived, but I'm really glad you're here," I say.

"I'm really glad I'm here too, Fin," he replies.

I like that Kian knows me well enough that when I don't answer something right away, he doesn't have to hurry and ask again. It's one of the few things that annoyed me about Auryn. She sometimes thought I was ignoring her, but really, I just got so far into my own mind that I didn't notice the things happening right around me.

By the time we get down to the lobby, Colere is pacing back and forth. I walk up to the three of them and introduce Kian.

"We know who he is. It's a pleasure to meet you Kian," Colere says, "we hope you understand that when we get to our destination, you will not be allowed to bring that knife in with you."

"Of course, I totally understand," he replies. After they turn away, he winks at me, proud of tricking them, no doubt.

We leave our apartment building and head east. A lot of the current population lives in the grouping of 120-year-old high rise apartment buildings close to the old water line of Lake Ontario. There are dozens of buildings, all at least 40 stories tall, and all in surprisingly good shape. I would be genuinely surprised if we had to walk very far to get where we're going.

Even in the shadows of all the buildings, it's hot today. Hotter than it's been the last several days. When the sun peeks through the buildings and directly onto my shoulders, they're hot to the touch almost immediately. After a few blocks, I wish more than anything that I had brought water.

"So, where are we actually heading to? Is it close? I'm getting kind of thirsty," I ask.

Unsurprisingly, it's Colere who answers.

"We're actually very close. You've probably walked by the building already. Once there, we can get the both of you some water."

After a few more blocks of walking, we turn left. The old street sign is still standing, and through the rust and dirt it says, "Church Street." The original people who named the streets were literal, it seems. A minute later we're in front of a gorgeous old building.

"This, my friends, is the Cathedral Church of Saint James," says Colere.

Kian and I are both impressed with how well maintained the building is. The entire front is symmetrical. It has three large windows on both the left and right side, each at least two stories tall. They look like slightly melted candles in window form. The entrance comes out from the rest of the building and forms the first of many peaks. The top peak of the building is probably 12 stories high, and the intricate concrete block work looks like it might stand another thousand years.

"We built this here almost three hundred years ago," Colere says. "Not the three of us, of course, but the Followers of the Five Stones. We initially settled here in the late 1700s because we could feel a special energy source in the area. Once we found it, we decided to build a building worthy of housing it."

At this point, I have so many questions, but before I can ask any, Kian says,

"So are all five stones here, in this building?"

Colere turns to Kian and laughs loudly. Zev and the third cloaked person also chuckle under their robes.

"I'm sorry, I don't mean to laugh," Colere says. "The five stones are actually scattered across the world. The power a person would have if they'd been in contact with all five stones. I mean, there hasn't been a Keeper of the Five stones in generations and generations!"

"Where are the others located?" I ask.

Colere stops laughing and gets a big smile across her face.

"Only select followers know the answer to that question, Finley, and seeing as neither of you are members, I'm not going to be able to tell you that," she says.

"Alright, well how about just one of the other locations then?" I ask back. What's the worst they can say, "no?"

"How about this?" She starts, "If everything goes really, really well today, I'll give you one of the other locations before you leave."

"You have yourself a deal," I respond.

We walk towards the front door, and as we approach, two more cloaked figures open the two large doors for us to enter. As I pass, they say in unison,

"Welcome, Finley."

A shiver runs down my spine as they say it. It was a friendly tone and pitch, but having these complete strangers greet me by name as we walk into this intimidating church makes this feel even more like a trap. As we walk down the hallway, Kian grabs my arm and stops me for a moment.

"I… I don't like this, Fin. I had a dream about this. I don't remember a lot of it, but I remember then pulling me away from you," he says.

"Well then, don't do anything that's going to get us in trouble here," I respond, half-jokingly, as the adrenaline begins pumping through my veins.

"You know that's not how it works," he says back, his voice now filled with anxiety.

I look him directly in the eyes. I love that he still worries about me, but sometimes, when I'm already dealing with the stress of a situation, I wish he could dial it down just a little bit.

"Listen," I say, "I promise that I'll be as careful as I can be. Plus, you're here with me, so I know things will be okay."

He looks at me for a moment and a small semblance of relief comes across his face. As I'm about to hug him, Colere says loudly from ahead,

"Please don't fall too far behind, we wouldn't want you two getting lost now, would we?"

CHAPTER 14: LUNA FINCH

"Well, everything you've said seems to line up. You two are free to go. Check down the hall in room 104 for apartment assignments before you head out."

Esha sighs loudly and looks over to Garven. They fist bump each other and nod in agreement with the panel of interviewers.

"Appreciate it," Garven says.

They turn and walk out of the room and down the hall towards room 104.

"I thought they might never let us out. Four days is too freaking long," Esha says.

"And they tried telling us it wasn't jail when we were walking there. Yeah right," Garven responds.

As they reach the apartment assignment office, there's a short line. The man in front of them turns around and smiles at them.

"Might be a little bit," he starts saying, "so many people have been coming here that there is always a line. At least that's what a couple workers told me on my way in."

As they settle in for a wait, there's a commotion across the hall. A couple patrol people are conversing in whispered yells, trying to not let others hear. Esha turns to hear them more clearly.

"What are they…" Garven begins to say.

"SHHH!" Esha says.

The friendly stranger turns towards the both of them and smiles at Garven, who rolls his eyes.

After 30 more seconds, Esha's expression begins to change from a look of concentration to a look of worry. Garven dares not say anything until she's ready to talk.

"Yeah, Luna Finch. That's her. She's just gone," a guard says.

"The damn Green Cloaks came in here, demanded to see her, and now she's nowhere to be found. Boss is gonna be pissed," he continued.

"I don't know. He might not be all that mad, if you get what I'm saying," a second guard says.

As they part and scurry in several different directions, she turns back towards Garven.

"Bad news," Esha says.

"What's going on?" Garven asks.

"Luna escaped from here. They also implied it was an inside job," Esha informs Garven.

Garven sighs deeply. Two steps forward, one step back.

The line moves slowly as they continue to discuss what it could mean.

"Hopefully we can find out where Auryn, Fin, and Kian, are staying, and let them know right away. They need to be warned," Garven then says.

Esha agrees, and they both stand in silence for a few minutes.

After 45 more minutes waiting in line, they reach the Office of Living and Zoning. They approach an older man, no more than 5'8, with a scruffy beard and salt and pepper hair.

"What can I help you with?" He says in the tone of someone who has said this exact phrase thousands of times.

"We were told by the Release Council to come down here and get our housing assignments," Esha says.

"Will you be needing one apartment or two?" The man asks.

Esha and Garven lock eyes and burst out laughing. Tears nearly come streaming out of their eyes. They then both look back to the man, who's expression remains unchanged.

"Two apartments, please," Esha finally says.

"Oh, also, we were told to ask if we could get our quarters in the same building as my sister. She just came back on the ship, and we were told she got housing already," Garven asks.

The man's eyes narrow. He looks both Esha and Garven up and down. After a moment, he lets out a deep sign.

"Great, more paperwork and approvals," he says while rolling his eyes. The sarcasm is not lost on Esha or Garven.

"Sorry about that," Garven replies. He then gives the man the name of his sister.

The man calls over someone else in the office, and after a brief discussion, the new person exits down the hallway. Esha notices a hand drawn name plate on the desk. Written on it is the name "Harry H."

"He's gotta go get proper authorization. I'll start the paperwork while he's gone so we can hurry this up a bit. Even if you can't stay in the same building, it'll be easy to assign you a different one," he says.

"What's the H in your last name stand for?" Garven asks, trying to make small talk and appear friendly.

"Hood." The man replies without looking up. That signals both the beginning, and the end, of the small talk.

Five silent minutes later, the coworker comes back into the office and lets us know that it's been approved, all of us can live on the same floor together.

"That's fantastic," Esha says, more exasperated than excited.

They finish answering the questions and are now free to head on out to their new building. They're told that it's a converted hotel building near the intersection of Peter St and

King West. The man gives them directions and a piece of paper he's drawn a rudimentary map on for them. He gives them a kind wink as he slides the map in their direction, the first feeling of warmth they've felt from someone in days.

"Thanks, Mr. H. We appreciate that," Esha says.

"Sorry I was so grumpy before. I appreciate you being patient," he replies.

As they leave the room, the line shuffles forward, and a sour looking man with jet black hair is called up to the window next. Esha and Garven look at each other after seeing him and give each other a "what's his deal" look, but decide to keep walking, out the door to freedom.

As they leave the building and exit through the large ornamental doors, which are as heavy as they are beautiful, a voice interrupts their walk.

"Hey stranger," she says.

Garven's eyes get big as he whips his head to the left. Ten feet away, sitting on the edge of a concrete flower bed, which hasn't seen any actual flowers in decades, sits the best thing he's seen in years.

"They were being weird about me coming to see you. I tried seeing you after I saw Fin, but…"

She couldn't finish her sentence because Garven had run up and picked her straight off the concrete to hug her. Swaying back and forth, Auryn's feet don't quite reach the ground. She buries her face into his shoulders, and tears start to make his shirt damp.

Esha stands by awkwardly for 20 seconds as they hug, and eventually Garven lets her down. Auryn walks over to Esha, and they embrace as well. Not with the same energy and enthusiasm as Auryn's first hug, but Esha appreciates it, nonetheless.

"Thanks for getting my brother here in one piece. I imagine it wasn't the easiest thing in the world. Probably some troubles on the way," Auryn says.

"Nothing we couldn't handle" Esha responds while smiling slyly.

Auryn laughs and hesitates for a moment before asking,

"Fin come visit you today?"

"Fin's out?" Garven says.

"I take it that's a no, then. That's so strange," replies Auryn.

"Why, when did they get out?" Esha asks.

"Well, Fin and that guy they were with were let out yesterday, and we met up and walked back to our apartment building together. We were gonna meet up this morning to talk but when I knocked on both their doors, no one answered," Auryn says.

"The four of you?" Garven asks.

"Oh, yeah," Auryn says, while a hint of red fills her cheeks, "Fin, their friend, me and Mina, a, uh, friend of mine from the ship."

"The same friend you seemed pretty dang close to when walking off the ship? That one?" Esha asks.

Auryn darts her eyes towards the ground before settling herself.

"Yeah, her. And now I can't find Fin or the guy."

"Kian. His name is Kian," Garven says.

Auryn wants to respond, *"I don't care what his name is!"* but thinks better of it before the words escape her mouth.

They walk back to the apartment building together, the map no longer needed because Auryn knows the directions. Along the way, Garven and Esha ask Auryn how the space flight was, how the colony setup went, and all sorts of questions over the 20 or so minute walk.

"Mom, Dad, and Forbin are all doing well. Mom was pretty bummed I was leaving, but dad was secretly happy I was coming for you," Auryn says.

"I had wondered how they would take the news. Gotta be hard traveling all that way, just to lose another kid for a while," Garven replies.

"Yeah, as soon as the colony was fully operational, Dad was talking about getting a part time job, on top of the part time jobs mom and him already have," Auryn says.

"That man cannot stop working. Probably for the best though, he'd drive mom crazy if he was in the living quarters all day," Garven says.

"That's EXACTLY what I said!" Auryn blurts out.

They both laugh as Garven throws an arm around her.

"I missed you. You know that right?" Garven then says.

"I know. I missed you too," Auryn replies.

"Well obviously, it's impossible to not miss me when I'm gone," Garven then says, trying to contain his smile and laughter.

"Yeesh, I shoulda left you here!" Auryn blurts out. They both begin laughing once again.

Once they approach the apartment building, Esha looks up.

"This building must be 30 stories tall," she says.

"Yup, and no working elevators. If your legs weren't strong before now, they're certainly going to be in a few days," Auryn responds.

"You got that right. Although some of us hiked from Cleveland to get here, while some of us got to fly around for a bit and then land like a mile away," Esha says, smirking at Auryn while saying it.

"Sorry, I was too busy setting up Earth's first permanent colony on another planet to count my steps. I'll make sure to keep track next time I'm out there," Auryn retorts playfully.

"Maybe the first colony, maybe the second, and I mean geez, who even remembers the second?" Esha says, making sure the sentence doesn't sound too mean.

Auryn cracks up before saying,

"I like this version of you. 'Sassy Esha' is much more fun than 'wouldn't ever really talk to me Esha.'"

"Well, it just wasn't a catchy enough nickname," Esha responds.

They both snicker and wrap one arm around the shoulder of the other.

After they pass through the lobby with two security guards, who also happen to live in the building, and show their paper accommodations, they begin the long walk up the stairs.

When they reach the 15th floor, Esha and Garven both find their rooms, Esha's room 1523, Garven's 1527.

They each stop in to check their rooms out briefly, but Auryn mentions that she would like for them to come to her room asap.

"1534," she says, as she walks in the direction of the higher room numbers.

They each nod and enter their rooms to place down their backpacks. Garven looks around his apartment, a one bedroom, converted from a nice sized old hotel room. There's a small dirty window on the opposite wall from the door, enough room for a small couch, two chairs, and a low table. A door to the bathroom sits next to a closet in the hallway. This building feels much more structurally safe than what they lived in while in Cleveland, but maybe not as nice as the building in Buffalo.

He exits back out the door and walks towards Auryn's room, and as he reaches it, Esha enters the hallway. He knocks on the door as she approaches, and he can hear Aryn yell out "It's open!" from inside.

As they walk in, it looks nearly identical to Garven's room, except sitting on the small couch is the woman who walked down the ramp next to Auryn a few days ago.

She stands up and introduces herself,

"You must be Garven and Esha, I've heard so much about you. My name is Mina, a traveling companion of Auryn's."

Esha and Garven share a quick side eye, then grin and walk forward to shake her outstretched hand.

"A traveling companion, you say?" Garven asks.

Mina's face doesn't change as she answers,

"Yes."

She motions for them to have a seat on the couch, and she moves around the low table to sit in a chair. She's wearing her ship's casual clothes, while Esha and Garven are still wearing their well-worn travel clothes.

"Do either of you know if there's a place to get fresh clothes?" Garven asks Mina and Auryn.

"Not sure, we haven't been out that long and haven't explored much. Just found where the food and water stands were and that seemed like enough for now," replied Auryn.

"Maybe that's what Kian and Fin are out doing, trying to find supplies and clothes and such," Mina says.

"Possibly. It's still a little weird they didn't swing by this morning though," Garven says.

"Well," Auryn begins, "everything is a little weird right now."

As she says it, she looks over to Mina, and Mina looks back and smiles warmly.

"Okay, so what exactly is going on with you two?" Garven blurts out.

"Well, it's a little complicated I guess," Auryn begins to say.

"Not really," Mina says, letting out a small chuckle as she does.

"Auryn and I were romantic partners on the way back here to Earth. I flirted with her until she got the point that I was interested. Which took FOREVER, by the way, and now, I'm hoping we can still date or somehow be together, but she needs to figure things out with Finley first."

Everyone else in the room freezes for a moment. A room on Earth might never have been more silent than it is at this moment. Esha and Garven once again look at each other, then over to Auryn. The entire time, Mina sits there with a smile on her face.

"Wow," Esha finally says, bursting with laughter as she does,

"Me caes bien."

Mina begins laughing along with her, and Garven raises his eyebrows and looks back to Auryn. Auryn can feel her cheeks burning.

"Yeah, well, I guess that about explains it," she then replies.

The four of them talk for almost two hours, about the journey from Cleveland to Buffalo, then to Toronto, and about the journey to set up a new colony.

"The most dangerous situation I was in? Maybe when I almost flew off the side of a spaceship as it was moving faster than any other point in the journey. Oh, my ribs were also broken during the first part," Auryn says, responding to a question by Esha.

"Wow, and I thought being tied up and blindfolded in the back of a van, and then running away from someone with a gun, oh also then escaping a burning building was going to take the 'Most Traumatic Experience' trophy," Esha responds.

"Gotta say Auryn, I think Esha and Garven win the award on this one," says Mina, prompting Garven to smile and yell out "Winner winner!"

They all laugh together, and Mina gets up to grab a water jug and fills everyone's glasses.

Another hour later, they hear a knock on the door.

"Oh! That must be Finley! I'll get it," says Auryn.

As she walks down the short hallway and opens the door, ready to give Fin a bearhug, she's surprised that it's not Fin and Kian standing in her doorway. He looks familiar but she can't quite place it.

"Hi all. Sorry to bother you," he looks around nervously in the hallway while saying it.

"Would you mind letting me in for a moment? I have some information about your friends that I think you should know."

Auryn looks him up and down and realizes that she could certainly take this man in a fight. She motions for him to come in and closes the door behind him as she does.

He walks down the hallway, and as he enters the main room, Garven says,

"Harry?"

He smiles at Garven and Esha.

"It's good to see you! What brings you by?" asks Esha.

He walks over to the window and closes the dust covered curtain, even though you could barely see through the dirt and grim on the window anyways.

"Sorry I came to visit you in your apartment, I know that's weird. But I had to tell you as soon as I overheard," Harry says.

"Heard what?" Asks Auryn.

"The Green Cloaks. They have your friends. I guess they came to their apartment early this morning and all walked out together. They were brought to the cloaks main building, an old church over on Church and King Streets."

"Why would Fin go with them? They had to have been coerced," says Esha.

"Who are these Green Cloaks?" Auryn asks.

"These zealots that tried to kill Fin on the way here," replies Garven.

"And Finley just, what, willingly walked out with them? Why?" Mina asks.

"From what I was told," Harry says, "they all looked to be in good spirits on the walk over. Nobody like, tied up or anything."

"Alright, we need to head over to the church and see what's going on," Auryn says.

"From the tone he was using and the way they were talking, it sounded to me like once they were in the church, they were not getting out," Harry replies.

"Why are you telling us this?" Esha asks.

"Well, the two of you were nicer to me than most people, so I made a note of your names and the names of the people you asked about. Plus, a lot of us here don't exactly like the Green Cloaks, they've infiltrated all aspects of the government here. I have friends of friends who vanished after saying or doing something the Cloaks didn't like, and I didn't want that to happen to your friend," he responds.

Everyone looks around the room towards each other with renewed concern. Garven rubs his eyebrows with his thumb and forefinger, Auryn clenches her jaw and stares hard at the floor.

"I've drawn you a little map of where the church is located. I don't know if it'll help, but it's at least a start. I have to get out of here before I'm seen, but good luck to you all, you're going to need it," Harry says before giving everyone a head nod.

With that, he leaves the room and closes the door behind him. Gone with him is the jovial spirit that once inhabited the room.

CHAPTER 15: WHISPERING STONE

Kian and I walk towards two giant ornate carved wooden doors. Ten feet tall, four feet wide each. Colere grabs my hand and says,

"It's only you beyond this point. Kian can stay out here. We'll grab him some water and he can relax."

I turn and look at Kian and he ever so lightly shakes his head no. Colere reassures him I'll be out in a couple minutes. For the first time I've been here, I can't seem to tell if someone is lying or not. There's a fog around her thoughts.

What I do know is that I am being drawn to this room. I know it's not a great idea to separate. I know none of this was a good idea to start with, but the call has overtaken my rational thinking. All I want in the entire world is to know what's behind these doors.

"I'm sure it'll be alright, Kian. I'll see you in a few minutes," I say to him, before I nod at Colere.

The doors open and the room is dimmer than I would expect. There are some torches on the wall, and I can see dozens of Green Cloaks standing around in a circle. I take a few steps before my heart rate quickens and my palms begin to sweat. The vision around the edge of my eyes begins to blur.

Something isn't right.

As I try to stop, Colere loops her arm through my left arm, and another Green Cloak loops their arm through my right, and they begin to drag me towards the middle of the circle.

I am about to call out to Kian, but before I can the doors behind me slam shut. The weight of the wood hitting the frame echoes through the chamber. They drag me up to a stone pedestal. A pedestal that looks vaguely familiar from my dreams. It's about three and a half feet tall, and on it is the largest gemstone I have ever seen in my life. It must be a foot wide and almost as long. It's easily 8 or 9 inches tall.

The Emerald Stone. I can feel what it is, its history, and its importance, immediately. It feels like it is whispering to me secrets only I am allowed to know. I don't have any idea how long it's been when I am interrupted by a rhythmic chanting. I look up to see 30, maybe even 40 Green Cloaks surrounding me in a half circle. Chanting in unison, the words I cannot make out, bouncing around the old stone walls.

They stop, and Colere steps forward.

"Finley of Cleveland, do you believe that you are the Emerald Stonekeeper?" She asks. The room is now quiet, except for the whispering of the stone.

"I'm sorry, I don't know what that is," I respond.

Before I can ask what any of this means, I am interrupted.

"Keepers of the Emerald Stone, we have upon us someone who lays claim to the stone. It is now time to find out if, after 100 years without, we have another," Colere says.

"I don't know what you think I am, Colere, but I want to leave. Now," I say, voice rising with each word.

She ignores my pleas. They all do.

"Tell us Finley. What is the stone saying to you? What does it whisper into your ears?" Colere asks.

"I, I don't know. I can't tell. I don't know what it's saying," I plead.

The crowd of cloaks gasps. They look back and forth to one another. Some even take a step towards their neighbor and whisper.

"So, you admit the stone speaks to you?" She asks.

I look around the room, I notice the rings around everyone's eyes, a small sliver of green, like mine, but glowing. They're all staring at me through the dim lighting of the room.

"Tell us what it says and become who you are supposed to be. Listen closely now, you don't want to get this wrong," Colere says with a stern tone.

I want to run away. I want to break through that door, find Kian, and hide. I want to let whoever is in charge of Toronto know that there is a cult operating right under their noses. I want, in so many ways, to not be standing where I currently am.

But unexpectedly, what I really want, above all else? I want to hear what the stone has to say. The draw is powerful, intoxicating. The whispers grow louder every second I stand here, until they are drowning out Colere entirely.

Finally, I give in and close my eyes.

"There is only one way to know the truth, Finley. Place your hands on me, and become who you were always meant to be," a thousand voices whisper to me and only me.

It's coming from the stone, that much is certain, but how? I do not know.

"Do not tell them the words I say to you, for they are not worthy to know. They hold within them darkness. Do not let them use my power. Come closer, place your hands on me, and become my Keeper."

The voice sounds like a combination of a hundred different people, adults and children. Whispers upon the wind, carried through branches and strengthened by gusts. The sounds of a hundred Stonekeepers, telling me I am the chosen one.

I cannot tell if this is real, a dream, or something in between. What I can tell is that I am going to touch this stone. I am going to place my scratched, scarred hands onto it, and I have come to terms with whatever happens.

I scan the room one last time before I do. People are yelling in my direction, but they refuse to move any closer. I notice a stronger green hue to the room, casting dark shadows onto the walls behind them. I can hear nothing but the sound of the voices floating on the wind. Luna was right all along, I am powerful, and she was right to be scared.

I do not know what comes after touching the stone, but I am no longer afraid. Much like Kian's knife became my knife, so too shall this stone.

I look back towards the stone, take one step forward, and place both my hands on it at the same time.

In an instance, I feel a power surge through me. My adrenaline pumping through these mortal veins, my heart racing at near unmeasurable beats. The surge I feel through me is what I would imagine a thousand suns would feel like coursing through my veins.

I look up, my hands still touching the stone, and see a sea of faces, contorting in slow motion, some trying to run for cover as the room fills with the emerald green light. The man with jet black hair, who I hadn't noticed before now, shields his face and turns away. I see Colere, stunned and standing in place only six feet away. Her hair begins to blow back, away from me. Each millisecond another strand wafts in the wind.

I try to say something, but instead of my voice, a noise I've never heard before comes out. I wonder if I look confused to the few people left in the room still looking at me. I try to form words, coherent syllables even, but nothing human comes out.

It's like the stars themselves are screaming from the depths of me. Both high and low pitched, it echoes around the room. The few small stained-glass windows, no more than a foot tall, located near the ceiling, shatter into thousands of tiny, sharp pieces. I watch in slow motion as they fall towards the floor. I see people throwing their arms up over their heads, trying to protect themselves, as several of them push for the door to open.

"Let go, and become the Stonekeeper," the voices whisper to me.

I don't want to let go. I want to feel this way forever. I am intoxicated with the power I feel in myself, and enchanted with the terror these cultists feel towards me. I would live the rest of my life in a single instance if it meant keeping my connection to this stone.

"This is only the beginning, Finley," it whispers.

I take one last look around the room, and as the voices whisper to me to release my grip on the stone, I finally listen. I remove both my hands at the same moment, and when I do, an explosion of light fills the room, blinding me momentarily.

As my eyes struggle to see anything, I feel myself weightless for a brief moment. As if I am floating on the clouds themselves. Am I flying? Is this an unexpected power from the stone? A half second later, as my eyes try to refocus, I can feel myself not floating but falling.

What hits the stone ground first is my shoulder, and the pain shoots through to my neck. Immediately after, my head hits the stone, and before I lose consciousness, I see the aftermath: People huddled against the wall. Some knocked unconscious, some cut from the exploding glass windows.

What I see last, though, is Colere, still standing there, jaw dropped, eyes locked onto me, hair slowly falling from the effects of gravity. Hers is a face filled with awe and wonder.

It's as if she's seen a ghost.

Or perhaps, the ghosts of a thousand Stonekeepers.

CHAPTER 16: RESCUE PLAN

"Alright, we need to go get Finley," Auryn says.

"They're not gonna let us waltz through the front door and grab Fin and Kian," Esha says.

"Maybe we don't use the front door," replies Mina.

Auryn, Esha, and Garven all turn to look at her.

"Let's go tonight and scout the church out, find a way to break in, and get them," Mina says.

"Shouldn't we tell the council? This is basically kidnapping!" Garven says.

"I mean, you heard him, they've infiltrated all layers of the government here. Telling the council would make us lose the element of surprise. I agree with Mina, let's go scope it out, then try to break in," Esha says.

Auryn nods in agreement.

"Okay so tonight we head out, get the details, and then put a plan together. Tomorrow night we break in. Would that make everyone feel a little better?" Auryn says.

Garven, Esha, and Mina all nod their heads.

"I'm gonna get some food and then take a nap this afternoon. See everyone around 10:00?" Garven says.

Auryn nods, and Esha and Garven both hug Auryn before they leave. Mina gets a polite if not standoffish feeling head nod before they go.

After they leave, she says,

"Your friends don't like me too much, I think."

"What do you mean? They've been nothing but nice to you?" Auryn responds.

"Yeah, I guess. I think maybe they're just upset that you came home with a girlfriend, all the while Finley was here the whole time," Mina says.

"Well, Finley also got themselves a boyfriend while I was gone so it's not like they can be mad at me for it,

" Auryn replies.

"We haven't had much time to talk about how you feel about that either, Auryn. I'm a little worried you're keeping this all inside, and that you might be making some rash decisions today because of it," says Mina.

Auryn gets quiet for a few moments, and Mina gives her the time to think it through.

Outside the windows, the fading light from the soon to be setting sun is filled with lush oranges and purples. It's beautiful. On the ship there were always bright lights, generators humming, and all sorts of activity, but here in this quiet room, overlooking a few city blocks, with a colorful sky. It's strangely peaceful.

It's amazing how different the darkness of space and the darkness of Earth are, Mina thinks to herself.

"I guess it was just the shock of seeing Fin with someone else that bothers me, and I know I'm being a hypocrite about it, because I found you, and you and I are so good together. I'm just torn because I still love them, and at the same time I really like you, and I'm just not sure how fair that is to anybody," Auryn finally says.

Mina smiles and looks at Auryn with a softness in her eyes.

"Not everything in this world is black and white, Auryn. You can love Finley and like me. It's not a character flaw to have these feelings and emotions. What is a character flaw is not setting whatever boundaries you need to set. Or not having the tough conversations you need to have. You know?" She pauses briefly, then continues.

"Are you okay being in love with Finley and being in, um, like with me? Because I'm fine with that. But when we rescue Fin, you both need to talk and decide what you're both okay with."

"But what if you're fine with it now and not fine with it in a day, or a week, or a year?" Auryn asks.

"When that bridge is built, and it's sturdy enough to cross, we'll talk about it," Mina replies, "but right now, in this moment, I would really like to not be alone. That's not meant to pressure you, but I am going to head to bed and relax for a bit and, if you want, you can join me. Tonight's going to be a late night, so don't take long to make your decision."

Mina walks towards the bedroom, Auryn's bedroom technically, and gives one last look over her shoulder before she closes the door behind her. Auryn sits on the couch, unsure of how she feels about all this.

She feels selfish because she wishes Fin didn't have Kian, and guilty that she didn't seem to care about rescuing him earlier. She feels in awe of Mina's emotional maturity, but a small part of her wishes Mina was loud, angry, and upset, because an argument is easier than processing how she really feels.

Mostly what she feels is an immense sense of nervousness, and a large dose of fear that tonight and tomorrow are going to be even more dangerous than they are imagining.

As she stands up, looking first at the direction of the door leaving the apartment, then at the door to the bedroom, she sighs a deep, guttural sigh. She then smiles, because something she hadn't been thinking suddenly crossed her mind:

How lucky she is that she found two amazing people to be with. Especially considering how few people there are left in the world.

As she turns towards the direction of her bedroom, the slowly fading light of the sun barely illuminates the path down the short hallway. She grabs the hand crank light that had been flickering the last rays of its own energy for the past several minutes, and in the growing darkness of a once again quiet building, she walks over to the bedroom, turns the handle, and enters the safety of her newer relationship one more time.

THE TENTH DREAM

I have been in a dream-like trance for what feels like an eternity, and I cannot figure out how to get out.

As I sit here, in an empty, light gray colored room, I'm having a hard time concentrating. There are no doors, no decorations, no furniture. It's the most nothingness I've ever experienced. I've never had to describe nothingness before, and it's difficult to fully wrap my head around. If it wasn't for the light reflecting off the corners, creating some semblance of defined space, I honestly think I would lose my mind.

I can't think about nothingness forever, so instead my mind reminds me how much I miss Auryn and Kian both. I miss everyone, and I don't even know if they're alive, or if I'm alive. Is this death? It doesn't feel like death, but it doesn't exactly feel like life, either.

I lay as still as I possibly can and once again close my eyes tight. I've tried everything to cure my boredom, and as a last resort I figure I can chant a phrase, or mantra, over and over. The first little while I try "Let go or be dragged," but nothing happens. I open my eyes to see the gray nothingness once again.

I decide to try a new phrase that's been rattling around in my head today, seemingly out of nowhere:

I am one with the stone.

I repeat four times, then eight, then twelve, with no luck. I am still lying here, on a surface that is neither comfortable nor uncomfortable, in a place that is neither hot nor cold. It's not humid or dry, it is actually kind of bright, which is the only "something" I can describe it by. But there is no light source. I sigh loudly and think to myself that I should try something else.

Um.

"The stone is one with me."

How unoriginal.

"The stone is one with me."

This is never going to work, I think.

I take a deep breath and try to clear my thoughts. The room is blank, my mind can be as well.

"The stone is one with me."

Maybe while I'm asking the impossible, it could also call my friends for me. Like one of those ancient phone booths that we'd see outside some gas stations on the way from Buffalo to Toronto. Tiny little glass booths with phones long ago ripped out.

I chuckle for a brief second before I open my eyes. As I do, a flash of light fills the room, and my body sinks further into the solid ground. It engulfs me, surrounds me, hugs me even, then breaks beneath me. It now feels like I'm falling through the infinite abyss.

There is no resistance to my fall, no wind whipping by. My arms flail, my legs kick, but I'm not sure why, there's no way to steady myself. I'm not even sure if down is the way I'm falling. It's a sensation more than anything palpable.

After what feels like no time, and all of time, my free fall is interrupted by the sudden appearance of a floor under my feet. I don't slam down into it like I would expect. Instead, it's just suddenly there, and I'm suddenly here, and where any of this is I have no idea.

I look down, and my body is my own, I think. If I stare too long at my grungy shirt, it feels off in a way I can't quite describe. Real, but as if parts of it were generated by something.

I look up and see a mostly gray room.

"Great, I teleported to the same exact spot," I say to myself out loud.

But as my eyes focus more, the room is different, and filled with 2 things: In one corner, a hibiscus plant. In another, a piece of cloth pinned to the wall. It depicts a rhinoceros enclosed by two palm-trees and olive branches.

I look around to find something, anything else, with no luck. No windows, no doors. A gray box. I take a few steps forward, then a few more to one side. If I knew how to whistle I would, just so the endless quiet would cease.

I am startled as I hear a voice. It is not my own. It's deep, but frail.

"Could it be? Could it actually, really be?" He says.

I don't know where it's coming from. It sounds an awful lot like the speaker to my dad's old record player, but I see nothing in this room that would make such sounds.

"Hello?" I say back, unsure of who I'm talking to.

"I KNEW I wasn't imagining things! I think it's the same person who popped in a few days ago and vanished quickly," the voice muses, seemingly to itself, or is it talking to someone else?

"HELLO!?" I yell, my voice showing definite signs of frustration.

"Oh, my goodness! My apologies!" The voice starts, "It's very rude of me not to acknowledge you. Welcome to my waiting room, Stonekeeper"

I stagger a bit over the pure shock of this. A strange room, with a strange voice, who knows who I am. My mind is racing and having trouble keeping up with what's happening.

"Are… are you the stone? Are you the whispers?" I finally respond.

"The green in your eyes, it glows with the brightness of a youthful Stonekeeper. It's been a long time since I've had that same glow," he says.

"Are you a Stonekeeper? Were you a Stonekeeper for the Emerald Stone?" I ask

He bellows a big, hearty laugh, and says,

"We can do many things, but speaking to the past versions of ourselves isn't one of them. You're close though. My name is Abdo, and I am the Ruby Stonekeeper."

A door appears out of thin air in front of me. I walk towards it. As I get close, it has a bronze knocker on it. It's intricately made and depicts a Secretary Bird with small red rubies where its eyes are.

" It's okay, come on in," the voice says.

As I turn the handle, he says.

"It's been a while since someone besides Sun-young has visited. We're the only two left."

I don't know what any of this means.

The door swings open and inside is a new room, filled with vibrant tapestries and vivid paintings. There's a stunning iron sculpture in one corner, and a man sitting on a comfortable looking rocking chair beside it.

"I know the rocking chair probably makes me look ancient," the man says as he chuckles, "and I am!"

I take a few steps towards him, further into the room. He waves his hand in the air and a second, identical chair appears in front of him, directly across from the rocker.

"Please, have a seat. I know when I was in your position, I had so many questions," he says.

I sit down in the rocking chair and lean back and forward a few times. It's soothing, and I immediately understand why he likes it.

"They help old bones like mine feel a little better, even in this pretend world. I spend most of my time here now anyways," he says.

"Pretend world?" I ask.

"Ah yes, you are in a trance right now. Your body is wherever you left it, but by the looks of it well taken care of. You don't seem to be struggling while here, so that's good. May I ask your name?" He responds.

"Yes, of course. My name is Finley. It's really nice to meet you, Abdo. I didn't even know there were other stones, let alone other Stonekeepers," I say.

"That's not unusual. What's unusual is how long it took for another Emerald Stonekeeper to appear. I've been hanging on as long as I could so Sun-young wasn't the only one left. That is too heavy a burden for one person to carry."

"So, she is another Stonekeeper?" I ask.

"Indeed. And in time you'll get to meet her too," he says.

He then leans forward and asks:

"So, how did you get to be the Emerald Stonekeeper?"

I rock back and forth a few times. The wooden bottom of the chair glides smoothly on the floor of the room. Right before it feels like you're going to tilt over backwards, it stops and starts moving forward again.

"It wasn't on purpose, really. There's this cult in Toronto that hides it or protects it. I'm not sure how to describe it really. But they made me do it," I say.

"Those Green Cloaks are still around? Even after all this time? Even with the world in this much despair?" Abdo asks.

"You know of them?" I say.

"Know of them? The last Emerald Stonekeeper couldn't stop complaining about them!" he says.

"But," I pause for a moment, "didn't you say the last Emerald Stonekeeper died a hundred years ago?"

Abdo smiles. The lines from his eyes stretch out almost all the way to his gray hairline. His eyes soften, his rocker chair slows to a stop. He leans towards me slightly and stares into my eyes for several seconds. It's then I notice that they are not dark brown, as they appeared at first glance, but a deep, beautiful red.

"It is true that she died a hundred or so years ago, yes. It is also true that I was around when it happened, when her connection with the stone ceased. A sad time indeed. Maybe sadder than that, though, is that there is so much for you to learn, and so little time left for me to teach you."

CHAPTER 17: THE PLAN

Garven, Esha, Mina and Auryn all meet in the lobby of their apartment building.

"Why am I the only one wearing a backpack? Don't you all have supplies or anything to bring with us?" Garven whispers.

"We figured if we were all wearing backpacks, walking around as a group in the dark, it would look suspicious," Auryn responds.

"You know, that's actually kind of a good point," Garven says, eyebrows raised as high as they can go.

As they head through the door of the building, the lobby watchman says,

"Up to anything fun tonight?"

"Eh, not really, so we're just gonna wander around and learn the roads," Esha says.

"Alright, stay safe," he replies, narrowing his eyes as a saccharine sweet smile spreads across his face.

They exit the heavy glass and metal doors, out into the warm nighttime air. It's still so warm, even at night, even this far north.

"I don't like the way the lobby guy was looking at us," Mina says.

"Normally, I'd say you're being paranoid," Auryn says, "but Harry has me so freaked out that I think you might be right."

"Alright alright, everyone calm down. We're just four friends heading into the evening to explore the city. There's nothing unusual about that," Garven says.

"There is if you know our friends have been kidnapped," Esha replies.

They all nod and walk in silence for a few minutes. As they pass the never-ending skyscrapers, they make sure to look around plenty. At street signs they stop and write down the names in a small notebook Garven has. They zigzag through the streets and try to make it look like they just came upon the big, old church.

As they approach, they slow down. Even at a distance, and even in the dark, they can see several Green Cloaks walking around the front of the building.

"You think they do that every night?" Mina asks.

"No freaking idea, but we're not going to be able to casually stroll up and scope the place out," replies Esha.

Here they notice the first problem: It's surrounded by nothing but dirt fields. There are no buildings close by to hide them, nowhere to sneak between. Just a hundred or so feet of open space surrounding the front doors of the building

"Well damn," Auryn begins, "what do we do now?

"They can't be surrounding the entire building, let's go out a block wider and head towards the back of the church, maybe there won't be people back there," Garven says.

They walk carefully but quickly to the next alley and turn down. Darkness makes it hard to avoid garbage and debris on the ground. Garven hits his foot on some concrete that had broken off the building, and he muffles his yelp to not draw attention.

As they reach the next road, Mina looks around and says,

"There's nobody out. It's so much quieter around here than where we're living. It's not like it's that late."

"Well, it is pretty dark around here. Maybe when it's cloudy, less people are out?" Auryn responds.

"It is kind of eerie." Esha says, "In Buffalo there were always people out until pretty late. Maybe we're just not in the entertainment area?"

"They had an entertainment area?" Auryn asks.

"Oh yeah, it was cool. A stage where musicians and poets performed, right around food vendors and tables. Even when there wasn't a professional performing, someone would get up there on a Friday night and try singing or telling jokes," Esha says.

"That sounds awesome," Mina replies.

"Probably not as cool as whatever was available in the spaceships, though," Garven says, with a hint of jealousy in his voice.

"It was really cool for a while," Auryn begins, "then everything started to break, lines were so long, and the feeling of being stuck in that giant tin can for years started to creep in."

"I know it sounds whiny, but it wasn't nearly as cool as I thought it might be," Auryn finished.

"At least you found me on the way back, didn't need the halo games when I'm around," Mina says as a smile spreads across her face.

"Well, I mean, uh," Auryn staggers while talking, "Yeah, that was nice."

"Loosen up, man," Mina replies while laughing to herself.

Garven and Esha laugh too, and the mood lightens.

Under the cover of night, with a partial moon obscured by clouds, they see a building across the street that looks like it might be attached to the church.

"DIO ESE CE RE" letters spell out across the back.

"Finley would love trying to figure out what that says," Garven says.

Esha chuckles quietly and smiles at Garven. She nods her head and turns her focus back to the building.

"It looks like there's a bunch of windows along the ground, behind that half wall that separates the property from the road. What if we try to break into one of those?" Esha says.

"We don't even know which building they're in. What if we break into this one and they're kept in the church itself? We'll alert the Green Cloaks and then we'll never get them back," Auryn says.

They all stand staring at the building from far across the intersection, peering out of an alley that stays dark even as the moonlight occasionally flitters through the cloud cover.

"Well, I guess we'll have to break into this building really quietly and then go from there. I mean, what are we going to do instead, nothing?" Garven asks.

Nobody says a word for a full minute, each person with their own thoughts surrounding them, their minds trying to determine what the right course of action is.

"Well, I guess it's settled then. Tomorrow night the four of us come back, break in, and get Finley and Kian outta there," Garven replies.

CHAPTER 18: OLD HEADACHES

"Everyone who ever thought they were 'The One' is down here now, turned to dust by the power of the Emerald Stone," a familiar voice from the shadows says, awakening Kian.

The once dark room is now illuminated by a torch, and the woman who was speaking reveals herself. This is the second time he's been checked on since being pulled backwards from the large ornamental doors as Finley walked through them. Then being punched in the face. He's mad at himself for allowing it all to happen. He's also thinking how familiar the voice sounds.

She's wearing a green cloak, of course, which covers everything but the upper part of her face. As Kian looks around, he tries to focus. What he thought were gray floors and grayer walls are actually much more horrifying: Skulls and bones from dozens of bodies.

"Almost all of them are men, no surprise," she continues.

"It's always a man that thinks they're all-powerful. That's why everyone else was happy to see Finley come through. Often those who don't want power are the ones who are most justified to receive it."

"What have you done with Finley!" Kian shouts, voice rough, chest burning, and head aching.

"Well, if you must know, Finley is in a transitive state. They touched the stone and didn't die, which is good, but they've been unable to communicate for a day and a half now, from what I've been told," she says.

"Maybe they'll end up here, amongst all the bodies of the once hopeful. I can only hope," she says, shrugging as she does.

The shrug sends shivers down Kian's spine.

"Bring me to Finley right now!" He yells, becoming more frantic by the second.

He tries to stand, but the chains around his arms won't let him rise above a kneel. In this old church, it feels intentional.

The woman chuckles to herself. She lowers the bottom portion of fabric covering her face and takes the hood of the cloak completely off. She has long, platinum blonde hair and eyes that have the faintest sliver of glowing green. Part of her forehead is wrapped in gauze. Flames from the torch reflect in her eyes, flickering with any breeze that passes through.

"Luna," whispers Kian.

"You are in no position to make demands, Kian, the traitor of Buffalo. You're only allowed to live right now because I allow it, and because of your closeness to Finley. If they do become the Emerald Stonekeeper, we'll need to make sure they don't do anything," she pauses for a moment,

"Hasty."

"Why are you doing this to us?" Kian pleads.

"Oh you poor, poor simpleton. You've come all this way and had no idea about the power you were traveling with. Didn't you notice any changes to Fin once you got here? Not just dreaming the future anymore, right? They could tell when you were lying. When was anyone lying? This is all just the start of the power of the Emerald Stone, Kian," she replies.

Kian stops struggling with the chains, and rests back down on the ground.

"If Finley wakes up, and that is of course a very, very big if, they will be one of the most powerful people left here in the Great lakes, maybe in the world," she says.

"And I intend to kill them."

Kian, covered in dust and dirt, sitting on the cold stone floor of this nearly 300-year-old church, surrounded by bones and darkness, remains silent for a moment. After 15 or 20 seconds of staring into the abyss, he looks up at Luna. Slowly, a smile creeps across his face. He locks eyes with her, flames still dancing, and says,

"You can't, can you? Otherwise, you would have already," He smiles as he says it.

The delight he finds from telling her this is immense.

"Above all else, Fin is a survivor, and when they wake, you might wish you hadn't pissed off the most powerful person on Earth," he then says.

"For as long as you've known me, do you think me to be an impatient person, Kian?" Luna asks.

He refuses to answer.

"My family has been hunting Stonekeepers for generations now. It's been lonely the last hundred years, I can admit. My mother had very little to do before me. But imagine my surprise when I saw all the signs of it from your little lover."

Luna takes a few steps towards Kian and crouches down.

"You've led me to Fin time and time again now. I noticed them in Buffalo because of you. I followed you to your apartment here in Toronto and found them because of it, and you were dumb enough to leave space between the two of you as you were walking down the hallway into the Stone Room," she says.

"All that might be true, but the Green Cloaks aren't here to kill Finley, they could have done that already. So how would you even get past them?" Kian asks.

"Past them? I am *one of them*. Besides, I am not here to reveal my plans to you. This isn't some 20th century detective novel," Luna answers.

"Why didn't you just kill Fin when you had the chance? In the van when we were kidnapped?" Kian asks.

"A combination of hubris on my part, which I will not let happen again, and I wouldn't have been able to infiltrate the Green Cloaks up here if I had," Luna says.

Kian, eyes now adjusted, notices a small bit of light coming from where he thinks the door is. He takes one deep, burning, full breath, and starts to yell,

"YOU HAVE A TRAITOR IN YOUR MIDST! SHE WANTS TO KILL FINLEY!"

Luna's smile is erased from her face immediately. She grabs her hood from behind her and brings it over top of her head. Kian can once again only see her eyes, and they glare at him for a moment before she turns around, torch in hand, and leaves the room, slamming the large wooden door behind her.

Pitch black once again engulfs him. His head still aching from being knocked unconscious yesterday, surrounded by horrors he wished hadn't been illuminated. He notices his stomach pang for food for the first time. Everything that could be wrong in the world, currently is, but still, he couldn't help but keep smiling.

The Green Cloaks thought this would be easy. Capture Fin, figure out the true power they wield, and use it for whatever nefarious reasons they want.

Luna thought this would be easy. Let the Green Cloaks capture them, and kill Fin.

But Kian knows it won't be easy for either of them.

It's with that thought he lays all the way back onto the cold floor and closes his eyes. The darkness he experiences changes very little, but listening to silence around him, he knows he'll be free soon.

THE TENTH DREAM (CON'T)

Abdo and I have been talking for a few minutes before I admit, rather sheepishly, that I was actually stuck for what seemed like a VERY long time in absolute nothingness.

"I think all of us get stuck in our own waiting room the first time," Abdo says, grinning.

"That's where I was before this? Why didn't it have anything in it? Yours has a plant and a flag, so why was mine empty?" I ask.

"Did you put anything in it?" He asks. He's smiling even wider as he says it.

It's the simplest explanation in the world, and I didn't think of it one time while I was there. Just use my mind, my imagination, to decorate the empty room I was in. I start blushing from embarrassment.

"Oh, don't even think twice about it. You never had the chance to learn from other Stonekeepers, how were you supposed to know? "Abdo says kindly.

"There's just so many things I don't know, Abdo. I have so many questions, but I don't even know if they're coherent thoughts," I say.

"Well, how about I start with a little explaining myself, and we go from there. That sound alright to you?" he replies.

I nod in agreement. My shoulders, previously so tight they might have been next to my ears, lower.

He then shares with me all sorts of information about the stones. There are five in total; The Emerald stone, The Ruby Stone, which is Abdo's and based in Khartoum, Sudan. Then there is Sun-young's, the Amethyst Stone.

There are also two other stones that don't currently have a Stonekeeper: The Topaz Stone, which he's said is near Perth, Australia, and the Sapphire Stone, which as far as Abdo knows is located in Bogota, Columbia.

"What do you mean as far as you know?" I ask.

"Well, Fin, the Stonekeepers for those two stones have been missing since around the time I was born. Last anyone can tell is that they vanished in the second half of the 1900s," he responds.

He then tells me that each Stone has special powers it gives to its Stonekeeper.

"The most important power your stone gives you is the ability to heal people. It's exhausting, from what Ava used to tell me. Which isn't a surprise. Most of our powers are exhausting," Abdo says, laughing quietly as he does.

"What do you mean I can heal people? How does that even work?" I ask, confused.

"Well, that's something we're going to have to figure out now, isn't it?" Abdo replies.

"From what's been passed down from Stonekeeper to Stonekeeper, what I can tell you is if you press down on an injury and channel all your energy into it, you can heal wounds, and cure the sick," he pauses for a moment.

"To a point, of course. There isn't enough magic in the world to save someone on the brink of death, but you can do a lot with your ability."

"So how do I do it?" I ask.

"That's the more difficult question, Finley. Every one of us uses our powers a little differently. When I go to start a fire, if there's wood around, I'll grab two pieces, one with each of my hands, and squeeze as hard as I can. Once I became good at it, I could start a fire in mere seconds." Abdo says.

"Whoa, your power is starting fires?" I ask.

"Kinda, yeah," Abdo smiles as he says this. He continues,

"It's actually that I can control heat, from warm to pretty extreme temperatures. I can also control the fires themselves. I've done all sorts of things to help my community, I've melted down busted and rusted metal pieces to help reinforce other structures, and I've contained wildfires during the last few decades of droughts. There's a surprising amount you can do with the ability to control heat."

"So, hypothetically, could you control the sun?" I ask, not sure if it's a dumb question or not.

Abdo lets out a hearty chuckle before collecting himself.

"There are stories, passed down through hundreds of generations, of a Stonekeeper long ago who was so powerful they could control the heat from the sun. But with all old stories, it's hard to tell what is truth from what is," he pauses for a moment to think of the right phrase,

"Exaggeration."

"Do you have any stories from the last Emerald Stonekeeper?" I ask, excitement filling my voice.

"Plenty, and we'll get to those in due time. For now, let me tell you a little more about the history of the stones."

For some unknowable amount of time, Abdo goes through the stories and history of the Stonekeepers. Like how during the Black Death the Stonekeepers had tried, unsuccessfully, to bring the Emerald and Sapphire Stonekeepers over to Europe to stop the spread. Or how in the late 1900s, when the previous Ruby Stonekeeper was nearing the end, how she constantly had to fly out to California to slow the spread of wildfires.

As travel became easier, Stonekeepers could help more people, but at the same time more and more people, and governments, cared less and less about the environment.

"Young me had so many conversations with Ava, and they were so depressing," Abdo says.

"Like what?" I ask.

"Like in the late 1900s and early 2000s, do you know who one of the largest polluters in the world was?" Abdo asks.

I shake my head no.

"It was the military. Specifically, the United States military. There were millions of citizens recycling, trying their best, and it didn't even make a dent in helping. Ava couldn't even begin to keep up with helping people, and the Saffire Stonekeeper was missing. They're the ones who could really help, from what I've heard.

"So, the Saffire Stonekeeper helps with pollution?" I ask.

"Partially, yes. They can help purify the air and control the wind. Helping people with all sorts of chronic problems," he replies.

Abdo tells me more about what he knows about the stones, the previous Stonekeepers, and more. We get to the point where my brain couldn't possibly absorb any more information, and I let Abdo know.

"Yeah, that tracks," he says, "besides, it's about time for you to wake up anyways."

"Before I go, I'm just wondering: Do you know where the stones come from?" I say.

"That's a good question, and something none of the Stonekeepers have ever been sure of. All we know is that for thousands of years, and almost certainly longer, we've been around, and we're not sure why we're chosen or why these stones give us powers," Abo replies.

"Well, I think I had a dream that showed me how they got here," I say.

Abdo's smile fades quickly, and he leans forward in the rocking chair once more. He gently places his elbows on his knees, and his hands under his chin. He looks at me expectantly.

"If I'm right, they came crashing to Earth millions of years ago, during the time of the last dinosaurs," I begin saying.

CHAPTER 19: BREAK-IN

"Okay, so Mina, you're the lookout stationed across the street, pretty much where we were last night," Esha says.

She continues,

"Garven and I will be the ones breaking into the building. We're going to gently knock out a window, crawl in, and use the hand crank light to try and find the two of them."

"Gently?" Asks Mina.

"As gently as we can, at least," answers Garven.

"Auryn, here are some rocks I collected this afternoon. If you start to hear a commotion, start throwing them through the windows of the church, they should be big enough to do some damage. We'll need time to escape and hopefully they run to protect the church instead of finding us. Once you hear them coming towards you, get out of there," Esha says.

"Did everyone pick up what we needed today?" Auryn asks.

"Yeah, I was able to find some rope, and we each have a crank light. I also took some of my old clothes and tore them up into strips, in case they're in bad shape we can use them as bandages or tourniquets," Esha says.

"I also found some old leather gloves. They're in pretty bad shape, but they should help me break the window without gettin' sliced," says Garven.

"Nice score. Where'd ya find those?" Mina asks.

"I was asking around at the food stands today. Someone was just gonna give them to me because they said they hadn't used them in forever, but I gave them my tomatoes as a trade instead. I felt too bad just taking them," Garven answers.

"What a big ol' softy you've turned into!" Auryn says, smiling as wide as she can.

"Well, when you've seen what I've seen, it's hard not to," Garven replies.

"Fair," Mina says.

Not only do they toss their gear into the backpacks, but also anything of value to the six of them. This means breaking into Finley's room and grabbing their notebook and other important items, same with Kian's room.

"Only what can be carried in a backpack," Mina reminded everyone an hour ago.

Her and Auryn had to pack their spaceship issued clothes and documents, while Garven and Esha packed what little they had, and some food they saved over the last day.

Once done, they all looked around the room.

"If things don't go well tonight—" Auryn begins saying.

"Don't worry, sis, they will," Garven says, cutting her off.

"I know they will, but I'm just saying, if they don't," Auryn says.

"We don't really do 'worst case scenario' speeches in these parts, amiga. We're gonna be fine, let's head out," Esha says.

Auryn looks over at Mina, looking for a sympathetic eye, and Mina instead chuckles.

"What? I like the way they operate," Mina says, while shrugging and heading towards the door.

They walk down the stairs, staying mostly quiet as the stress from what's about to happen washes over them. Four different patterns of echoes bouncing off the cement stairs and concrete walls, Esha slightly ahead of the rest of them.

Over the course of the last few days, all four of them have managed to pick up or trade for, a black shirt. Garven and Esha's both a t-shirt, Garven's slightly too small, Esha's slightly too large. Mina and Auryn both have long sleeves, which they're already regretting with how hot the stairwell is.

Mina and Esha are still wearing their spaceship issued boots. They're both supposed to check back in on the ship at the one-week mark, and in a few months, begin living on the ship part time while it gets ready to leave once again.

In all the commotion of the past two days, no one's been able to give much thought about heading to the colony, or what Earth is going to look like when the ship leaves.

How many people are going to leave with it? Will there be enough people left to maintain the momentum that the city has built? Is the Earth even salvageable?

There are supposed to be meetings in a few months, when the spaceship and crew have ample time to read the climate patterns and see if anything could be done to save what's left of humanity on Earth, but that's a long way away, and they have to get out of this night alive first.

They reach the lobby, and the same doorman as yesterday is there, sitting on an old barstool.

"Two nights in a row heading out late, huh? Even later tonight. Not getting into any trouble, are we?" He says.

"Not us!" Mina says cheerfully. "We're just night owls and love scoping things out when it's a little quieter."

"Planning on staying somewhere else tonight? Those backpacks look pretty full." He then replies.

"None of your—" Esha begins to say before being cut off by Auryn.

"We made some friends, and we might stay the night over at their building! Can't hurt to bring a change of clothes, you know?"

The doorman narrows his eyes as they glide quickly across the rest of the lobby, pushing open the doors without looking behind.

"Okay, that guy sucks, right? Think he's a Green Cloak?" Garven asks.

"I don't know what his deal is, but we certainly can't trust him," Mina responds.

As they spill out onto the sidewalk, the tension continues. When they reach the end of the first block, Mina turns around and notices the doorman outside their building, looking in their direction.

Not much is said as they zigzag around blocks and loop towards the old church, and it's no longer attached back building. As they get in the neighborhood of the place, Auryn once again mentions how quiet it is.

"Yeah, you mentioned that last night," Mina says.

"Sure, but we weren't trying to quietly break a window last night," she replies.

Garven and Esha glance at each other with a look of worry.

"Well, we have these leather gloves, and some fabric strips Esha's gonna wrap around her hands. As long as not too much of the glass breaks inwards, it'll be fine," Garven says.

"Famous last words," Esha mutters under her breath.

"Okay, so we all know the plan. Auryn, listen for any commotion and if it happens, make a diversion," Esha says.

"I still think I should be going in with you both," she replies.

"We've been through this, you're too close with Fin and your decision making might be…" Garven pauses before continuing,

"Compromised."

"And I still call bull—" Auryn starts to say before being cut off by Esha.

"Look, let's all do our jobs, not argue, and get everyone out of here alive."

Auryn purses her lips together tightly, wanting to say so much, but realizing in this moment, it's not productive.

They approach the corner where Mina will be stationed, and she drops behind a brick half wall so that only the top of her head can be seen. As she scans the area, she notices a Green Cloak doing a full walk around of the property, which is different from last night. She heads back over to the others and tells them what she saw.

"Damn, if they're doing that all night, then we only have a short amount of time to break that window and get in and out. Why would they have one tonight but not last night?" Auryn says.

"I bet that doorman ran over here to tell them. We took so long getting here, there would have been plenty of time for him to get over here," Mina says.

"The damn doorman!" Garven says.

"So, what do we do now?" Asks Mina.

"We have to do it anyway, they've been trapped in there too long, and we don't even know if Kian is still alive," Esha says.

"Auryn, can I have a couple of those rocks?" Mina asks.

"Sure, what for?" Auryn responds.

"I just think I might need them, is all." Mina says cryptically.

"Uh, sure," Auryn says as she moves her book bag to the front of her body.

As she reaches into the bag, a light clinking noise comes from the bottom of it. Her shoulders tense up as she waits for someone to ask about it, but nobody does. Everyone is too distracted by the task at hand. She quickly grabs three rocks and hands them over to Mina.

Mina puts one into each pant pocket of hers and holds onto the last in her hand.

"After they pass far enough away, we've got to go quickly, so Auryn, head down and over to the alley lookout. We're counting on you if things go south," says Garven.

"I've got this, Garven. Love you and be safe," Auryn responds.

"Love you too. Now let's go," replies Garven.

Auryn takes off running into the darkness immediately. She loops around the back of a block and down an alleyway to get eyes once again on the church from the side.

Once the Green Cloak guard is far enough away, Esha, Garven and Mina look at each other and nod their heads, unsure if they'll be able to pull off this ridiculous plan. If the night were anymore quiet, you could hear each of their hearts racing.

As Esha and Garven spring across the road and crouch down next to the street level basement windows, Mina moves to a location where she'll be better able to see when the guard is coming back. Still hidden behind the four-foot-tall brick wall, she has several tall buildings at her back. The one farther down, in the next lot and over a short fence, looks mostly abandoned, and worse for the wear. She takes note of this as the perfect building to slip into if things go south.

"Well, no turning back now, I guess," Garven says, wrapping an extra piece of cloth over the palm of his left hand.

"I'm going to crack the glass with a light punch and try to grab as much as I can with my left hand," he says.

Esha nods. Her wrists, palms, and lower fingers wrapped in what was once a shirt she wore for weeks on end. Stained with sweat and dirt from the miles between Cleveland and Toronto, it's one last life giving them an opportunity to save two of their friends.

Garven begins his swing towards the glass, and a warm breeze floats through the air. It feels like forever before Esha hears the first piece of glass crack across the window, and the small echo bounces off the building behind them. It's not a large window, just three feet across and about two feet tall. When she looks, she sees the growing crack, splintering across the whole thing.

"Man, I thought that would do it. We gotta hope this huge piece doesn't fall in now," Garven whispers.

He puts his fist a couple inches away from the window, and gives it another solid punch, this time the break happens immediately, and as he tries to grab a piece before it falls, it slices him on the side of the wrist.

From how long it took to crash to the floor of the basement, Esha guesses the height down to the floor is around eight feet. Before she has a chance to say anything, Garven says,

"Damn, that really got me."

Esha looks down at his hand, and the side of his wrist is bleeding already. She takes another piece of the cloth out of her pocket, grabs Garven's hand, and wraps it tightly around the wound.

"That'll have to do, you okay to go on?" She asks him.

"Yeah, I'm fine," he answers dismissively.

"Alright then, let's hurry it up."

This time, with a clear hole in the window, Garven grabs the edge of a piece of the remaining glass, holds it securely, and pulls it towards him. It breaks off in a large piece, which he's now holding in his hands.

"I guess I didn't really think this part through," he says while staring at it.

"Gimme," Esha orders quietly.

"You take care of the smaller pieces, I got this," she then says.

As she takes the glass, she looks around and notices a small patch of dirt right next to the short brick wall between the property and the sidewalk. She walks a few feet over and places it gently on the ground there. As she crouches away, she notices how much it reflects the moon's light, and stops.

She turns back to walk towards it and gently steps on it, the glass making a satisfying and quiet crunching sound beneath her boots. She does this several more times to really grind the glass into the ground.

As she's doing this, she can hear small pieces of glass falling to the floor in the basement from where Garven is. She looks over and sees most of the window has been broken out.

"Time to go in, I suppose," Garven says as he turns to look at her.

"I guess it is," she says as she crouches low to walk back over.

As she does, she notices the bandage around Garven's wrist already soaked with blood around the wound.

As they're both close to the window, across the street on lookout, Mina notices the Green Cloak guard turning the far corner and heading back right past where Esha and Garven are.

Hurry UP people, she thinks to herself as she watches Garven trying to lower Esha down through the window.

If the Green Cloak walks by right now, they're done for. Garven hasn't even finished lowering Esha as far as he's able, and this guard is maybe 15 to 20 seconds away. He's gotta get in there.

Mina's heart is racing. *I can't be responsible for them getting caught*, she thinks to herself.

She can't yell to them; it'll blow their cover. She can't go out and talk to the guard in case it was the doorman who warned them. They would have her description.

Think. THINK! Her mind yells at her. The Green Cloak is a mere 15 feet from seeing most of Garven's body still sticking out the window, which would be tough to explain under even the best circumstances.

As they get to seven or eight feet from turning the corner, Mina takes the rock still in her hand, winds back while trying to stay below the four feet tall wall and launches it as hard as she can.

As it hurdles through the air, the moon illuminates it so she can see it perfectly. It's sheen piercing through the darkness, with a velocity that surprises even herself. As it makes contact, the noise echoes through the street and down the block.

Mina looks over to Garven, his arms and head still exposed while trying to lower himself into the building, shock shown across his face. He looks towards Mina as she makes a *hurry up* motion with her hand just above the brick wall.

"Who goes there!" An unfamiliar voice yells out.

The Green Cloak is stopped in the middle of the street, hand cranking the flashlight he's walking with. The light, pointed at the window that was just shattered by Mina's stone throwing, causes the light from the flashlight to peer straight through it. A mere 25 feet from where Mina is crouching, the broken-down building stands there, with no other movement or noise inside.

The Green Cloak also continues to stand there long enough for Garven to slip inside the basement. All that's left now is a missing window, which if anyone looks in that general direction, will notice immediately.

"If anyone's messing around out there, better cut it out, you don't know who you're dealing with," the Green Cloak yells.

After shining the light on several windows and floors of the building next to Mina, he continues his walk in the same direction as before. By continually shining a light on the buildings across the street, it keeps him from seeing the window Garven and Esha have just finished climbing through.

As Mina stays crouched against the wall, she turns to slowly move and head towards the original lookout point, closer to the intersection. As she does, one of the rocks in her pocket falls out and makes a loud enough noise for the guard to hear.

"I heard that! Is somebody out here? You can't be hanging out by our church like this," he says.

Mina freezes, hoping he ignores it and continues on his way. Instead, what she hears is the footsteps of a loud and frustrated pair of boots heading her way.

Inside the old building, Esha and Garven land mostly unscathed on the floor of the basement. Esha's hands landed in some of the shattered glass, but besides a few minor cuts, she's all good.

"My knees are not meant to drop that far," Garven says while getting back onto his feet.

"The good news is, it looks like it's just us down here," Esha says as her eyes adjust to the darkness.

She begins turning the handle on the flashlight and as she does, a low light projects out into the basement. As she scans the large room, she notices a door 25 feet away. She looks over to Garven, who nods at her, and they both walk in that direction.

"You should turn the charging wheels a bunch and then shut it off, so we have it when we need it," Garven says.

"Yeah. That makes sense," Esha whispers back quietly.

When they reach the door, Garven turns the handle, and the first bit of good news happens: It's unlocked.

They slowly open it, and begin to walk down a long, dark hallway. At the end they see a half flight of stairs, just five steps, and keep heading in that direction. When they reach the bottom step, they both stop for a second to listen for footsteps.

Ever so faintly, they hear a voice. Garven puts his ear up to the wall next to the stairs and listens intently.

"I think I hear something through this wall," he says quietly.

"How? Isn't that stone?" Esha asks.

"No, looks like someone built it out of old cruddy drywall well after the church was built, maybe even recently," Garven answers.

"What are they saying?" Esha asks.

Garven once again puts his ear to the wall and listens carefully. Faintly, a voice comes through.

"Is someone else down here? I heard a noise," the voice says, followed by a pained cough.

"Somebody sounds really rough. I can't make out much though," Garven says.

"Is it Kian and Finley?" Esha asks.

"It's too faint, I can't really tell. Think we should check it out?" Garven says.

"Yeah, I mean, it's at least a lead," Esha answers.

As they begin climbing the stairs to find a way to get into the room, Mina begins to hold her breath as best she can.

She very slowly lays down and moves herself against the wall. Mina reaches into her pocket and grabs the last rock, ready to use it in self-defense if she has to.

The footsteps are close now, and the amount of light being reflected off the building behind her illuminates a surprisingly large area. Definitely enough to see her if he peeks over the wall. His foot scuffs the sidewalk as he gets close to it, and Mina can tell he's right above her.

She takes one more slow, steady breath in, and can feel her heart beating an uncountable number of times per minute. It hasn't pumped this fast since she and Auryn shared their first kiss. In that moment, she thought she might pass out before even reaching Auryn's lips, it's all she could think about. But here it's beating out of fear and danger, not excitement and nervousness.

The light shines back and forth on the building once more, and she can hear the loud breathing of the man standing no more than a foot or two away from her now.

"These damn kids, think they can break anything they feel like and cause a scene," he says softly to himself.

"We're gonna find you one of these nights, I can promise you that!" He then yells into the darkness.

At the same time that the guard mutters to himself, Garven and Esha discover two sets of doors at the top of the staircase: One door is partially open, and they can see stairs leading up towards the first floor of the building. The second door is locked, but from their side, so they easily turn the handle and hear the pop of mechanism unlocking.

They slowly open it, and there is an almost pitch-black staircase down into a room. Garven nods at Esha, and she turns the flashlight on and points it down the stairs. They slowly begin descending the steps, and make sure the door closes almost all the way, but not enough to lock them in.

A few steps down, and the light from the flashlight is now illuminating the rest of the stairs. A voice can be heard talking to them.

"What do you want with me now? I'm still not gonna help you."

"That's Kian," Esha whisper yells to Garven.

Garven nods and a smile spreads across his face.

"It sure is," he replies.

They make it to the bottom of the steps and shine the flashlight at him.

He recoils immediately from the brightness and buries his chin in his chest.

"Kian, buddy, it's us," Esha says in a soft voice.

His head whips back up, eyes wide and a little crazed.

"I can't see you behind the bright light. Are you captured?" He asks.

"No," Garven says, "we're here to break you and Finley out."

They lower the flashlight so it's not pointing directly at him, and instead at the floor, where it illuminates enough of the surrounding area to show Kian that it is just the two of them. Garven shudders as the light also allows them to see the skulls and bones littered along the floor surrounding him.

"We're here to break the two of you out. Are you okay? Where's Finley?" Esha asks.

Kian tries to talk again but begins coughing badly. His face winces in pain as he does, before he's finally able to get out,

"Do you have any water?"

Garven walks over, kneels down next to him, and pulls his water bottle out of his backpack. He puts it up to his mouth for him as Esha comes over to unbind him from his chains.

After a couple small sips, Kian says,

"I don't know where they took Finley. They knocked me out cold and then dragged me down here."

"Damn. So, you're not sure whether they're here or in the church?" Garven asks.

"I'm not in the church?" Kian asks, confused.

"No, you're in the basement of a building next to it," Garven replies.

"How long have I been missing? They boarded up all the windows in the room, so I haven't had any way to tell. I'm freaking starving though," Kian says.

"Almost two days you've been gone. They haven't even fed you?" Esha asks.

"No, one of the Green Cloaks said I wasn't getting any food because they wanted Finley to heal me when they were awake. They hit me in the chest and back with some sort of rod… and gave me the tiniest sip of water. She said they needed me to be in bad shape, to test Fin," said Kian, slowly and with labored breath.

"Heal you? How? That doesn't even make any sense?" Esha asks.

"They," Kian begins saying, starting to gasp for air even worse, "were bringing Fin to a stone… I could see it when the doors opened…glowing green, they were all in there," Kian says.

He begins coughing hard, and his face winces again and again as he does.

"Okay, let's get you outta here and then figure out where Fin is," Garven says.

"You sure that's what we should do?" asks Esha.

"We're not going to be able to sneak around with Kian when he's in this state," Garven replies.

Esha nods, and they both help him to his feet.

His feet scrap along the sidewalk as he continues to move the flashlight back and forth across the buildings. The longer the Green Cloak is standing there, the more Mina wants to clear her throat or itch her nose. She closes her eyes and takes a slow, quiet, deep breath in to try and get her heart rate under control. It just makes her want to cough more.

At some point in the next few minutes, if all goes well, Garven will be popping his head back out of the window, and this guard cannot be standing there when he does. Mina feels helpless, and very, very alone at this moment.

She's been alone for most of her life, and finding Auryn on the ship seemed like an end to that feeling.

I guess it never really goes away though, she has thought to herself time and time again.

But having someone in her life she cares about, someone she likes, and maybe even… no. Not the thought for right know. Right now, she needs to wait out this guard, get Kian and Finley out of the building, and get the heck out of here.

As she finishes her thought, the guard mumbles,

"These damn kids. We should just have the spotlights on all the time. We've got more than enough power for them."

Spotlights? Mina thinks.

With that, the guard begins to walk away. He's far enough beyond the broken window that after a few steps the half wall blocks his view of it. Mina breathes a gentle sigh of relief. She tries to get up to her crouching position and struggles.

The struggle is exasperated by having to carry Kian up the first set of stairs. When Esha and Garven reach the top, they make sure to close and lock the door behind them.

"No way you can make it down these stairs on your own right?" Garven asks Kian.

Kian barely has the strength to look up at Garven and answer.

"How are we gonna get him out of the window?" Esha asks.

"We'll cross that bridge in a few minutes. No way we can just go up to the first floor," Garven replies.

"If I could have a small bite of food, I think it would help," Kian says, voice raspy.

"Let's get to the door at the end of the hallway, then you can have a bite. When we climb out of the window, you're gonna need all your strength that you have left though, Kian," Garven says.

"I'll do what I can so you can come back and find Fin," he replies.

Slowly, with each arm of Kian's wrapped over a shoulder of Garven and Esha, they make their way down the hallway. He stumbles often, and every time he does, they get more and more nervous about getting him out of here.

The thought of the Green Cloaks checking on him— and him not being there, setting off all their alarms— hangs over the three of them like a dense fog. Nobody wants to say anything, but this is taking longer than they thought it would, and with a guard making rounds outside, the timing to get out of this building and not get caught is tiny.

They reach the larger, empty room they first dropped into through the window and close the door behind them. Kian drops to one knee while Garven grabs a tomato from his backpack.

"Here," Garven says, and Kian looks up.

"This is the happiest I've been in days," Kian replies while grabbing the tomato.

He takes a small bite first, and a small smile creeps across his face. His next bite was much larger, and the slurping noises that come out while he's chewing gross Esha out a bit, but she doesn't say anything.

After a few more quick bites, he finishes. Just by his body language, Garven and Esha can tell he feels at least a little better.

"Let's get the heck outta here," Kian says.

They all stand, Kian on his own, and quietly walk over to the window. When they get below it, Kian says,

"How the heck am I gonna get out of that?"

"First, we're gonna boost Garven up, then he's gonna pull us up. Easy," Esha says.

Kian stares at the both of them for a second before saying,

"You're joking, right? I can barely hold myself up, and now I'm supposed to shove Garven? And my ribs, I can't even lift my arms above my head."

"Well, I'm going to lift Garven, you're going to stand there and let him climb on you on the way up. Then we'll figure out the best way to get you out," Esha replies.

Kian lets out the longest sign of his life.

"Unless you have a better idea," Garven says.

Kian shakes his head and then stands as close to the wall below the window as possible. Esha begins to hoist Garven up, and Garven puts a knee hard onto the shoulder of Kian for support. Kian grunts loudly.

"Shhh," Esha whispers.

Garven grabs ahold of the edge of the window and can feel small, leftover shards of glass pierce his gloves. He winces slightly but pulls himself up. As he looks out the window and across the street, he sees Mina, peering slightly over the half wall in front of her.

When she sees him, she flashes her flashlight one quick time at him, while making sure the guard, now 50 feet away, walking down the sidewalk of the long block surrounding the church, doesn't notice. Garven sticks one hand out the window and gives a thumbs up.

When he does, Mina takes one more glance down the street, then hops over the half wall and sprints across the street, simultaneously running as fast as she can, with the lightest footsteps she is able to muster. She crouches next to the window and grabs Garven's under arm and shoulder as he's trying to push himself up. Legs still in the basement, she pulls with every ounce of strength she has, and Garven gets to the point he can lay his stomach and hips on the ground. He's out.

"Please tell me you have good news. That feels too quick," Mina says.

"Half good news. We've got Kian, but Finley must be in the church," Garven replies.

"Damnit," Mina mutters.

They both turn around and see both of Kian's hands trying, in vain, to grab at the window. Mina and Garven each grab one and begin to pull.

"God. No. Oh my. Please. Oh god," Kian whispers yells as he's being pulled up.

He gasps for breath in short, staccato inhales as his head reaches the opening. The two of them grab under his arm and begin pulling up. Mina feels a pop from around his ribcage, and Kian snarls his lips up and lets out a deep, guttural breath.

"I know man, we're close. Stay with us," Garven whispers, with a rare sympathy towards Kian.

They grab him by the pant waist and pull him the rest of the way out of the window. Getting Esha out has its own challenges, but she runs towards the wall, jumps up, and grabs Garven's arms hanging down into the opening. Mina, now grabbing Garven's shoulder so he doesn't slip down farther, pulls again, and slowly Esha appears in the opening.

Mina crouches, then stands up farther to look around. The guard has made it to the other end of the block and turned the corner. They're free to make it across the street. With the help of the three of them, Kian manages to cross the empty street back to where Mina was originally hiding.

"What," Esha begins to say, "the frick are we gonna do now?"

CHAPTER 20: THE AWAKENING

I wake up with the worst headache of my life. It feels like I've been sleeping for a decade. My mouth tastes like something died in it, and my breath is terrible. As I begin to look around, I realize I don't know where I am.

I sit up on the bed I'm on, which is surprisingly comfortable, in a medium sized room, maybe 12 feet by 14 feet. Walls made of large gray stones, one stained glass window that looks like it has metal bars on the outside of it, and a large wooden door. I try to stand up and stumble before catching myself on the large wood bedpost. My head pounding, my eyes sensitive to the light coming from the half dozen candles that are lit around my room.

I gently walk over to the door and pull the handle, but it doesn't budge. I steady myself and take a deep breath, then pull harder on the handle. Still, no movement.

My eyes begin to focus more, and I look around the room. There is a small nightstand next to the bed, and a single sheet of paper on it. I walk over and pick up the paper.

"Finley, if you're reading this, congratulations. You lived. There will be many things to learn moving forward, and with our help, you will become The Keeper of the Emerald Stone.

P.s. There are some snacks across the room."

I look around the room, feel the wall with my bare hands, and search for an exit other than the door. Every time I turn to look in a different direction, the edges of my vision get fuzzy, and my head pounds like a rhythmic drum.

Across the room, on the opposite side of the door, and several feet away from the end table, is a small table with a pitcher of water on it and some small square bread pieces, an inch thick and about 3 inches long. I recognize the bread from Buffalo, it's a travel bread, packed with nutrients.

The other thing I remember about the bread is how dry it is. I might need this entire pitcher of water just to down one slice. I pour myself a cup and throw caution to the wind. Why would they poison me now if they're happy I'm awake?

I don't know how long I've been out, or how long I was talking with Abdo. Could have been a few hours, could have been a few days, but the way my stomach is currently growling makes me believe it's more time than less. I down the first cup of water in three huge gulps. I can feel each gulp slide down my desert dry throat, and my stomach gurgles as it reaches it. It's probably the fastest I've ever drank in my life, and it didn't even make a dent in how thirsty I am. I fill the glass a second time, and about half the pitcher of water is gone. I down that nearly as quickly. When done I gasp for air like I've just escaped drowning.

I sit on the edge of the bed for a moment in the hopes my headache subsides, even a little bit. To my delight, after two or three minutes, it does. The light doesn't feel so bright, and I can open my eyes a little wider.

I fill my cup one more time and grab a piece of bread. I walk back over to my bed once more and sit on the edge of it.

I replay the last few moments before I blacked out again. It plays in my mind like a dream. The green hue casting shadows across the entire room. The whispers speaking to me, and only me. The explosion of energy that erupted after I placed my hands on the stone. It all feels so impossible. From one dream to another I then think about the time I spent with Abdo. I feel a warmth inside me, fortunate to have someone to guide me.

A thought crosses my mind and startles me. Was any of that real? Was Abdo just a figure of my imagination? It felt real, that's for sure.

I take a bite of the bread, and it seems to absorb the small amount of moisture right out of my mouth. It feels like I'm torturing myself, but I need the food. The noises coming from my stomach are so loud I'm afraid they're going to echo off the cold stone walls and through the building.

As I'm finishing the first piece of bread, I hear voices outside the room.

"I'm not even sure they're awake yet. It's been almost two days, and they haven't moved an inch," I hear the familiar voice say. It's Colere.

"Well, if they're not, I have no problem coming back later," a second, cheerful voice says.

As she speaks, all the hairs on my arms stand straight up. My eyes widen, and a shiver runs down my spine.

"It can't be," I think, lying in the hopes of convincing myself.

I hear the familiar noise of a large piece of wood being removed from the front of the door. I then see the latch lift, and I am panic stricken as it slowly opens.

Strangely, I don't have the same fight or flight feeling I would normally under these circumstances. It's been replaced by a weird calm I find hard to process. Physically, I feel ready to jump out the window, or lunge towards the door, but mentally I feel a strange peacefulness.

I see Colere's head peek through the door and smile as her eyes meet mine.

"Oh good, you're awake. You had me worried there for a bit," she says.

"I don't want Luna anywhere near me or this room," I say, calm yet forceful, my eyes narrow and staring at Colere.

"Oh? So, you remember Luna? That's fantastic, she said she knew you," she replies.

As she does, the door swings open all the way, and standing right behind Colere's shoulder is her, the most evil and heartless person I've ever known.

"Hello Finley, it's so good to see you again," she says, as she shows me a pretend smile that makes me want to vacate this bread from my stomach.

I am filled with white hot rage. Everything I just thought a minute ago, about a calmness washing over me, is gone.

"Luna wants to talk to you for a few minutes. She tells me there was a misunderstanding on both your trips here to Toronto, and would like to clear the air," Colere says.

"There was no misunderstanding," I say, my throat dry and my voice crackling, "she tried to murder me and my friends."

"That doesn't sound like Luna. She's been nothing but a huge help to us. She told us that you came here to Toronto because of her, which I think is just perfect. I'll leave you two alone for a moment to get this figured out," replies Colere.

I'm about to protest again, and to ask about Kian, when Luna takes a few steps into the room and smiles at Colere as she does.

"Thank you so much, I think this will be really great for the both of us," Luna says, keeping her fake smile the entire time.

Colere puts her hand on Luna's shoulder, whispers something in her ear, and then grabs the door handle and starts to exit the room.

"DON'T leave me alone with her," I yell again, but the door closes with a loud *thud*, stranding me here with this murderer.

The smile immediately vanishes from Luna's face as she stares daggers in my direction.

"You have made this so much harder than it needs to be," she growls at me, keeping her voice too low for someone outside the room to hear.

I stand up off the bed to confront her, and in doing so I realize how weak my body feels. Whatever I've gone through the past few days has taken its toll on me. Still, a small dose of energy surges through me. I can feel it in my veins, like nothing I've ever felt before.

Luna walks slowly and aggressively toward me, and I look around the room for anything I might defend myself with. It's been cleared of any items I could have used to break out or defend myself.

As she gets close, she says,

"I'm going to kill you before your powers grow too strong. This is for Allison."

Who is Allison?

As I'm thinking that, she lunges at me and knocks me back onto the bed. She grabs something from her pocket and puts it in the palm of her right hand. I try to get up, but she's quick, and before I can free myself, she jumps on top of me on the bed.

She has her left hand on my neck. As I try to scream, she cuts the airway off, and almost no sound comes out. In my weakened state, I try first punching her in the head and neck area, and when that doesn't work, at her left arm that's holding me down.

Her legs are on top of mine, so I can't get much strength behind the punches. As I flail, her right hand comes towards my mouth, and instinctively I close it.

"You're…gonna…have… to… open… eventually…" she says through the fighting, each word dripping with hate.

She then pulls her hand away from my face, and in one swift motion punches me in the side, next to my stomach. The combination of the blow, with her other hand still on my neck, causes me to gasp for air, and when I do, she shoves a capelet in my mouth.

Without even biting down it's leaking a liquid over my tongue. It's bitter, and as I'm about to spit it out, she takes her free hand and covers my mouth again.

"The great thing about this poison is it doesn't have to be swallowed, only absorbed. You're already too late," she says.

With her hand covering my mouth, I do the only thing I can think of doing, which is bite down.

Hard.

I break skin as I close my mouth, and Luna yelps loudly.

"Help!" she yells, in the same fake tone she used when entering the room. She's jumped back off the bed, holding her hand up as the blood drips down to her palm, and then her wrist.

The door opens almost immediately.

"Oh my god, they ATTACKED me!" She yells as she stumbles back towards the door.

"Oh, my goodness, Luna, are you okay?" Colere says as she hurriedly enters the room. "You need medical attention. Let me take you to one of our healers," she then says.

"Yes, please, I can't believe they attacked me like that," Luna says, her voice a full octave higher than normal.

"I didn't attack her, she attacked me!" I plead.

"She's poisoned me!" I yell.

"We'll deal with you later," Colere says, scolding me as if I were a bratty child.

As she ushers Luna out of the room and locks the door behind her, I feel increasingly unwell. The room starts to spin, and I feel lightheaded. I try to stand up, and as I do the tunnel vision starts. This feels like the beginning of my panic attacks, but worse.

My stomach makes loud, unhappy noises and I look around to find a bathroom. In the corner, I see a bucket with a toilet seat on it. Infuriating, but good enough. I stumble over and throw up into the bucket. The noise echoes inside and hurts my head.

As I lift my head up, I feel, for a brief second, a little better. It doesn't last though, and the room gets spinny again. I stumble over to the bed and notice on the end table a small pocket mirror. The mirror portion is cracked in several places, and the plastic handle and frame around the mirror is faded.

I hold it up to my face and as I stare into my own eyes, they are pulsing a bright, vibrant emerald green color. It's not just a small ring, but my entire eye. The colors swirl through my eye, and every time the nausea starts to return, the green becomes even more intense, like pulsing green waves in my eyes.

It's disorienting, and I blink hard to try and steady myself. As I wipe the back of my hand against my sweaty forehead, I lose balance and fall onto the bed. Now, even with my eyes open, everything seems dark. I can feel the poison slowly infiltrating my body.

I want to scream but no longer have function over my voice. After all this time, I still have one question.

Why me?

I don't even know Luna, other than in passing. Why does she have such a deep hatred for me that she would go these lengths to kill me?

I don't understand, and considering I'm a few moments away from the end, I guess I never will.

A PRETTY LONG TIME AGO

(235ish Years Ago)

Fifteen years after Allison Finch rolled into the train station in New York City, she did something she never thought possible: She gave birth to her son.

After being placed in custody of the state, and being separated from her brother, who she never found again, she never thought happiness would come to her. So, when she found out she and her fiancé were to have a son, she was elated.

It also then came as no surprise to her that her fiancé died a few months before the child was to be born.

This is the way my life is, she often thought, *because I've been cursed to this life by the Green-Eyed Lady.*

She was so filled with anger that she taught her son, John Finch, to hate the green-eyed woman, and whoever would replace her in the future. After her fiancé died, she gave the boy her own last name, to pass down through the generations.

"They doomed us to this horrible life," she would tell John often.

She did as much research as she could, and slowly figured out who the Green Cloaks were, and that this woman, the so-called Emerald Stonekeeper, was a member of theirs.

A whole group of people who could help, and just picked and choose who and where to help?

The thought infuriated her. So, it was no surprise that the hatred stayed strong in her son.

In turn, when he had his first born (William, 1882), he passed on that hatred as well.

So it went, through Charles (born 1911), Frank (1939), Henry (1965), Thomas (1993), Joshua (2020), Ethan (2048), and Anthony (2075). Even when the Emerald Stonekeeper vanished from the Earth, they were taught to hate whoever eventually came back. Some, like Frank, took it more seriously, and others, like Joshua, thought it something of a silly family lore.

When, by 2103, an entire family history of men did nothing to avenge Allison, it was now up to the newest member of the family: Luna Finch. Luna, with a single poison pill, just might have finished the job that eight sons in two and a half centuries couldn't.

CHAPTER 21: BREAK-OUT

"We broke into one building, I guess we gotta break into another," says Esha.

"I'm coming this time; you're going to need all the help you can get," says Mina.

"We're just going to leave Kian here? He's in rough shape, Mina," replies Garven.

"There's no safer place for him than outside the building. He can't come with us, and I'm not staying here as a lookout any longer," Mina says.

There was no talking her out of it, Esha and Garven could tell.

"Look, I know I don't know you all that well, but I do know Auryn, and this is the most important thing in the world to her right now, so it's the most important thing in the world to me as well," Mina then says.

"Alright, let's figure out how to get in there," Esha says, with resignation in her voice.

They stay crouched down behind the wall and walk back and forth a bit. After a few minutes, the Green Cloak turns the corner again and shines his flashlight at all the buildings, as he had last time. In doing so, he's paying no attention to the building they just escaped out of and its broken window.

Once he's far enough away again, the three of them crouch and quickly walk across the street. They stay tight and low against the building, making sure to peek around each corner before moving further. Some clouds begin to cover the moon, and the night becomes dark.

As they peek around another corner, they see a separation between the two buildings, and a door leading into the church.

"What are the chances that door is unlocked?" Esha whispers.

"I don't know, but we should find out," replies Mina.

They continue to stay close to the wall as they approach the door. Garven tries the handle, and it's open. He slowly and quietly opens it far enough for Mina and Esha to walk through and then enters the church himself. As he tries to quietly close it, the handle slips out of his hand.

CLANG.

The door closes loudly, echoing through the long hallway they entered. Esha whips her head around, eyes large, and mouths the words,

"Come on, man."

They stay silent for a moment, and down the hallway and around the corner, they hear footsteps. There's a coat room right next to the doorway that the three of them shuffle into quickly.

Large, old wooden coat closets line the walls, with a few long coats hanging on hangers. As the footsteps approach, the three of them get into different sections and hide behind already hanging coats. If anyone were to really look for someone in the room, they'd see their feet below, or notice the backpacks pressed against the sides. Not an ideal hiding spot.

Halfway down the hall, the Green Cloak says,

"Is that you, Maxwell?"

No response.

He walks further towards the doors, and when he gets there, places a hand on the metal push bar that opens them from the inside. He opens the doors a foot and looks around outside.

"Weird. I could have sworn I heard this door shut," he says.

He lingers for a moment, looking out the narrow window of the door. Esha sneaks a quick look out from behind one of the jackets and see's he's wearing a full-length green cloak with green hood.

They really live up to their name, she thinks to herself.

As he turns away from the door, Esha ducks back behind the coat. If it were daylight out, with the sun shining into the building, he might have noticed the gentle sway from the coat and wondered why there was movement there. Instead, the dim, solar powered lighting hid the three of them well enough for him not to notice and simply begin walking back down the hallway.

As the footsteps become quieter, the three of them removed themselves from the coat area and peek around the corner. With no one in sight, they huddle back up.

"Okay so what's the plan here? We try each room? These doors are heavy and loud, and Finley's is going to be locked, right?" Garven says.

"I don't really see any other way. Make the rounds, try the handles, see what happens," Esha says.

"I don't like this at all," Garven replies.

Esha shrugs and says,

"We've come too far to give up now, especially breaking out Kian. It's only a matter of time before they realize what's going on."

Garven sighs, nods, and peeks around the corner again. They slowly make their way down the hallway. Esha tries a doorknob on the right, and it opens. Inside the room are a couple of couches, a table, and nothing else. She quietly closes it, and they move forward.

"What if we open someone's bedroom?" Mina whispers.

"Do people sleep here?" Esha asks.

Mina shrugs.

Garven tries a handle for a door on the left, and it doesn't budge.

"We'll come back to it," he says.

They all nod and keep moving.

As they reach the end of the first hallway, there are options to go left and right. They listen for a moment and hear two voices coming from the left, down a ways and around the corner.

"We should avoid that way," Mina says.

Esha and Garven agree, and they head towards the right. After a few steps Esha looks beyond them and sees some shadows being cast from the opposite direction. The shadows are slowly getting larger.

"Someone's coming," she whispers.

They try the first door. It's locked. Esha's heart begins to race. The voices are getting closer, the shadows larger on the walls.

Garven crosses the eight-foot-wide hallway and tries the door on the left. The handle turns and they rush to enter the room. Once in, they slowly and carefully close the door behind them, then turn the lock. The clicking noise echoes into the hallway.

"Why is everything so loud in this place?" Garven asks to no one in particular.

They take a quick look around the dimly lit room while waiting for the people to pass by. Mina notices a wall with a bunch of writing on it. She slowly walks over and sees Finley's name, along with Kian, Garven, and Esha's.

"Uh, guys?" she says.

"What?" Esha replies.

"You might want to see this," Mina says, voice hushed but nervous.

Esha and Garven walk over, and as their eyes focus on the dark wall, they see it. Finley's name in big black lettering, in the middle and circled. A line off of it to Esha's name, another to Garven's name, and a third to Kian's. Under Kian's name it says "BUFFALO" in big bold letters, and under the other three it says "CLEVELAND."

"What the hell is this?" Garven asks.

"I think it means they've been tracking all four of you the whole time," Mina says.

There are two longer lines coming off of Finley's circle as well, each with a smaller circle at the end of them. They reach out farther than Esha, Garven, and Kian's names, and then have faint lines to each other as well. Both of the smaller circles contain the same writing:

?

Woman

20ish

Relationship?

"Well, if there was any doubt before, there's no going back to our old life knowing this," Esha says.

"Yeah. Yeah, that's correct," Mina replies.

"Well, as creepy as this is, there's nothing we can do about this now. Let's find Fin and get outta here," Garven says.

Mina smirks for a second as she looks at Garven and Esha. She grabs the marker on the small ledge below the dry erase board. She writes "Sarah" next to one of the question marks, and "Caia" next to the other. She puts the marker down and chuckles to herself.

"Well," Garven says, while smiling, "sure."

The three of them laugh quietly and head back towards the door. Esha puts her ear up to it to listen for any noises coming from outside. After hearing none, she slowly opens it.

Once in the hallway, they continue heading in the same direction as before. The lights on the walls are dimming even more the later into the evening they go, some of them out completely, creating long stretches of darkness through the halls.

After 20 feet of careful walking, they get to another intersection. They can keep going straight, but as they get towards the corner, they hear voices from the hallway branching off to the left. Esha puts her finger up to her lips to make sure everyone is quiet, and then she slowly, and just barely, peeks around the corner.

"My god, I can't believe they attacked me like that," Luna says to Colere, acting surprised by it.

Esha whips her head back around to look at Garven and Mina, eyes wide, teeth gritted.

"What?" Mina mouths.

"It's Luna," Esha angry whispers.

Garven's face changes immediately. Mina's never seen him so angry in the short time they've hung out together. Concern, worry, maybe even anxiety filled, but never like this. Even in the low lighting she can tell he's pissed.

"Are you sure you're telling me the whole truth, Luna?" Colere asks her, eyes narrowed.

"I swear it on my family's name," Luna replies.

"Well, let's give them some time to cool down then," Colere answers, still looking wary of Luna.

"I think that's a good idea," Luna says.

As they walk away from Finley's room in the opposite direction of the three of them, Esha turns and says,

"I know what room Fin's in. They're right down this hallway."

"How can you be so sure?" Garven asks.

"There's a large wood bar across the front of it, locking it closed," Esha replies.

"That does seem promising," says Mina.

Esha waits for Colere and Luna to turn the corner farther down before she steps out into the hallway. In this hallway there are extra lights set up, and even a small, lit torch on the wall. After she takes a few steps, she hears footsteps from down past Fin's room. She backs up immediately, slamming into the front of Mina.

"Um, ow," Mina says.

Without saying anything, Esha looks around the corner just a sliver, and a Green Cloak guard is walking down the hallway towards Fin's room. They stop for a moment in front of the door, turn around, and walk back down the hall.

"They have a guard patrolling the area," Esha says.

"How many guards to they have in this place?" Garven asks.

"We should time how long it takes for them to come back, so we know how long we have to get Fin and get out," Esha says.

"Smart, but what if someone comes from the other way?" Garven asks.

"We'll burn that bridge when we come to it," Esha says, a smile on her face as she does.

"I like that, I'm gonna steal that. I love bridge related sayings," says Mina.

Esha watches the hallway waiting for a Green Cloak guard. After four minutes, the guard returns, walks down the hallway, checks that the lock is still on the door, and walks away.

"Now," says Esha.

They quickly walk to Finley's door, and Esha puts an ear up to it. She can't hear anything, so she and Garven carefully lift up the heavy piece of wood that lays between the two metal pieces bolted to the door, keeping it closed from the outside. They then turn a smaller standard room lock and carefully open the door.

CHAPTER 22: THE RESISTANCE

I'm struggling to maintain consciousness as I look toward the door, where I think I just heard a sound.

"She…." I try to get out, voice muffled and quiet, "poisoned me."

My heart is pumping furiously, trying to combat the poison running through my system. I want to pass out, but I can also feel something besides the poison coursing through me.

Several figures rush to me on the bed. My vision pulses between blurry and black, and my brain isn't filtering the words being spoken to me clearly. A hand grabs my wrist, and I do what I can to pull away, slapping my other hand at the arm of the intruder. Without warning, I am picked up off the bed and slung over someone's shoulder.

My head is pounding, and the sudden rush of blood to it makes it unbearable. I start sniffling and then crying.

"Please, please be quiet" someone whispers in my ear several times. It's a familiar voice, and my brain tries desperately to place it.

"Esha?" I ask, blood pumping through the front of my head.

"Yes Fin, it's Esha, please be quiet," she whispers right next to my ear.

After walking a few more steps, the lighting changes from my overly lit room to a darker surrounding. At first, I thought it was just my tunnel vision again, but I'm starting to be able to make out lights on the hallway walls. I lift my head up and see behind us is Mina, putting a large piece of wood up against the door to the room I was just trapped in.

I look to my right and next to us is Esha, moving her hand in a motion that says *hurry up* to Mina. She finishes and quickly walks towards us. As she meets up with us, everyone starts quickly walking away from the door.

Each second my vision and hearing are improving a tiny amount, enough for me to see, right before we turn the corner, a blurry figure at the far end of the hallway.

"HEY!" she yells, "STOP RIGHT THERE!"

"RUN!" Mina yells, and suddenly the three of them start sprinting.

The bouncing from Garven running is excruciating, his shoulders repeatedly pummeling my lower rib cage, forcing breath out of my lungs. We make a turn, and then after a few more hits to my ribs, another. By now, chaos has spread through the building. People are yelling, someone is ringing the loudest bell I've ever heard in my life, although that might be my headache talking. I don't know how much farther we have to get out of the building, but I know we don't have much time.

After one more turn, I hear Mina say,

"There's the door, go go go!"

We sprint down a long hallway, and I can hear Esha push open a door ahead of us. As we go through the door, my shoulder slams into the metal stanchion in the middle of the double doors.

"Can you watch it, please," I say as loud as I can, which is still quite soft.

"Sorry!" says Garven.

We start sprinting away from the building, and when we reach 45 feet outside of it, I look up to see a half dozen Green Cloaks spill out of the building after us and look around. With my vision still improving, I see one of them stop, lift a bow up, and take aim at us.

They let go and it whizzes by Garven's ear.

"DAMN, was that an arrow?" he asks.

"HURRY UP!" Esha yells.

As we do, suddenly the area is flooded with bright, harsh lights. On top of the church are two large spotlights, both pointed in our direction. We don't even have the cover of night on our side anymore.

We reach the intersection and keep sprinting. On the road behind and to the left of us, four more Green Cloaks rush out into the street. Some with torches, another with a bow. They're only 60 feet away, and with Garven carrying me, they're gaining.

Another arrow flies by, this time clipping Esha in the arm.

She mutters something that I can't hear, and as we reach the other side of the intersection, I hear Mina yelling at Kian.

"Get up! We gotta go!"

I look around and see Kian trying to get up onto his feet. He looks like he's in bad shape, stumbling as he stands, then limping badly as he starts to run.

He's not gonna make it, I think to myself.

We make brief eye contact, and he begins to smile at me as he's trying to pick up speed. The Green Cloaks are getting closer, only 35 feet away now.

As Kian turns to run alongside us, he suddenly lurches forward and lets out a scream. The type of scream I've heard very few times in my life. The last time being outside Cleveland, when the wall was pushed on that Raider. A horrible, agonizing scream. As I look down at his abdomen, I gasp.

"LET ME DOWN!" I yell at Garven.

Startled, he throws me off his shoulder, and the pure adrenaline pumping through my body I half jog, half stumble over to Kian, who is now down on one knee. I see the arrow firmly stuck into the side of his lower back, blood beginning to pool out.

"SOMEBODY HELP HIM!" I yell.

"You have to let me go, Fin. I'm not going to make it," Kian says.

"But you can't just give up. You need to fight. I NEED you to fight," I say.

"And I need you to live, Fin," he replies.

The guards are even closer now, and two of them are drawing their bows. I turn my head as they do, and attempt to cover Kian, hoping that maybe they won't want to kill me.

"I need you, Kian, please don't give up," I say to him, tears streaming down my face, making his shirt wet.

Even if Garven or Esha could help Kian to his feet, where are we going to run to, where are we going to hide?

As the guards' arms are pulled nearly all the way on the bow, I see the light reflecting off of something behind them.

Someone dressed in dark clothes is holding a bottle that glistens in the reflection of the spotlights, then, the top of the bottle ignites in a small flame. In one smooth, beautiful motion, it's being launched in the air and towards our direction.

It flips around while mid-air, and while it does, more and more of the inside of the bottle lights on fire. A beacon in the sky, hurtling toward the group of Green Cloaks, who are completely unaware of the impending impact.

A split second before the first bowman is about to release an arrow aimed at Mina, the bottle hits his shoulder, explodes on impact, and lights his cloak on fire. The impact causes the arrow to fly forward but just misses because of the Molotov cocktail.

He lets out a blood curdling scream and begins flailing his arms around trying to put out the fire. For a brief second, I laugh, thinking about all the times my parents told me about "Stop, Drop, and Roll," something I'm sure he wishes he knew about right now.

With the sudden commotion, most of the guards turn around to see what's behind them, and as they do, the figure lights another bottle on fire. This time, instead of launching it in our direction, they turn, take aim at a church window, and launch one through one of the stained-glass windows.

"What the hell?" Mina asks no one in particular.

"Auryn?" Esha asks.

Garven, now only a step away from Kian, laughs as he begins to pick him up off the ground.

"I should have known," he says.

Four of the guards split off and begin chasing Auryn, and four more turn back around and head towards the Church. The one who's lit on fire is currently being helped by the last guard, who ripped off their cloak and wrapped it around them.

By now we're all on our feet, Kian with an arm slung around Garven's shoulder.

"Where do we even go?" I ask.

As the guards running back towards the church get halfway there, Colere starts yelling,

"Do NOT let them get away. Get back over there and GRAB FINLEY!" The four of them pause for a moment, confused about what to do.

At this moment, Auryn disappears into an alleyway. As the guards chasing her get towards the opening, another lit bottle crashes into the ground in front of them, immediately halting them. If they think they're going to catch her when she has that far of a head start, good luck.

"PSSST," someone yells down the street half a block from us, in the opposite direction of the guards.

I turn my head away from watching Auryn and see the person peeking out from an alleyway. They are waving for us to follow them. Generally, I wouldn't recommend following a stranger in the middle of the night, but we're all out of good options.

Kian takes a couple of steps with Garven but can hardly even stand.

"This is gonna hurt," Garven says, before he then picks Kian up and flings him over his shoulder, careful to not disturb the arrow still sticking out of him. Kian makes an audible groaning noise.

Garven has gotten strong the past few years, I think to myself.

We all jog the best we can towards the person peeking out from the corner. I'm expecting to stumble as I do, but to my amazement, I feel…fine?

How is that even possible? Luna just attempted to poison me to death. I think.

When we reach the corner, she says,

"Follow me, we have a hideout in this little maze of alleys."

A hideout, for what?

I don't have time to think about it as we keep running down the alleyway. We make a left, followed by a quick right. Another 30 feet down, we start to turn the corner as we hear a couple of the Green Cloaks yelling far behind us.

"They can't have gone far. Split up and FIND THEM."

That's Colere's voice, and to say she's mad would be an understatement.

The person leading us slows down, looks back behind us to see if anyone is close, then knocks on a door.

Tap (short pause), tap tap, (short pause), tap tap tap.

"You need a shorter secret knock," says Esha.

I have to stifle a laugh after she says it. The eye hole slides open and then slams shut no more than two seconds later. The door swings open and the man inside quietly yells,

"Get in, quick!"

Once we're all in, he locks and closes the door behind. They put out the candle in the window and close the dark curtains over the large bay window in the front of the apartment.

"Everyone's going to need to be real, real quiet for a minute," the woman says.

Kian grunts and slowly gets down to his hands and knees. He then lays all the way on the floor and begins to say,

"What are we…"

But gets cut off by the woman placing a hand on his shoulder, and then the sound of people yelling outside.

"No, I don't know where they went! They disappeared when they turned the corner!" a man's voice says.

"Keep it down out there, we're trying to sleep!" Another voice yells out.

"Ma'am, get back inside your home, this doesn't concern you," the man's voice yells back.

"You're not the police, and you can't tell me what to do, so: Shut. Up!" She yells in return.

Over the next minute, lots of footsteps go running by the alley in front of the home, mere feet from where we're all sitting on the ground.

As the voices dissipate and quiet takes over the night, the man lights one single candle and places it on a small table nearby.

"My name's Elim," the man begins saying, "that's Albie."

He points to the woman who helped us.

"I suppose you're wondering why we helped you," he begins to say.

"I'd love to hear all about it, but he's been shot with an arrow," I say in a panicked voice.

Elim's eyes get wide, and he brings the candle closer. I nudge Kian to move into a different position so we can better see the wound, but he doesn't respond.

"Kian? Kian!" I say, tapping on his leg.

Nothing.

"He's lost consciousness, we have to do something," Mina says.

"That's a lot of blood, I don't know if we have anything that can help with that," Albie says.

"Do you have a shirt or something we can use to try and stop the bleeding? Everything we have is dirty," Esha asks.

Albie quickly grabs a shirt and tosses it to me.

"We have to get that arrow out of him, I think. Right?" I ask.

"I don't know, I think it depends on if it hit an artery," Garven says.

"How would we know that?" I say as I lift up Kian's shirt and start pressing the clean shirt around the wound.

"He probably would have bled out by now if it had. Take out that arrow and I'll try to patch him up," says Elim.

"You a doctor?" Garven asks.

"Uh, sort of," Elim responds.

"If someone can help me take the arrow out, I think I got this," I say, mustering as much fake confidence as I can.

"What do you mean you 'got this,' Finley?" Esha asks.

"Just, give me a sec. Help me get this arrow out and trust me," I reply.

Elim bends down next to me, and as I hold Kian in place, cloth ready, he grabs the arrow. He looks at me, I nod, and he yanks the arrow out of Kian. The blood pours out faster as I cover it and press my hands down firmly.

I close my eyes and think of what Abdo told me. I have the power to heal people, I just need to figure out how, and quickly. I close my eyes tightly and try to concentrate. I feel a calmness start to wash over me.

"Whatever you're gonna do, you gotta do it fast," Esha says.

"Yeah, come on Fin, he's dying," says Garven.

"Look, I can get my tools, I can stitch him up if the internal bleeding isn't too bad," Elim says.

"I need everyone to do me a favor and please, please shut up for two seconds," I say.

"He might be dead in two seconds!" Albie says.

"SHUT. UP!" I respond.

I take a deep breath as the room falls silent again. I can feel the warm, stagnant air surrounding me. I hear the labored breathing of Garven, and can feel the stares of the entire room, especially Albie's. Kian's breathing is shallow, and any moment now, he might reach the point of no return. Abdo warned me that people close to death cannot be saved. I am running out of time and have no idea what to do.

I remove the cloth between my hands and Kian's wound, putting my fingers directly on it. I can feel the blood covering my fingertips, I breathe in deep and try to feel a connection, any connection, to myself, to Kian, to the stone. As I imagine the stone, I feel a tiny, brief surge of energy pulse through me.

I take another breath, steadying myself, and imagine placing my hands on the stone, the power I felt coursing through me, the way I felt more powerful than the sun itself. I open my eyes and direct all my energy towards Kian's wound. My hands, bloody, begin to tingle. In my peripheral vision, I see the room has a green tint to it.

I can hear the muffled voice of Albie saying,

"What the hell?"

I close my eyes once again and feel a connection to Kian's body, like I've welded my hands onto his side. I go deeper into my mind and can picture his insides, where the arrow hit, what inside is bleeding. I can feel the pain he's feeling, and it's excruciating. I want to yell, I want to take my hands off him, but I want most of all to save him.

What I said to him before was true, I do need him, even if I didn't realize the full extent until now. Not for survival, or because I couldn't make it on my own, but because I'm strong enough to admit to the people I love that my life would have less meaning with them not in it.

In my mind, I can now see the vein that was pierced. I imagine myself repairing it, I can see the scarring over top, I can feel the blood loss slow, the tissues around the area start to repair. Finally, I can feel the pierced skin mend itself back together.

I open my eyes and look down again, seeing the wound closed, and the skin scarred around it, and I marvel at what I've just done. A split second before I lose consciousness, I can hear them. I can hear a thousand whispers once again,

"We knew you couldn't resist."

THE ELEVENTH DREAM

I open my eyes, and I am no longer in the living room of a stranger's apartment, I am in my Stonekeeper's room. It's empty, like it was before, but now I know I have the power to change that. Along a wall I imagine a bunch of stone blocks with some pillows on top, and they appear. On the floor, there are a couple of mats to sit or lay down on. The ceiling turns dark, like the night sky.

A few feet away from the mats I place an old metal table and chair set, weathered by years of being outside. I smile as I look around.

"Yeah, this looks almost exactly like my rooftop in Cleveland," I think to myself.

I then imagine the door to the room as the door to my family's apartment, a worn-down kick plate and all.

I walk through the door and into my waiting room, where I imagine an old, 20th century style phone booth I saw in some of my dad's old magazines. What a cool concept, having your own little space in public to contact someone you need. By the time I was around, cell towers weren't functioning anymore, and reaching others was tough. Before the ships took all our main technology with them, people were re-building old telephone landlines again, but with not enough experts and not enough people, they gave up on it.

I walk into the booth and pick up the phone, a pleasant-sounding voice comes on the line and says:

"Would you like to reach Abdo, Sun-young, or someone else at this time?"

"Someone else, please," I say, interested in what that means.

"We're sorry, no one else is available right now," the kind voice replies.

"Abdo," I then say, and I am immediately teleported into the waiting room of Abdo.

I walk over to his door and knock on it. It pops open slightly, and I push it open further as I enter the room.

"Ah, Finley. I trust you found your way here easier this time?" He says with a smile.

"That is an understatement," I reply.

"I'm glad to hear it. I'm also glad I happen to be here! Although the older and weaker I get, the more time I spend here. It's nice not feeling the aches and pains of the mortal world," he says.

"How are things going for you Abdo, in Sudan?" I ask.

"Oh, you know. They're alright. For some reason the Red Cloaks have been in a little more of a tizzy the last little bit, asking people if they know where I am, but I just lay low and stay unassuming," he replies.

"So, they don't know your whereabouts?" I ask.

"Not exactly, no. In my younger days, when they were especially bold, they'd try to kidnap me or steal the stone. On their worst days they'd try to convince me to join them, but controlling fire and heat has always allowed me to protect and defend myself. If they found me now though, they would find the stone, since I always keep it on me. I'm old now so I don't think I'd be able to do much to protect myself anymore," he says.

"Why do you keep the stone on you? I only touched the Emerald Stone once and I was just able to heal someone a few days later," I say.

"Well, it's different for all the Stonekeepers, but the longer you're away from it, the weaker your connection to it is, so since I'm as old as I am, I just keep it on me. Wouldn't be as easy for you though, since your stone is so dang big," Abdo says.

He laughs as he says it, and I do too, picturing that giant thing sitting in a backpack, me lugging it around.

"So, when you're not near the stone, it doesn't whisper to you anymore?" I ask him.

"Oh, my stone hasn't whispered to me since the first day I touched it. That's how it usually goes. Sun-young and I sometimes get to talkin', and wondering if it ever even really happened, it's been so long," he says.

I look down at the ground and my face scrunches slightly. *They don't still hear the whispers?* I think to myself. Maybe I just heard them again because I'm so close to it? But Abdo has his on him, so that can't be it.

"What's got you troubled, Fin?" He asks.

"So, you have never heard the whispers from your stone again. Like, *ever* ever?" I ask.

"Not since the few seconds before I touched it for the first time. Why do you ask?" he replies.

"Well," I pause for a moment, "right before I came here and saw you, someone close to me was shot with an arrow, and in really bad shape. I was able to heal them by picturing the stone in my mind, and focusing on the connection to it," I say.

"Well, that's great!" Abdo replies. Before he could continue, I cut him off.

"But after I healed him, and right before I passed out, the whispers spoke to me."

There's an uncomfortable moment of silence between us, with Abdo staring at me intensely. I break eye contact and look around the room, waiting for him to say something, anything really.

"You're telling me that the voices from your stone still whisper to you?" He finally asks.

"At least this one time, yes," I say.

He raises his hand to his face and rubs his temples. He then shakes his head and mutters,

"Ieu tiasa janten masalah."

"Um. I have some things I need to look up, and to discuss with Sun-young. You mind giving me a little time?" He asks.

"Of course, sure, yeah. Should I go back to my place, or wake up, or…" I say.

"That part is entirely up to you. Let's meet back in a day," he says, obviously distracted.

I leave his room without him saying anything to me, and stand in his waiting room for a moment, wondering what all that just was. He's never been so short with me before, and certainly never kicked me out.

It's only felt like a few minutes here, but I wonder how long I've been knocked out in the real world. I'm also left wondering how I got here without specifically concentrating on it. Do I now come here every time I sleep? I guess I won't know until I try and pass out again later.

CHAPTER 23: NADIRA'S FRIENDS

I close my eyes and allow myself to come back to the real world. I am no longer on the floor, but instead laying on a small loveseat with a thin blanket draped over me. I open my eyes, and sitting on a chair next to me is Kian, looking exhausted, but smiling.

"Hey there," he says, "I hear I owe you a big ol' thank you."

"You don't owe me anything. I would have done whatever I could to save you," I respond.

He stands up, having difficulty as he does, and comes to sit down on the couch next to me. My legs wrap behind him as I lay on my side. He puts his hand on my leg and rubs it gently.

"I'm really glad you're okay. I was really worried about you in there. I didn't know what they were going to do to you," he says, making direct eye contact with me the whole time.

"Me? I was worried about you in there," I say back to him.

As I do, Albie, Elim, Garven, Esha, and Mina all walk back into the room.

"What. The hell. Was that?" Albie asks out loud.

"I can't believe it. It's true. The rumors are true," Elim says, disbelief splashed across his face.

"What's true?" Mina asks.

"You're the Emerald Stonekeeper, aren't you?" Elim says.

I push myself up onto one elbow, and then all the way up to a seated position, sliding my legs out from behind Kian.

"That's the stuff of myths," Albie replies.

Elim ignores her entirely.

"Yes," I say, not sure how to continue.

"I KNEW it! Elim shouts. "The Green Cloaks have been so much more unbearable recently. Walking around with weapons shown. Yelling at people, acting like they own the city. I KNEW something was up with them. Totally makes sense why you all were fleeing from them." Elim says.

"They kidnapped me a few days ago. Me and Kian. Garven, Esha, Mina and Auryn came to—" I freeze mid-sentence.

"Where's Auryn?!" I ask loudly.

"Don't worry, we have people out looking for her," Albie says.

"What? What people? She has nowhere to go. We gotta find her. I have to go now," I say as I start trying to get up from the couch.

As I do, I get light-headed and stumble for a moment.

"You cannot go out there. Not in the shape you're in, and not with every Green Cloak in the city looking for you," Esha says.

"But we have to find her!" I plead.

"She'll be found, Finley. Elim, Albie, and us have been talkin' while you've been passed out the last half hour. They're members of the Green Cloak Resistance. They call themselves 'Friends of Nadira,'" Garven says.

"Nadira was one of the first people in this neighborhood kidnapped by The Green Cloaks, never to be seen again. She was a shining light, and we will not let her disappearance be for nothing," Albie says.

"Why'd they kidnap her?" I ask.

"She was a beacon for those in need. Feeding people who were hungry, finding abandoned apartments for people to live in who the city didn't think worthy of being here. She was truly here to help others, not just those who bow down to the Cloak," Elim says.

"They've really infiltrated every level of the government here in Toronto. City board members, police officers, even random citizens will narc on others just to try and gain favor. They control so much of the food, and even the technology here downtown," Albie says.

"We've seen them fiddling with the old phone towers and wires over the past year. We think they might be trying to get communications back online, but only for themselves I'm guessing," says Elim.

I sit back down on the couch as they talk. I knew the Green Cloaks were bad news, but I didn't know it had gotten to be this bad. I thought it was just me and my friends that they were trying to take down, I didn't know it was anyone who disagreed with them.

"The good news, strike that, the GREAT news, is that we now have a secret weapon," Elim says excitedly.

"What weapon?" I ask.

"You."

CHAPTER 24: AURYN'S CHAPTER

After tossing her third and final Molotov cocktail at the guards chasing her down the alley, Auryn turned and sprinted. Things went downhill quickly, and she doesn't know if the rest of them are going to get away.

"There were so many Green Cloaks so quickly," she muttered to herself when she reached her third block of running.

After hopping over an old chain link fence between two more run-down looking buildings, she checks behind her. She doesn't see anyone but can still hear voices in the distance. She runs another block, then turns right to start heading in the direction of the rest of the group.

As she approaches a corner, she hears more shouting. She slows up and briefly checks around the edge of the building, and as she does, she sees two more Green Cloaks down the block, shining flashlights in each direction.

I have to get off the streets, she thinks to herself, as her back is against the wall of the building.

She also wonders if the rest of them made it. She could tell that she peeled off a bunch of Green Cloaks who were chasing them, but they all looked in such rough shape, she can't be sure it's enough.

She waits a minute before peeking around the corner again, and sees this block is all clear. She sprints across the wide, pothole ridden street and down another narrow alleyway before noticing a row of connected buildings with the front door propped open. In the cover of the dark night, she slides inside and sees a hallway with even more doors. It's too dark to see so she grabs her crank flashlight, turns it a few times, and as it begins to light up, she sees a half dozen men standing outside a door at the end of the hallway.

"Turn that off, who's shining that at us?" A voice asks.

"Sorry, no one," Auryn says as she turns it off.

"Oh, a lady, well damn I didn't know we were gonna have a visitor," one of the men reply in a tone unsettling to Auryn.

She sighs deeply.

I can't go anywhere on this forsaken planet without running into jerks, she thinks to herself.

With that, she starts walking backwards. With it being as dark as it is, she can slip out quickly and without them seeing. As she's about to turn back into the vestibule, she hears footsteps squeaking towards her from down the hall, and the group of men are shouting at her.

"Where ya going, beautiful?" One yells.

You don't even know what I look like, you idiots, she thinks to herself.

She exits out the door and notices some old boards leaning up against the wall of the building to the left. She quickly scans the area, and the street is too wide open, she'll be seen. She's already so exhausted, the adrenaline quickly fading from her body, that she decides to take a calculated risk and try hiding.

She slips behind the boards and slows her breathing down.

I hate this stupid planet, she thinks, as a couple of the guys come streaming out of the door.

In the next few seconds, all half dozen guys come pouring out of the building. In the illumination of the night sky, she can see they range in age from late teens to early thirties.

"Where'd ya go, sweet thing?" One of them calls out.

Auryn shudders at the thought.

As they make more and more noise, hollering and asking where Auryn went, a voice from down the street yells out.

"You gentlemen shouldn't be out this late."

It was a stern voice, a man, probably in his 40's or 50's, sounding exactly like every security guard Auryn's ever heard talk.

"Yeah? Says who?" One of the guys responds.

"Says us," The man replies.

Auryn can't see who the man, or "us," is, but the guys that were just harassing her are awfully quiet now.

"Come on man," one of them mutters under their breath.

In the quiet of the night, Auryn can hear multiple footsteps walking down the street in their direction, echoing off the dilapidated buildings.

As they get closer, the new voice says,

"You know you shouldn't be out this late, making all this noise, waking people up from their sleep."

"Not a problem GC, we're heading back in now," one of the half dozen of them replies.

"Maybe we would have let that go, but you know how much we hate being called Green Cloaks, so we're going to need you all to stick around a minute and have a little discussion," the man replies.

Auryn peaks out slightly from behind the large, partially rotted old sheets of wood. From the looks of the buildings across the street, it looks like these were torn off the roofs sometime in the last year or two. Maybe it's how they're keeping this place standing, by harvesting materials from other buildings nearby.

She sees a group of four Green Cloaks walk up to the guys. One of them has a crossbow, another a crowbar.

"Any of you happen to see a young woman run in this direction recently?" The main Green Cloak asks.

Auryn was right, he looks to be about 40, with a strong jaw, and a scruffy beard. He's 6'5, much taller than anyone else around him, and even under his cloak you can tell he got serious muscles.

The guys all look at each other and don't say anything.

Why wouldn't they just say yes? Auryn wonders.

"I asked you all a question," he says, increasing his volume.

"Nah man, we haven't seen anyone," one of the guys reply.

He's 5'9 and wearing a grey hoodie and dark jeans. As he says it, he's looking at the ground.

The tall Green Cloak walks up close to him and says,

"Oh, so you were all yelling out here for who? No one? Just yelling into the night sky for an invisible, no wait, imaginary person?"

"No man, it was no one. We were all just joking around," another man says.

He looks like he's the oldest of the group. Wearing a black long sleeve shirt and lighter jeans, hands inside his pant pockets.

"Ohhhh!" The Green Cloak begins to say.

"Just joking around! That's all? Well then, I guess we're all good here!"

The second he finishes the sentence; he takes a baton he had hidden under his cloak and strikes the guy in the gray hoodie right on his thigh. Its impact is loud, and Auryn can only imagine how much that must have hurt.

Gray hoodie guy yells out in shock and pain as he takes a knee to the ground. The Green Cloak leader raises his arm in the air, and right before he brings it down to inflict even more pain, the older guy says,

"Wait! Wait. Yeah, she came into our building a few minutes ago. We told her she should wait around and hang out, but she ran back out the door. We were coming out looking for her when you guys arrived. That's it, I swear."

"She should hang out?" He responds.

"Yeah, that's all. Then she ran out here and vanished in thin air." The gray hoodie guy says, the pain he's experiences seeping through each word.

"Alright. Fair enough, I guess. Maybe next time don't go around scaring our suspect, got it?" The Green Cloak asks.

"Of course. We had no idea, won't happen again," the older guy replies.

"Yeah man, it was an accident. Won't happen again," the gray hoodie guy replies.

As the Green Cloak leader is about to turn around, he takes the baton and swings at the gray hoodie's upper arm, hard once again.

The baton makes contact and the noise echoes off the buildings.

"What the hell was that for!?" he asks, grabbing his arm.

"For lying to us," Green Cloak replies.

The group of guys lifts their fallen friend off the ground, and they slowly walk back into the building. Once there, the Green Cloaks start talking.

"She couldn't have gotten far," the woman carrying the crossbow says.

"Alright, let's keep looking, two teams of two. If you see her, shoot her with an arrow on the spot. Everyone remember where?" The man asks.

"Not in the heart, head, or stomach, boss." The three others reply in unison.

"That's right," he replies.

CHAPTER 26: SAFE HOUSE

"We can't stay here much longer," Elim says.

"There's so many Green Cloaks on patrol, how are we going to sneak Finley out of here?" Albie replies.

"I'm not going anywhere until we find Auryn," I demand, feeling slightly better after a night of restless sleep.

"We'll find Auryn, but we absolutely cannot stay here. They know you're in the neighborhood and they'll do anything they possibly can to find you. I wouldn't be surprised if they go door to door, demanding entry soon," Elim replies.

"They can't do that, can they?" Esha asks.

"They do pretty much whatever the hell they want, unfortunately," replies Albie.

"So, what's the plan if we do leave? There's five of us, plus whoever leads us. It's not like we're a small group and can sneak around," Garven asks.

"Great question," Elim replies.

He then proceeds to go over the plan with us. He's put out a call on some old handheld radios for as many Friends of Nadira people to meet up in the early evening around the corner from the house we're currently in. The fact that they have a couple of working communicators, even as old as these are, is an awesome surprise.

We'll all walk together in a huge group, and if we happen to get spotted, which is likely, we'll break into three or four groups. Then, one of the groups will purposefully walk a little slower and fall behind, so when they get questioned by the Green Cloaks, it'll give us time to get away.

He also explains that the safe house we'll be going to is actually closer to City Hall, which feels like the opposite direction we want to be going in.

"We'll try to see the council in the next day or two, explain how bad it's become, and see if they can do something about the Green Cloaks finally," Elim says.

"Do something about them? Half of them ARE them," Albie says.

"We don't know that for sure," Elim replies.

"Sure enough to make it a bad idea," Albie replies.

"And Auryn?" I ask.

"We already have people out looking for her. Someone thinks they saw her slipping away` after there was a ruckus with some Green Cloaks and some local guys," Elim responds.

That's not good enough, I think to myself. Instead of protesting I nod my head in their direction. If she's strong and resourceful enough to manage two space missions, I'm sure she'll be okay.

Over the next few hours, we all talk, nap, and eat. Albie explains the hierarchy and structure of the FoN, and how many people they have.

"Almost 500 total, but I only trust about a quarter of them," she says.

Albie is in her late 30s and has been living in Toronto most of her life. She's around 5'6, with vibrant red hair and eyes so green I'd almost think she was a Stonekeeper herself. She tends to wear a lot of head scarves because otherwise she'll be noticeable to anyone who pays attention. She looks a little like a much younger version of Salia, my mom.

Her great grandparents moved to Canada from Ireland when things first started going downhill for Europe. They could see the writing on the wall about the upcoming water and crop shortages, and wanted to move closer to the Great Lakes of Canada and the United States. With the three largest freshwater lakes in Europe being on the other side of the continent in Russia, including the biggest, Lake Ladoga, they knew they wanted to travel over the ocean and settle here.

The great lakes have the second (Lake Superior), fourth (Lake Huron), fifth (Lake Michigan), 11th (Lake Erie), and 13th (Lake Ontario) largest freshwater lakes in the world all huddled together, so a lot of people tried making their way here, including Albie's family.

Elim's family have been in North America for pretty much as long as people have existed on the lands. His parents could trace their ancestry back to an area known now as Arizona in the mid 1800s. They know it goes back hundreds of years farther than that, but lineage documents have been lost over the years.

In the mid 1900s, one of his great uncles, or maybe great-great uncles (he can't remember exactly), was a council member on the Navajo Nation Council Chamber.

Elim is also in his late 30s, around six feet tall, and he has a long braid of black hair that he keeps wrapped and tied as a bun on the back of his head.

"From what my mother told me, much like Albie's family, they saw the water signs very early. Instead of staying in the American Southwest, they traveled up here around 75 years ago," Elim tells me.

At dinner, the hand radio crackles from the nearby countertop, and we get word that about 40 people will be coming this evening, even more than both of them imagined.

"We've got about an hour, so let's finish up dinner, get you all cleaned up one last time, and get all your gear ready," Albie says.

When everyone else leaves the kitchen, Albie asks me to stay behind.

"I have something for you," she says, as she holds out her hand.

I hold my hand out and in it, she places a small pin. It's a crude shape of an "N" with a circle around it.

"It's to let others know that you're a friend of Nadira. If

you're ever in trouble, place it near your heart," she says, smiling as she does.

I nod my head and thank her, letting her know how much it means to me.

Afterwards, I sit on the couch in their living room while getting my gear sorted and packed. Kian sits down next to me to do the same.

"So, still worried about Auryn?" He asks.

"Maybe a little, but she's one of the toughest people I've ever known, so I'm sure she's okay," I answer, wondering if he's asking out of care or jealousy.

"Maybe when we're all back together, you, her and I could sit down and have a conversation about…"

He pauses for a moment.

"Everything?" he says.

"I know, Kian, it's just been so crazy since they landed and—" I begin to say before he cuts me off.

"I know, I know, I'm not demanding answers out of you or anything. It's been absolutely nuts the past few days, I just want to spend some time and get what we can figured out," he says."

"Well, that makes two of us, at least," a voice says from the other side of the room. It's Mina.

"Didn't mean to interrupt or anything, but I can't seem to get an answer from Auryn what she's really looking for either, so you two mind if I wedge in and join that conversation?" She says, chuckling a little towards the end.

"I, uh, sure yeah I guess," Kian replies, a little annoyed.

"Great, cause if we're all just gonna be weird around each other forever, I'm just gonna head back on the ship," she says, a grin on her face the entire time.

A silence falls over the room for a second.

"No, please, everyone, stop trying to talk me out of going on the ship!" Mina says, slow and sarcastically.

"You're going back on the ship?" Asks Garven as he walks into the room.

"Originally that was the plan, but now? With us knowing this all-powerful celebrity, I'm thinking of staying," she says, not at all seriously.

"No, I was just saying if we don't get this whole love triangle… square? This love shape figured out I might as well," Mina replied.

Garven then proceeds to ask her about the ship, how the accommodation was, any travel sickness, did the ride feel like it took forever, and more. Passing the time with these questions helped, and hearing Mina talk about space travel in a way Auryn hasn't yet was actually really nice.

"Would you ever go back to the settlement and then come back to Earth again?" Garven asks.

"I can't imagine the ship can make many more trips, if I'm being honest. Not unless they pick up a lot of technology while back here on Earth, which they might I guess," Mina replies.

"Did they leave a lot left on Earth?" Esha asks.

"I think they had something of a secret stash left here, yeah," Mina says, surprising everyone in the room.

"Interesting," Albie says 'as she walks through the room and into the kitchen.

We all look around at each other, and the talking stops. We sit in silence for a few minutes before Elim walks back into the room.

"Alright, 15 or so minutes until we head out. You five are going to need these hoods to conceal yourselves," he says.

He tosses each one of us a hood the goes only down to our shoulders, it also covers the bottom part of our faces. Mine's dark blue, and it has seen better days.

"Albie crocheted them all. She's really good at repurposing old blankets and things like that, making more practical items," he says.

"I've made 'em for most of our friends," Albie says as she walks back into the room.

"Must have made 75 of 'em over the past few years," she says as she sits down on the arm of a plush chair in the living room.

I slide my dark blue one over my head and pull the face mask portion up to test it out. It's warm, maybe a little too warm, but I say nothing. Any way we can get out of here undetected is great, and if this helps then that's amazing.

The base of it rests on my shoulders, and I tuck it under the thick straps of my black tank top. I look around the room as the rest of us do the same, including Albie and Elim.

The radio communicator crackles from the other room, and Elim walks to grab it. After a moment he comes back in and says,

"Alright, let's roll out."

I sling my backpack over my shoulders, slip my knife into the pocket of my green pants, and the seven of us quietly leave the place, closing the heavy wooden door behind us.

As we quietly walk down the narrow street, the sounds of the city in the evening overtake me. The wind whistling between buildings, a woman yelling at someone inside an apartment with the windows open, two people having a quiet conversation on a bench on the sidewalk. It all seems so normal, and yet I'm here trying not to get kidnapped or killed.

We round the corner onto a larger, more populated thoroughfare, and I see them; 40 or so Friends of Nadira, all wearing the same dark colored hoods and face coverings that we were given a few minutes ago. Everyone is wearing backpacks, and lots of people in long sleeves, no doubt covering any markings they might have on their arms and legs.

We walk up to meet with them, and without saying a word, they swallow us into the group, like a school of fish reuniting with a few who took a wrong turn at the last underwater ship.

The sun is slowly setting as we all head in the direction of city hall, and people of all ages, hanging out on porches, walking down sidewalks, begin to take notice of the nearly 50 people walking together down the middle of the road.

My anxiety starts to ramp up, and I'm overcome with worry.

Shouldn't we have just tried to sneak over? The five or six of us could have done it without being noticed, right? This seems like we're calling for attention.

Is that what they want? Not to help me, but to get attention? Or is this a trap and they're not actually here to save us.

As my breathing begins to intensify, a hand squeezes mine. I look over and see Kian walking next to me and smiling.

"It's gonna be okay. Safety in numbers, if not in stealth," he whispers quietly to me.

"I don't know, I have a bad feeling about all this," I respond.

"Has there ever been a day that you've had a good feeling?" He asks, smiling the whole time to let me know it's a playful barb.

He has a point though. I'm not sure the last time I've had a good feeling about anything, except maybe him. Even Auryn landing I had a bad feeling about, and now I know why.

As I let my mind wander, I think of how much easier everything would be if I hated Mina. If she was a horrible person, or at least super annoying. Instead, she's thoughtful, smart, and beautiful. Of course she is, Auryn wouldn't pick someone who was a jerk.

I can absolutely see why she would find companionship with Mina on the ship. Selfishly, I just wish it had ended when they both stepped back onto Earth. But here I am, holding hands with Kian, so how mad can I even be?

"Green Cloaks, two of them, a few blocks down on the left," a quiet voice says, breaking through my thoughts.

"After we pass them, you five break off down an alleyway, hopefully they follow you," Elim says, pointing to five people to the left of us.

We shuffle slowly to the right as we keep walking, away from the breakaway group. We march slowly through the impossibly long shadows of the buildings. Long broken streetlamps, some in surprisingly good shape, rise up out of the sidewalks every 60 or 70 feet. I feel my heart racing as we slowly approach the Green Cloaks. They stopped what they were doing almost a minute ago, and keep their eyes focused solely on us.

"I would guess they don't have any handheld radios, otherwise they would have called this in already," Albie says.

As the large group of us walks by, one of the Green Cloaks asks,

"What's going on here?"

"Just out for an evening stroll. Safety in numbers, ya know?" Elim replies back, head still down, hood still up.

"We can't be having this large a group walking around at night," the Green Cloak says back.

"Sounds good," Elim says.

We all keep walking, and around 25 feet later, a group of five people veer left, down a smaller side street. I look behind me as the Green Cloaks start following us. After the intersection, they stop and look down the alleyway, then back at us, and have a brief discussion.

A few moments later, they head down the alley after the smaller group.

"It's working so far," Albie says, with a hint of surprise in her voice.

"We've got a long way to go," replies Elim.

We walk several more blocks with no issue besides stares and concerned looks from people on the streets. That is until we get about 10 blocks from city hall. Straight in front of us appears a half dozen Green Cloaks along with eight to ten security guards. I guess word got back that a large group was walking around.

Elim and Albie get close to us as we continue walking.

"We're close enough now. Let's split into four groups of ten each and head down different side streets. As soon as you're out of sight, start sprinting. Mass confusion is what we're going for here. Everyone understand?"

Low mumbles of "yes" fill the air, and as we reach five blocks away from the guards, two groups, including ours, split off. Our group to the right, the other group to the left. Myself, Kian, Esha, Garven, Mina, Albie, Elim, and three other people I have never seen before turn the corner and almost immediately begin running.

"Alright you five, you have to follow us and do everything exactly how we do. The safe house is only a few blocks from here, but I'm sure the guards and Cloaks will be fanning out, looking for everyone," Albie says loudly while running down the alley.

Two blocks down, they turn down a small passage between two buildings, with only crumbled sidewalks underfoot. When they get to the far edge of the building, they peak around the corner, then give the signal for us to sprint across the street.

As we do, my foot slips off a curb and slams down hard onto the road below. I panic a little thinking I've injured myself yet again while trying to flee, but thankfully everything seems alright for now.

"You gotta work on your coordination, Fin," Garven says as he catches up to me, laughing a bit as he does.

"I can't even argue, you're right," I say back.

As we cross the street there is a row of large office buildings directly in front of us. Shattered windows line most of floors two through four, which is probably about as high as anyone can throw a rock. Sickly looking overgrown weeds grow up the sides, and the double doors on the front of the building look partially caved in.

When I reach the sidewalk, I look towards the left, and at the intersection about a hundred feet away, I see a security guard and a Green Cloak staring at us. Albie notices at about the same time and yells,

"Into the building, NOW!"

I dare not disobey the order, and start sprinting towards the caved in doors. Esha and Elim reach them before the rest of us and fling the right door open. All of us stream through quickly and Albie grabs a chain and lock out of her bag, loops them through parts of the damaged doors, and clicks the lock tight.

"Won't hold forever, but we don't need forever" she says as she joins us in the former lobby.

"Is this where the safehouse is?" I ask, hoping it's not because they definitely saw us enter here.

"No, but we can cut through to come out on a different block," Elim replies.

"First, let's take off the hoods you're wearing and stash them in your backpacks. At this point we want to look different," Albie says.

I nod my head in understanding, as do the others, and then begin to walk through the lobby. We pass by a grand old desk, covered lightly in moss and heavily in water damage. I look up and see the ceiling above it with a large hole in it, and scattered debris on top of the desk. I wonder how long ago it all caved in.

We walk through a wide doorway that hasn't seen its matching doors in decades. My parents told me that taking doors from offices and hotels was popular when people were first trying to fortify their own homes, since they were almost always made of high-quality metal or wood.

Down the hallway, the last soft rays of light come through the windows and barely have enough strength to illuminate the hallways.

"Everyone watch your step," one of the people I haven't met before says.

"Try not to fall through the floor into the basement," he says.

Not exactly what you want to hear while running from security and in a dim hallway, but I take note accordingly.

Everyone spreads out so there's not too much weight on any single spot on the floor. The carpet, old and crusted with dirt and grime, flexes with each step I put on it. It all feels soft, like a couple of steps in the stairwells in the old apartment I grew up in.

I flatten my feet to distribute the weight the best I can, and after a hundred feet of slow, steady walking, we all make it to the end of the hallway. There's a large, mostly broken out window that Albie hoists herself up to. As she carefully begins to peek her head out, she quickly pulls it back in.

She mouths the words *They're outside* to us, and we all remain as still and quiet as possible. After another few moments, she checks again, this time keeping her head out the window a few seconds longer. She then pops back in, flattens out one of her hands, and uses two fingers from the other hand moving back and forth to signal that they're walking away.

She hops back off the windowsill and has us huddle up.

"Okay, so, the safe house is across the street, but the area is going to be crawling with guards and Cloaks. Elim is going to crawl out through the building first to look around. One person won't look so suspicious. Once we get the all clear, I'm gonna hop out with Fin, Garven, Mina, and Kian, and we're gonna walk, not run, across the street. We can't look like the group that just broke in through this building.

As she's talking, I notice for the first time under her extra-long shirt, three knives strapped to her upper thigh. They're definitely throwing knives. She sees me checking them out and says,

"Just in case, ya know?" And smiles.

As she's saying it, the floor creaks loudly behind us. Everyone turns around to see what it was, and as I do I see Albie grabbing one of the knives, and in one almost impossibly smooth motion, she throws it hard.

I can hear the sound of it piercing the air as it speeds past my face, and as I turn to watch it, the person who snuck up behind us drops to the floor, barely missing it.

In barely another second, Albie has a second knife in her hand, but right before she's about to throw it, the person on the ground lifts their hood off their head and throws their hands up. As they do I move in front of Albie and blurt out,

"DON'T!"

More loudly than I should. The singular focus in her eyes disappears and she jumps back a half step, startled.

"What are you doing Fin, get out of the way!" She yells.

"I'm friendly! I'm friendly!" Yells Auryn.

"Yeah right," Elim says back.

"That's Auryn!" I say, and the people in the group that don't know us well look confused and a little skeptical.

Before I have the chance to explain further, Garven has ran the 20 feet between the group and Auryn and picked her up off the ground, wrapping her in a bearhug.

"How the hell did you find us?" He asks, barely loud enough for us to hear.

"Yeah, how did you find us?" Asks Elim, with more than a hint of suspicion in his voice.

"I saw the large group walking through the streets from the second story window of the place I had broken into. It was luck, mostly, but when I saw the five of you" Auryn says, pointing at us,

"I knew I had to follow you,"

"But we were all in cloaks with our faces covered?" Albie says.

"Sure, but I know what their bodies look like, how they move. All of it matters when tracking." Auryn replies.

"Well damn, she's pretty good. I could see why you were so insistent on reuniting with her, Fin." Albie says.

I blush after she says it. Auryn and Garven walk back towards the group, and as they reach us, I give her a big hug. After letting go, so does Mina.

"Glad you're back," Mina whispers in her ear. No doubt meant only for Auryn, but with the silence in the hallway, everyone hears.

"Alright, back to business. We have to get across the street and to the safehouse. Fill Auryn in quickly while Elim slips through the window and scopes the area out again. Once he gives the signal, we gotta go," Albie says.

I do as Albie says and fill Auryn in on the plan, if we want to call making it across the street a plan. About a minute later, we get the thumbs up from Elim, and we start to exit through the window.

Before I go, Albie reaches into her backpack and pulls out a pair of sunglasses in surprisingly good condition.

"Aviators. We can't have anyone seeing your eyes," she says as she hands them over to me.

"These are nice. Thanks!" I reply.

She nods her head and hops up onto the windowsill.

When it's my turn, I place my hands up on the narrow concrete inside ledge and jump up, twisting my body midair to land on my backside. I then flip my legs up and over, so they are facing outside. I look down and the drop is farther on this side than it was on the inside.

Here goes nothing, I think to myself as I use my hands to shove myself off.

I land hard and nearly stumble, but Auryn is there to catch me. The now eight of us crouch low against the building and slowly get as close as we can to the road. The three others we didn't know stay back in the building in order to change the group size. Elim stands up and casually walks out onto the sidewalk, trying not to look suspicious as he clears us again. Once he does, we all stand up and walk out onto the sidewalk.

Once we're all there, we casually walk across the street in two small groups of four. The very last dim rays of sun are now falling over the horizon line, and the presence of night is helping us remain unnoticed. We reach the opposite side of the street sidewalk and the first group of four, Garven, Esha, Kian and Elim slip down a narrow walkway about 20 feet ahead of us. As they leave our view, I hear a noise coming from across the street.

"Hey! Hey! You four! Stop right there!" A man calls out.

"Everybody stay calm," Albie says in a hushed but serious voice.

"Shouldn't we run?" Mina replies, the nervousness dripping through every word.

"We're too close to the safe house now. They'll see where we go," Albie replies.

I can feel my heart pounding in my chest. My hands get sweaty, and my vision ever so slightly begins to darken around the edges.

The man across the street jogs over to us.

"Where are you all headed?" He asks us in a stern voice.

"Oh, we're headed to the food stalls around city hall. Wanted to get out and stretch our legs, have a bite," Albie replies.

The man stares at us without saying anything for what feels like an eternity. His posture is stiff, and while he's not wearing a cloak, he's dressed pretty closely to how the downtown security guards regularly dress.

"You wouldn't happen to be a part of a large group that was walking around here earlier would you? Cloaks over their heads. Probably 40 or 50 of 'em?" He then asks.

"Geez, I don't even know 10 people, let alone 40," Mina says cheerfully.

"We just got back from space a few days ago, not a lot of time to make friends," she then says.

"Oh, you folks were spaceship folks? Any chance you could put in a good word for me, lot of rumors about not being

enough spots for everyone who wants to leave. Not sure how much I believe that, but a good word couldn't help,"
 he then replies.

"I'd be happy to! I've got a little bit of pull on the ship, being an engineer, so I'll do what I can for you," Mina replies, her voice an octave higher then she usually talks, smile plastered on her face.

"Well, we're pretty hungry, we should get taking off. If we see that large group you were talking about, we'll make sure to report it!" Albie says.

We take a few steps before the man yells out,

"Wait!"

My heart sinks. I close my eyes for a second, try to reset my face, and turn around with everyone else.

"How are you gonna put in a good word for me if you don't even know my name?" He then says while looking at Mina.

"Oh my god! I swear I'd forget my head if it weren't attached to my body!" Mina replies, still using the voice I've never heard her use before.

She's good, I'll give her that.

He proceeds to give her his name and security rank, and she promises to remember and put in a good word first thing tomorrow. He winks at her, because of course he does, and begins walking away. After he's far enough away, I can't help but laugh, and once I do, the rest of the group does as well.

Albie, Auryn, Mina, and I are cackling away as we walk towards the narrow alleyway and turn down it. A few steps down, Garven is standing there with a confused look on his face.

"What took you all so long, and what's so darn funny?" He says.

For reasons none of us can explain, his posture and question all made us laugh even harder. I am doubled over in laughter, tears streaming down my face. I try to stand up and make eye contact with Mina. This sets me back to square one and I am desperately trying to wipe the tears from my eyes yet again.

"I didn't know you were such a good flirt," Auryn finally says to Mina.

"How could you not? It worked on you," Mina replies.

A day ago, or heck maybe even 15 minutes ago, I think that phrase would have stopped me in my tracks. Now? I don't know, now I kind of get what Auryn sees in her.

THE TWELVTH DREAM

A fireball shoots across the daylight sky, brighter than the sun. Blinding to the point of needing to shield my eyes, I lose track of it for a brief second. I look up again just as Auryn begins to say,

"What the f—"

She's cut off by the sound of it, getting shriller by the second.

It came from west of the city and is streaking towards downtown. It's the fastest thing I've ever seen in my life, rising into the air as it screams by. I look in the direction its heading and see smoke filling the downtown corridor already.

How can downtown be on fire when the object hasn't even gotten there? Is this the second one? Why would we have been so calm in this moment?

No answers come as I jolt awake.

CHAPTER 27: THE DISCUSSION

The safehouse is surprisingly nice, for modern standards at least, and very large. It's an actual house, which feels rare for downtown, and has seven total bedrooms. Each of us gets our own room, and Albie and Elim are staying in the last bedroom "For a day or two, until we get everything sorted on what we wanna do."

What's quickly becoming obvious to all of us is that Toronto is another city we probably can't stay in, and there might not be anywhere left for us to go. Maybe we can eke out a life in hiding, but it feels like a real waste of my healing abilities, if I can harness them. I should be out there, helping as many people as possible, and not stuck running from shadow to shadow, trying not to get captured.

My frustration grows by the minute. If I don't stop this downward cycle I'm going to be infuriated beyond the point of no return in short order. I move from the comfortable oversized chair in the main living room, to the equally as comfortable couch, as if a 10-foot change in scenery will do me good.

I look up and around the room and see the dust from the seat floating through the air, illuminated by the light from a new day filtering through the windows. It reminds me a lot of our old storage and record room. The dust falls in such a similar pattern, gently swirling whenever someone downstairs moves around.

I hear footsteps coming from the kitchen. They're heavy, and sound like Garven or Kian's. I look up as Kian enters the room. He gives me a shy smile, and raises his eyebrows as if to ask,

You mind if I sit next to you?

Selfishly, I'm a little annoyed. I know it's for no reason; I'm just in a sour mood in general, but I would love to become progressively more upset in the silence of this warm, comfortable room.

"So, now that we've had an evening and morning to relax, I was wondering if we could have that conversation I mentioned yesterday," Kian says.

I know he's being reasonable here. I know it's been exceptionally weird since Auryn's been back, and I know we're going to have to talk about all this at some point, but I really, really just… don't want to.

"Yeah, I guess. Do you want to grab Auryn and Mina?" I respond, fighting my instincts to stop after every word.

"Yeah, I'll be back in a minute," he says.

As he walks away, I take a deep breath. When he's out of earshot, I sigh the longest, loudest sigh of my entire life. I know, mentally, I'm crashing out at Kian here when I'm not actually mad at him. I'm mad that I'm in this position. If I hadn't fallen for Kian while Auryn was gone, I'd have the moral high ground, and it'd be so much easier to get mad, yell, and be immature about this.

Unfortunately, that beautiful, kind man walked into my life and here I am, in a surprisingly well-furnished living room, waiting to have a conversation with my first love, her girlfriend, and the man that's made it extra complicated.

What I would give to be literally anywhere else on this planet right now.

I sigh a second time and adjust myself so I'm sitting more upright in the chair. A voice startles me,

"Two full sighs? You must be really dreading this conversation, huh?" Mina says.

I sit up abruptly, startled at the noise.

"How long have you been here?" I ask.

"Like, the whole time. This room is huge, and I've been on this couch in and out of sleep for a while," she says, genuinely surprised that I hadn't noticed her.

"I guess I've been in my own head a bit," I responded.

"And now you have to have 'The Talk' with your girlfriend, her girlfriend, and your boyfriend, what could you possibly be preoccupied about?" She replies.

She's so effortlessly funny, it's annoying.

It doesn't surprise me, though. Auryn is beautiful, strong, smart, and adventurous. Of course she was going to find somebody amazing. I never asked her to wait for me, just like she didn't ask it of me, but I just thought we'd be that rare couple that makes it long distance, I guess. Really, *really*, long distance.

I can't wallow for too long, because I hear the footsteps of Kian and Auryn walking towards the room.

"I couldn't find Mina upstairs," Kian says.

"Am I invisible? Is that what's happening?" Mina says, exasperated.

"Well, I wouldn't say that he looked particularly hard for you, if I'm being honest," Auryn then says.

Kian laughs, which surprises me a little.

"There's just so many layers to this, I wasn't sure if having all four of us was really needed," he then says.

"It is," I mumble.

Kian and Auryn both raise their eyebrows in surprise. Kian sits on a plush chair right next to the side of the couch I'm sitting on. Auryn takes a seat next to me, and Mina walks over and grabs the last available chair, a few feet across from us. Theres a low, small table between Mina and me.

"So, I wanted us all to gather…" Kian starts saying before Mina mutters under her breath,

"Most of us."

Kian pauses for a second, then keeps going.

"I thought it would be a good time to talk about what all this is. What we are all to each other. How this all is going to work. What I want everyone to know is that I really, really like Finley, and I want them in my life. After that, I don't know." Kian says, shaking his head back and forth towards the end.

"My part is the easiest. I really like Auryn, and I'd like to be with her. If that includes her being with other people, or us both being with other people, that's fine with me," Mina says.

Auryn and I turn to look at each other, and stare in silence for a moment into each other's eyes. It feels so… intimate. Since she's landed, it's been such a whirlwind. Me in jail, then kidnapped, then the breakout and safehouse, it's been a thousand miles per hour nearly every second we've spent together.

Here, in the calmness of the room, with the sun beams highlighting her stunning cheekbones, a smile overtakes her. It starts small and she tries to stop it from happening, but it's a train that's left the station. It grows wide, and I see the same Auryn I fell in love with before the world ripped us apart.

I can't help but smile just as wide as her, and as I do tears well up in the corners of my eyes. Before I can wipe them, she extends out her hand and with the back of her pointer finger, gently wipes them away for me.

"Oh, so you both like, *love* love each other. Damn," Mina says.

"Shut up," I whisper softly, beginning to chuckle and sniffle as I say it.

She's right, of course. I do *love* love her. I've never stopped, but how this affects Kian and Mina matters too. Like it or not, we're a big, weird family now.

"I'm okay with that, as long as I'm not completely neglected," I hear someone say.

My brain wants to pin it on Mina, since she seems so free and easy with all this, but after a moment I register that it's actually Kian who said it. My dad used to do this corny impression when I was young. When I said something he pretended not to understand, he'd talk like an old movie robot and say,

"Does. Not. Compute."

Does not compute indeed.

It snaps me out of the trance that I'm in while staring at Auryn.

"Wait, you are?" I ask.

"Yeah. I didn't think I was, even up until a minute ago. But the way you two look at each other, I don't know. I don't think I've ever loved anything that much in my entire life. But I'd sure like to," Kian says.

I am blushing uncontrollably at this point, and at a genuine loss for words. We all sit in silence for a minute.

"So, all this for nothing to change?" Mina asks.

"I mean, I guess Auryn and I haven't talked about what we are, and what we want," I say, trailing off towards the end.

We once again look at each other. With subtle cues like raising my eyebrows slightly, I try to get her to start talking first, but she doesn't take the bait.

I sigh.

"Do you two want to be left alone for this conversation?" Kian asks.

Before I can say yes, Mina says,

"No no no, we said our part in front of the group, let's just get this all settled here and now."

I take a slow, steady breath in. I notice my chest rising, and the gentle pause in movement before it lowers back down. A few stray dust particles fall in front of Auryn's face, and a shadow from the top of the open window has creeped onto her forehead.

I would do anything to be with my big penguin, and I suppose if that means that I occasionally have to share her, I guess I'm okay with that?

"Look, Finley, you know how much I love you. I've literally traversed the galaxy and back for you. There's nothing in the world I wouldn't do for you," Auryn says, now pausing.

A wave of nervousness consumes her. She lifts her hand up to her face and starts biting her thumb nail. It looks like she's going to cry.

What she wants to say is that, if I demanded her stop seeing Mina, she would, but she would be hurt and probably hold it against me for a while. Honestly, I would feel the same way if she wanted me to stop seeing Kian. I would do it, ten times out of ten, but why should I have to? The days of settling down with one person, getting married, having kids, all of that is long gone.

That time and era of opportunities no longer exists. They were on an Earth that burned to rubble decades ago.

Before she can finish her thought, I interrupt her.

"I think we should try to keep things how they are. I can get used to you seeing Mina, if you can get used to me seeing Kian. Seems fair, I guess?"

"Hypothetically, what if I also find someone else," says Kian, a huge grin stretched across his face.

"Oh my GOD, dude," Mina says at the exact same time as I say,

"NOT now, man!"

Which is also the same time Auryn happened to say,

"Read the room, Kian!"

"Alright, alright! We'll talk about it later, geez!" he replies.

With that, we all begin an uncontrollable laughter. Within mere seconds, tears are streaming down our cheeks. I am shoving my face into the couch cushions to try and hide. This conversation that I've been dreading for days, thinking about endlessly, worried about in the back of my mind during every part of my existence, ends with a joke.

My heart swells as I realize how fortunate I am that I still have a family like this after everything that's happened to me.

I stop laughing for a moment and lock eyes with Auryn once again. I lean in and kiss her. I kiss her like we're making up for 3 years of lost moments, because we are. I put my hand on the back of her head, run my fingers along her neck, and close my eyes tight as a small tear escapes the corner.

After maybe 15 or 20 seconds we release to a suddenly quiet room. I smile at her, and she does the same.

I then look at Kian, lean over, and give him a soft, short, kiss on the lips.

"This is going to take some getting used to," Mina says

CHAPTER 28: A CONVERSATION

Later that same evening, I walk into my room and close the door softly behind me. I slowly stroll over to my bed as if I'm floating on air and sit down with a smile still plastered on my face. I'm shocked at how everything went today, and while I'm sure there will be some tough days ahead while we figure out how to make all this work, I cannot help but smile at the calmness and positivity of today.

I take a deep breath in, smelling the mix of centuries old wood floors, blankets that need an airing out, and extra clothes shoved into the drawer of an ancient looking dresser across the room.

Is this peace? However temporary it is, I'm enjoying every second of it. I start to take another deep breath in and close my eyes as I do. When I open them, I am on the top of an airplane hangar.

I look around, confused and disoriented. Mina, Auryn, and Kian are all having a conversation. They don't seem to notice that I'm not talking.

I try to speak for a moment and nothing comes out. I try again and my mouth is moving, and words pour out that I have no intention of saying.

"It is sad that it's only the five of us here," I say.

What I had actually tried to say was,

"Where am I? What's going on? What is this place?" or any of the other million questions I have right now.

Suddenly, without even trying to speak, I respond to something that Auryn had just said,

"It's tough, but I do understand."

Before anyone says another word, a fireball shoots across the daylight sky, brighter than the sun. Blinding to the point of needing to shield my eyes, I lose track of it for a brief second. I look up again just as Auryn begins to say,

"What the f—"

She's cut off by the sound of it, getting shriller by the second.

It came from west of the city and is streaking towards downtown.

I close my eyes hard to shield them from the light, and when I open them, I am sitting on my bed, with the smell of oak and old clothes once again filling my nostrils.

I jolt up out of bed and spin around, looking at the room. The lighting seems the same as when I came in, no one has come to check on me. Nothing like this has happened since first walking into Toronto.

But why is this flash mirroring my dream? I can't help but feel like this is especially troublesome, and I need to talk to someone who might understand.

Abdo and Sun-young.

I tentatively sit back down on my bed. I know it's unreasonable to think the bed had anything to do with that, but I can't help but be at least a little nervous. After a minute of nothing happening, I lay back down, close my eyes, and slowly drift into my own waiting room.

When I open my eyes within the trance, I see the door to my own place. I haven't spent much time here the last few days, so I open the door and peek in. Everything is still in the same place, and why wouldn't it be I guess, it's all imaginary.

I close the door and walk over to ring Abdo. The friendly voice lets me know he's in, and I transport into his waiting room immediately.

"Hi, Fin. Sun-young is here and we have some things to talk to you about as well," he says into the intercom of the waiting room.

The door opens and I walk through it and see the two of them sitting there.

I've never met Sun-young before. She looks very similar in age to Abdo, and she greets me with a warm smile. Her hair, a silver and gray combo, parted in the middle and down to her shoulders, except for some bangs across her forehead, near her eyebrows. She's wearing a warm forest green cardigan, pulled tight across her midsection.

"Finley, I've heard so much about you from Abdo. It's so nice to finally meet you in person," she says.

"It's so nice to meet you as well, Sun-young" I say in response,

"There's a few things I'd like to talk to you both about."

They both look at each other with a concerned glance, then back at me. It feels like my parents are about to talk to me about the birds and the bees again.

"So, we were talking about how you still have an intense connection to the Emerald Stone. Finley, that's highly, highly unusual," Abdo says.

"We've gone back through all the records we could find, which admittedly isn't a ton, and it seems there were only two Stonekeepers who have ever kept their connection as strong as yours," Sun-young says.

"So, what does that mean?" I ask, genuinely unsure.

"Well, it could mean nothing," Abdo begins to say.

"But it also could be really, really meaningful," he says.

"So, it could be every possible outcome?" I ask with a little more snark than intended.

They both laugh. It's the type of laugh only two old friends can share together.

"Well. There are stories, legends even, about these Stonekeepers. We don't want to burden you with too many details, but they happened to coincide with periods of great transition in the world," Abdo says.

"For one Stonekeeper, they lead a time of great prosperity for people all across the world," Sun-young says.

"The other tried to use their power for just themselves, and the world was thrown into great turmoil," Abdo then says.

"I guess what we're saying is that you have a lot of opportunities in front of you," Sun-young then says.

"Then why is every day of my life just a fight to survive? Why is everything so difficult almost every second of every day of my existence?" I ask, feeling increasingly frustrated.

"I would love to tell you that struggle brings understanding, and tough times make great leaders, and all the things people have said for hundreds of years about living through tough times. But if you want me to be truly honest with you, Fin, it's because sometimes the world sucks, and it's going to be up to you, at least a little bit, to make it a little better," Sun-young says.

"Up to me?" I ask, incredulous.

"Up to you," Abdo says as they both nod.

I take a few moments to myself to collect my thoughts. There are so many questions I have, so many thoughts scrambling around, but I need to ask them about these waking dreams I've been having.

"Okay. So… we'll get back to all that. But I have something I have to tell you about while you're both here," I say.

I go on to explain first what happened while entering Toronto, flashing forward by a bit to seeing Auryn coming down the walkway with who I later learned was Mina.

I then tell them about having this strange dream about an object heading towards downtown Toronto, and after having the dream, having the waking dream.

"How long has it been since you had the last waking dream?" Sun-young asks.

"A few minutes before I came here to see you both," I respond.

"Hmmm," Abdo begins to say,

"When you wake from your trance, if something has happened to Toronto, come right back to us. Then we know that these visions happen quickly. If you're not back in an hour or so, Sun-young and I will try to find any writing or passages talking about seeing the future while awake," he says.

"I know Ava could see the future in her dreams, but she never mentioned it happening while awake, we'll have to go further back to look for something," Sun-young says, more to Abdo than to me.

"Well, I guess we each have homework then," Abdo says, smiling at me.

Even though he's sitting in the same chair he's always sitting in, he seems older, frailer than even the last time I saw him. Maybe I'm just projecting, but it seems like all of this stress is getting to him, aging him even.

"Well then I'll see you soon, or maybe not," I say.

"Hopefully not, for everyone in Toronto's sake," replies Sun-young.

I nod in agreement and head towards the door. As I open it and start to leave, I see her put her hand on top of Abdo's and smile at him softly.

Old friends at the end of the world.

I close the door behind me and can no longer make out what they're saying. I want to open it and ask, but my mind is spinning. I head back to my waiting room before deciding whether or not to leave my trance.

Back there, if I were in the room with them, I would have heard them say:

"We should have told Finley, Abdo. They have the right to know," Sun-young says.

"I know, I know. But I just don't think they're ready to hear it yet. Those two Stonekeepers held so much power," Abdo replies.

"I don't think you get to decide that" Sun-young replies.

CHAPTER 29: A CHAT

As I wake up in the morning, I am thankful that nothing happened to Toronto last night. No loud explosions, no fires, nothing unusual at all.

Well, I guess that's not entirely true, there was one thing that happened in the City of Toronto last night for the first time.

"Hey, babe," Auryn says sleepily, as she notices me awake.

"Hey," I reply as I slowly stand up and put my tank top back on.

"Getting up so early?" She asks.

"Yeah, I've got some things I want to get done before we head to city hall. You should stay here and sleep though," I reply.

I lean over and kiss her on the forehead, and she turns on her side, tightly hugging a pillow as she turns her body into the shape of a shrimp. She makes a cute noise as I do, and then promptly passes back out.

I smile while looking at her. I'm not sure I ever really believed this was possible when I saw her blasting off from Cleveland years ago.

I walk silently across the hard wood floor and open the bedroom door as quietly as I can. I back out of the room in order to once again shut it without it slamming. Right as the door closes I accidentally back into someone in the hallway.

"Oh, sorry!" I say as I turn around.

When I do, I see that it's Mina that I bumped into.

"No problem, Fin," she says.

She then looks me up and down, starts to grin, and says,

"Looks like you had a great night last night."

I feel my cheeks get hot immediately, no doubt turning as red as the apple I ate when I first got to Buffalo.

"Um… I guess… I mean," I fumble out.

"Relax, Fin. We're cool," she says.

"Besides, it's not like I don't know how you're feeling right now," she then says, smiling once again as she does.

We both stand there for a moment, not looking at each other at all in the process.

"Alright, well, I made it weird so I'm gonna head to the kitchen and get some breakfast. Heading that way?" She asks.

I look at her for a second and chuckle.

"Well, it's too early for my brain to think of an excuse not to, so I guess, yeah. I'm heading that way too," I respond.

We walk through the hallway and down the sturdy old wooden steps. When we reach the first floor, I see Albie and Elim already at the kitchen table. They look up and smile at the both of us.

"Welcome to breakfast. Can I offer you some mushroom coffee and some bread?" Elim asks.

"Nothing in the world sounds better," I respond.

"Once everyone's up and fed, we have to go over our plan for City Hall," Albie says.

"Plus, we have some backup plans ready if the need arises," Elim says.

"The need is definitely going to arise," Albie softly snaps back.

The four of us chat for a while over breakfast, and eventually Esha joins us downstairs.

"I am not used to waking up later than people," she groggily says.

"I know, unless I had the third lookout shift, you were always up before me. Getting lazy when we have some actual nice beds, eh?" I reply.

"This might be the last comfortable bed I ever sleep in, so you best believe I'm gonna lay around an extra hour," Esha replies as she grabs a cup for coffee.

"Wow that bread looks good. What kind is it?" She then asks.

"It's sourdough. The starter for it has been in my family since the year 2020. It's more important to me than almost anything," Elim says.

"Including me," Albie says while laughing, "he brings that starter in his backpack literally everywhere we go."

Eventually Garven, Kian, and Auryn all come downstairs and have some coffee and bread as well. Once everyone finishes, Albie says.

"So, today is going to be pretty dangerous."

"What day around here isn't?" Garven replies.

"Fair, but we're literally walking straight into a place that is probably infiltrated with Green Cloaks, with the person they want most in the world," Albie says.

"So why," I begin to say, "are we doing it?"

"Gotta ask this idiot for that answer," Albie says, pointing at Elim.

Everyone turns to look at Elim, and he's a little startled at the attention.

"Okay, well. We've been looking for a way, any way, to get the attention of the City Council here in Toronto. We've been trying to let them know that the Green Cloaks have become out of control, basically acting as their own police force. We need them to finally listen to us," Elim says.

He continues,

"So, what better way to get the Council and the Green Cloaks attention than to have you with us. And a dozen or so more of our friends, as protection of course."

"So, you want me to go in there and, what, threaten them?" I ask.

"No, no, you have it all wrong. Let me explain," Elim answers.

He then goes into detail. He believes that one or two of the council members are Green Cloaks, and he wants the others to see how worked up they get, and how dangerous they are, when I'm in the room with all of them.

Once that happens, he believes, there will be a reckoning. They'll start confronting this growing problem and start listening to their citizens.

"All feels a little too easy to me, but what do I know?" Albie asks rhetorically.

"There's nothing easy about this, Albie," Elim replies.

"Is that the entire plan? Do we have a backup? What if we're arrested, or I'm captured again? What if they don't believe me and now, we have nowhere to go?" I say back, voice slowly rising in volume as I do.

Albie and Elim share a look for a moment. Elim subtly shakes his head to argue no, and Albie raises her eyebrows and slowly nods yes.

"What aren't you telling me?" I ask.

Elim lets out a long sigh.

"So, you have to swear that this doesn't leave this room. Under no circumstances do you tell anyone else. Not other friends, not people in City Hall. There's no using this as leverage, nothing," he says.

"I'm gonna be totally honest with you, Elim. None of us have any other friends besides the people in this room," Esha says.

"And the only other family any of us have is on a colony 15 months of space travel away from here," Garven says.

"Yeah, they're right. Everyone on Earth that I would share anything with is in this room right now," I say.

Elim and Albie share one more look before continuing.

Elim then tells us about an airport hangar, a decent distance away by foot on the outside of the city. They have a couple of electric 4x4 golf carts waiting only a few blocks away from City Hall, hidden in a rundown building.

If things go south at City Hall, we all need to book it to the rendezvous location, and then we're going to high tail it to the hanger.

"Why do you have a hanger? How many people are there? How do you have these carts?" I ask in rapid fire succession.

"It was originally set up as an alternate launch point for the ship, but once construction ramped up the government realized there was no reasonable way to get the ship there if something went wrong with the downtown location, so they took most of the stuff and left it abandoned," Elim says.

"Most," Albie repeats, adding extra emphasis to it.

"There are at least a couple hundred people there. Many of the engineers that decided to stay behind, some urban farmers, all sorts of people that didn't feel it was right to abandon so many people on Earth," Elim then says.

"Sounds a lot like Buffalo," Kian says.

"The one thing that really brings everyone together though, is that everyone there hates the Green Cloaks. We get one shot to build the world again, and we can't have these zealots running it," Albie says.

"Well, I can get behind that," says Esha.

"So, what are they doing there? Building stuff? Making things? Are they building another ship?" I ask.

"Not a ship, no, but—" Albie begins to say before being cut off by Elim, who says,

"You can find that out if things go as poorly this afternoon at City Hall as Albie thinks it will."

"Feels reasonable," Mina says.

Albie and Elam both smile, look around the room, give us an awkward head nod, and then walk down the hallway, leaving us to ourselves.

"So, there's no way this is going to go well, right?"
Kian says.

"I don't know, maybe it'll be okay?" Auryn half
answers, half asks.

"Nah, I gotta go with Kian on this one. This is gonna go
poorly," Mina says while chuckling.

A silence falls over the room for a solid minute.

"I mean, what else is freakin new. Let's go run headfirst
into a bad situation yet again," Garven says.

"Can't be as bad as trying to escape a building literally
in the middle of burning down, amiright?" Esha says.

"We really need to sit down and trade stories soon. I
need to know what ya'll were doing while we were flying
through space," Auryn says.

"Maybe when we're in the airplane hangar we can talk
about it," Esha says, a smile appearing as she does.

"My goodness, is Esha joking around now? It's official,
it really is the end of the world," Auryn replies.

With that, we all have a good laugh, and as it slowly
quiets down, I return to my room to begin packing what very
little belongings I have once again.

CHAPTER 30: HAIL MARY

I have a habit of fidgeting with my backpack strap whenever I'm wearing it. It makes it so that the ends fray sooner than they should. At least I no longer place them in my mouth as a nervous habit, as I did occasionally on the hike from Cleveland to Buffalo.

"Do you have any idea how gross that is, Fin?" Esha would always say.

"No more gross than 90% of the things we do," I'd often respond.

This isn't that type of trek though. Outside, there are a dozen or more Friends of Nadira waiting for us. Once we join up, it's a quick walk to City Hall, where we're going to interrupt a council meeting that's open to the public. Getting through the streets is one thing, getting into the hall they're having the meeting is another.

I take a deep sign as Albie announces,

"It's go time. Everyone ready?"

Auryn mumbles "I guess" under her breath. The rest of us don't really answer. We've all been in so many dangerous situations, it's hard to feel excited walking into another one.

She swings the door open and the eight of us all walk out into the sunny and hot mid-afternoon. We're single file until we get to the road, Auryn in front of me, Kian right behind. I have my head down, looking at the ground as we walk, and he places a hand on my shoulder, gently moving his thumb back and forth.

I put on my sunglasses as I turn to look at him.

"I'm okay," I whisper.

It's the truth, and it's something I've been thinking about often lately. I still get all the signs of panic attacks: Tunnel vision, tingly hands, racing heart, even sweating, but it never tips over into a full-blown attack. Ever since I touched the stone, things have been different.

I'm sure it's related, but I'm not sure why. It's nice, honestly, but I still feel like a full-blown attack is waiting for me, ready to infiltrate my brain at the first sign of nervousness.

We reach the road, and I see Albie and Elim looking over to our left, so I do the same. There, a dozen friends are hanging out, split between two street corners, probably to not look suspicious. One of the people from the closer groups nods their head at us, and begins walking in the direction of City Hall, just a few blocks away.

On the walk over, the three groups stay about half a block apart, the third group staying on the opposite side of the street from us. I was expecting to leave the house and be immediately swarmed by security, or Green Cloaks, but it's a big city, so I guess they can't be searching for us all the time. While walking, Elim describes to us how to get to the electric golf carts hidden a few blocks from City Hall, in case everything goes poorly.

Before we left, Elim told us that the building now used for City Hall was built in the 1880s and 1890s. Eventually, around the 1960s, they built a new building and left this one. That's the funny thing about a lot of the architecture that's still standing strong today, it was built in the late 1800s and early 1900s, meant to last the test of time, and they have.

As we round the corner, I see it. It's beautiful and reminds me just a little bit of Buffalo City Hall. The center section, which juts out into the air, is much narrower than Buffalo's. The intricate details along the front are as unique as I've seen in all my adventures.

Where Buffalo's was Art Deco, the Toronto building is considered Richardsonian Romanesque Revival, intricate details carved into the sandstone facade, with arched window tops and a triple arched main entrance.

Ahead, I see our first real obstacle: Two guards stationed outside the doors. Albie spins around and says,

"Everyone split up, groups of three or four. Look inconspicuous."

Garven, Esha, Elim and Albie form one group, and the rest of us, Auryn, Mina, Kian, and I slow up to create space between the two groups. I watch as they approach the doors. The guards give the four of them a once over, then nod to let them in. That was easier than expected.

As we approach, one of the guards looks at me, then

then pulls his handheld radio up to his mouth and talks into it. Kian grabs my hand and squeezes it, then drops it so he can put his arm around my shoulder.

"Purpose of being here?" The guard asks.

I'm about to answer but Auryn starts talking first.

"We're hoping to get some room assignments changed. Couple of us wanna move in together."

As she says it, she leans in and kisses Mina on the cheek. When she does, Kian pulls me into his body and kisses me on the top of the head.

"Wrong City Hall, that's at the newer building around the corner. The uh, less nice one," he responds.

"I TOLD you guys it wasn't this one! But noooo, you never listen to me!" Auryn says, creating an argument out of thin air.

"It's not a big deal, it's like a minute from here," the second guard says.

"It's more about the principle," Auryn replies, really hamming it up.

"Well, is there anything here we should see, or, I don't know, do?" I ask.

"There's a boring public meeting starting in a few," the first guard says.

"Ew, no. I don't want to do that," Mina says.

"Come on, we should know what's going on in our city!" Kian then chips in, full of extra cheer.

"Ugh, FINE. But if I fall asleep it's not my fault," Mina replies.

Every one of us should get an award for acting, I think to myself as the guard waves us into the building. When we enter, we rejoin with the other four and wait as the other groups filter in. Once together, we walk towards the auditorium in a large group, me once again in the middle, to make sure I'm not recognized before we get there.

We reach a large staircase, with eight steps straight up, then a T shape with steps to the left and the right. We follow a group of unfamiliar people to the right and reach the top of the steps. Not far down the hallway is the large room with a hundred or so seats in it.

"This didn't use to be an auditorium, they made it a few years ago to accommodate the new government, with a promise of being more open," Albie whispers to me.

"At first it was, but when the Green Cloaks started infiltrating, it became the same old, same old," Elim then says.

As we walk in, we find some seats about 15 feet from the stage where the council members will be seated. My seat is narrow and uncomfortable. Each row contains seats of varying shapes and sizes, different wood types and fabric colors for the padding. No doubt picked from the scraps of dozens of other buildings.

It's only a few minutes before the meeting is set to get started, and there aren't a lot of people here. Besides the 20 of us that came in the group, there's maybe 15 other people. Large swathes of seats are left unfilled, and it's dawning on me that I'm going to be very, very easy to spot if one of the Green Cloaks that captured me is here.

I lean over to whisper this to Auryn, who's sitting next to me, but as I do the first councilperson walks in, followed closely behind in a single file line. They walk towards a long rectangular table with nine seats all facing the audience.

One, two, three, four, five, oh god, six, I think to myself.

I tap on Auryn's leg hard to get her attention, my eyes as wide as can be.

"Geez, Fin, what?" she says.

"Six of those council members were in the room with me when I touched the stone," I say urgently, while still trying to stay quiet.

"Six?! Are you sure?" she asks.

"I remember each and every one of their faces," I respond.

"Okay, we gotta get out of here, now," she says.

"Tell Albie what's going on," I say to Auryn.

Albie, sitting next to Auryn, had noticed that we were talking and is already leaning forward. Auryn turns to her and puts her lips next to Albies ears.

"SIX!" Albie says, much louder than she should have.

I look up at the council members, then back at Albie. I nod to let her know I'm sure. She turns to talk to Elim, as I feel a tap on my shoulder. I turn to face Kian.

"What's going on?" He whispers.

"Six of those council members are Green Cloaks. I saw them in the room when I touched the stone," I whisper back.

"Well, we gotta get the heck out of here," Kian says.

"Yeah, Albie is just talking to Elim and then I think we're gonna leave," I respond.

"Back to the safe house, or to the golf carts?" Kian asks.

"Not sure, depends on if we can get out of here unseen," I respond.

Elim looks over at me and holds up six fingers. I again confirm that's how many Council members I know are Green Cloaks. He makes a hand motion meaning let's all get out of here, and quick.

About 10 of us all partially stand up and try to crouch our way to the aisle without being noticed. In a fully lit room with an entire wall of windows, it's just as impossible as it sounds, and one of the council members loudly yells,

"Where are you all rudely heading to?"

Out of shock, I swing my head to look at him, and as I do my sunglasses fall partially off my face. The council notices immediately, and two of them whisper to each other. The member who yelled at me was in the room the day I touched the stone. A mere ten feet in front of me.

I remember him staring at me as I placed my hands on it. As the force of the stone started moving people away from me, I remember his hair being blown back, and him shielding his eyes. Then I remember him as one of the dozen people flung away from me.

"We gotta go NOW" I say loudly to the group, as we stand all the way up and start running up the aisle.

"Security, stop them!" The council member yells frantically.

Two security guards at the top of the aisle turn and look at us. Now, all 20 of us are scrambling to leave, and the guards look at each other as if to say,

"What are *we* supposed to do?"

As the 20 of us rush towards the doors, the first two guards step aside, but talk into their comms device to call for backup. Elim reaches the guard first and swipes the com out of his hand and onto the ground in one motion, immediately returning to a run and bursting through the door.

Outside the auditorium it becomes bedlam. We go rushing down the stairs as four security guards come rushing up them, trying to grab anyone they can. Two of the guards grab one of the Friends of Nadira by both his arms, but two other Friends pull them off. As one of them is about to punch one of the guards in the face, Elim yells,

"No violence today."

The man stops his punch and lets the guard drop to the ground. The other two guards are shoved aside as we make a break for the doors, knowing there's at least two more out there.

"You know how to split up!" Albie yells out, I assume to the other Friends of Nadira that we didn't walk with.

Garven reaches the doors first and puts a heavy shoulder into it. The door swings open wildly and almost bounces back to hit him. I watch as he leaps down the couple steps and veers right onto the sidewalk. As I get closer to the door, the two guards are yelling,

"Whoa! Hey! Everyone stop right now!"

When none of us do, one of the guards reaches out for Esha, who is only a few feet in front of me. He grabs her arm and yanks her in his direction, and she yells,

"Get OFF of me!"

He isn't letting go, so in a snap decision, I run into him, dipping my shoulder down to hit him square in the chest. He stumbles backwards, hitting the wrought iron handrail, and then steadying himself with it. Esha looks at me and is about to say something, but I yell,

"No time!" as I keep running.

She joins me, heading to the right, along with the original eight of us. The others split in different directions, some heading directly across the street and down an alley, others to the left, and even some others heading out diagonally across the street.

For being only 20 people, it feels like chaos.

After 15 or 20 feet of running, I look behind us, and the security guard I shouldered has started to chase us.

"We've got company!" I yell out to the group.

"Stick to the plan!" Albie yells back.

We run down Queen West Street until we reach University Ave, where we make a right. Another block later we make another right on Amoury Street, then a quick left onto Centre Avenue. A half block down, I see the building. It has a large, faded sign that says "Textile Museum" on it.

There used to be so much stuff to do, you could go to a museum about textiles. Thats crazy, I think to myself.

We run under the outside archway, and there are some large, rotted boards up against the side of the building. Albie and Mina get there first and fling off the first board, exposing half the opening. They then grab the second board and toss it to the side. Inside the opening, I see two large golf carts, as Elim had described, and a woman smiling.

"Let's rock n' roll!" The woman yells out as she sits in the driver's seat of the second cart.

I hop in the first one along with Auryn, Garven, and Albie, who takes the driver's seat. Mina, Esha, Kian and Elim hop in the second cart with the woman.

"Aren't these things slow?" I yell in the direction of Albie.

"Nah! Besides, that's Biyu, the second-best driver in Toronto, behind me!" She yells back

She smiles at me, and the cart lurches forward quickly.

As it reaches the sidewalk, the security guard that was still chasing us screams at us to stop. He's ten feet away, and as we turn in the opposite direction of him, I turn around to look at the cart behind us. He catches it just as it exits and grabs onto a vertical bar on the side, slowing the cart but causing him to stumble as he runs behind it.

I then see Mina reach over and punch him, square in the side of the face. The first blow doesn't make him let go, so she winds up and hits him again, this time in the shoulder. He stumbles again, loses his footing, and falls, still hanging onto the cart, which is now dragging him.

I quickly look around, and we've drawn a lot of attention to ourselves. I don't know if it's for having these motorized carts, the dragging of that man, or some combination of both. What I do know is that if things don't settle down soon, we're never going to escape this as quickly and quietly as we need to.

Albie makes a sharp left turn when we reach a T, onto Edward Street, and as the cart behind us does the same, the security guard finally lets go and gets flung several feet. We make another right, ending up back on University, and then a quick left.

At this point, I lose track of streets as I scan all around us for Green Cloaks, security guards, and anyone else who looks like they might be extra interested in what's happening. In all fairness, I hadn't seen a motorized vehicle in a while myself before Buffalo, so I would definitely be staring at us if I were a random person on the street.

After another 10 minutes, I feel myself relaxing ever so slightly. The buildings are starting to be shorter, older, and spaces often filled with empty parking lots. Less and less people are around, until the point we see almost no one.

"Everyone's so concentrated in the city center, there's barely anyone out here," Albie says while driving.

"Are we much farther from the hanger?" I ask.

"If I really punched it, maybe 15 minutes, but it'll probably take us a half an hour so I can conserve the battery a little," Albie replies.

I turn and look behind us to make sure the others are still following close behind, and when I do, Mina smiles and waves at me. I smile back and give a little wave.

If you would have asked me a few days ago, I wouldn't have thought I could ever tolerate Mina being in my life, but now, in this short amount of time, I've actually grown to kind of like her. She lightens the mood, she's funny, and she's also willing to throw a punch, apparently. I would never admit this out loud, but I'm glad she was there for Auryn on the ship ride back.

It also makes me think about how much I've really neglected Kian over the past few days. What he went through at the Green Cloak's church might be even more horrible than what I went through, and we've barely had time to discuss it. When we get settled in at the hanger, I have to do a better job of making time for him. He deserves that.

We ride in silence for a while. The farther we get from the city center, the worse the buildings look, and the higher the weeds have grown. It reminds me more and more of the outskirts of Cleveland. Buildings empty for 50 or more years, the dirt and grime from windstorms pummeling it over the decades. Windows broken and doors smashed in, or missing entirely.

A strange sense of nostalgia washes over me. For as tough as Cleveland was, there was also a comfort there. It's where I grew up, where I knew my parents for the entire time they were alive. It's where I met and fell in love with Auryn, and it's where I was fortunate enough to get to know her brother and Esha. This entire new family I have is because of that city, and I'll be forever grateful.

As much as the landscape here reminds me of it, it does feel very different here. Two carts speeding down an empty street, heading to yet another place I've never seen in my life, to be surrounded by more people that I don't know if I can trust or not.

It's all, once again, a lot.

As we near, Albie turns to me and says,

"I really think you're all going to like it. I've been here a few times, and it's really quite cool."

"Cool, how so?" I ask.

"There's a lot of different projects going on here. So many people decided not to take the shuttles, and when the Green Cloaks started bossing everyone around, they decided to start new somewhere. This just happens to be the place," she answers.

"That actually sounds a lot like Buffalo. When we were there, they had these amazing, giant greenhouses, and were working on getting larger vehicles going. It was cool to see," I say.

"Yeah, we actually have had a couple people from Buffalo join the group recently. They've been a huge help!" Albie says.

My heart sinks. There were a lot of good people in Buffalo, but there were also some people I'd like to never see again. Not knowing who's here and who isn't makes me feel uneasy.

"I know it's a long shot, but any names you remember?" I ask Albie.

"Nah, sorry, hun. I've never been great with names if I'm being honest," she replies.

As we drive, I start obsessing over who could be here. It would be so easy for a Green Cloak to pretend they're not one. Maybe one of Luna's group found this place and snuck over to infiltrate?

"Hey, Fin?" Albie says, breaking the silence.

She looks uncomfortable, which is new. She's carried herself with confidence every moment of the short amount of time I've known her.

"I was wonderin' if I could ask you a favor, once you're at the hanger and settled in a bit?"

"Of course, Albie. I mean you did just help us escape almost certain kidnapping, and probably torture for me," I say.

"I know, it just, it feels so selfish even asking this," she replies.

"Albie, come on now, just spit it out," I say.

She takes a deep breath while still looking at the road in front of her. I give her the time she needs to be brave enough to say whatever it is she wants to say.

"So, about a year back, Elim got hit in the shoulder with an arrow from a Green Cloak. We healed up the outside of it, but ever since then he's just..." Albie trails off for a second.

"He doesn't really have any strength in it. He never complains or anything, but I can see how hard it is for him to do the things he used to. I was wondering if, maybe..."

She trails off again.

"Albie, if there's any way I can figure out this power I have, Elim will be the first person I heal," I say.

Her lips curl up into a smile, and her eyes start to water.

"I don't even have the words to thank you, Fin. I really don't," she replies.

She loves him so much. You can tell just by looking at her face right now. She only had the courage to ask me for a favor because it was for him. This type of love, I understand.

"Don't thank me yet, he might have to be the person I practice on," I say, laughing after I do.

"As many tries as ya need, hun," she responds.

"I'll let him know you volunteered him," I say, still chuckling as I do.

She takes her right hand off the steering wheel and places it gently on my knee, squeezes it twice, and removes it.

"We almost there?" Garven yells out from the seats behind us.

"Yup!" Albie replies cheerfully.

As she does, she turns the corner and in the near distance, we see it: An airport.

What's left of the airport, anyway. What was once stories and stories of glass windows, is now shattered and broken. The metal looks worn and rusted.

"Is that where we're staying?" I asked.

"No, no," Albie says.

"That would be too obvious. Plus, there's no protection from the windstorms that kick up out here. There are a series of hangers at the far end of the airport that we're at. They've spent a few years fixing them back up, but not making 'em too nice, so nobody get suspicious," she says.

"Smart," I reply.

"This doesn't look very inviting," Auryn yells from the back seat.

"We're heading farther down, not at the main building itself!" I yell back.

"I'm' really glad we didn't have to walk all this way," Garven then says, and I agree with him wholeheartedly.

We drive by the main airport terminal, slowly dodging long abandoned vehicles, stripped for parts just like all the ones we saw from Cleveland to here.

We drive through the opening of an old chain-link fence and onto the tarmac of the airport. Potholes cover large swathes of the ground, along with the stripped-down shells of a few 21st century airplanes. Gigantic in size, I wonder how they possibly stayed in the air for hours on end.

How could anything that heavy stay up that long?

Conceptually, I know the answer of course: Huge engines, forward motion, wing drag, all the kind of stuff my dad used to talk about, but seeing how large one is in person, it's shocking.

"Hey Fin, look at the tail of that one! The first good fill-in-the-blank since we came to Toronto!" Garven yells.

I look over and see an old plane, body resting entirely on the ground, with just a portion of the tail paint still left. It starts with part of an "S," then a letter missing. Then it looks like part of an "I" or maybe a lower case "l," followed an "RI" and then a letter missing.

"S lRI "

"I have no idea! I'm much better at gas stations I guess!" I yell back to Garven.

He laughs loudly and yells back,

"Someone here will know, I'm sure."

As we drive alongside the dilapidated airport building, it occurs to me that I've never actually been to an airport before, and everything is so much larger than I could have imagined. The buildings tower over us, the planes easily fitting hundreds of people, the length of the runway being a mile long. It's all so gigantic, and to think millions of people took these every day at the height of aviation is truly astounding.

"Alright, we're getting close. I'll pull over soon and introduce you to some of the security here," Albie says.

"Security?" I ask, nervous.

"Yeah, but it's not like all the armed guards and Green Cloaks wandering around downtown. These are volunteers who take shifts and walk around the premise," Albie replies.

Albie slows the cart to a stop right before we reach a couple large pieces of rusted out machinery. I can see the outline of the hanger behind them, but not anything that's inside. Albie sees me craning my neck to look around.

"All this stuff's been moved so it's hard to see back there. Pretty good job, eh?" She says.

"Absolutely." I reply.

THE THIRTEENTH DREAM

A fireball shoots across the daylight sky, brighter than the sun. Blinding to the point of needing to shield my eyes, I lose track of it for a brief second. I look up again just as Auryn begins to say,

"What the f—"

She's cut off by the sound of it, getting shriller by the second.

It came from west of the city and is streaking towards downtown. It's the fastest thing I've ever seen in my life. Slowly rising into the air. I look in the direction it's heading and see smoke filling the downtown corridor already.

I wake up, as I have many nights recently, with my heart pounding, sweat running down my face. Kian, lying directly next to me in the cots we moved together last night, doesn't wake when I jolt up, and I'm glad for it. It's been a stressful few weeks for all of us, and everyone needs their sleep.

CHAPTER 31: A FRIEND

Yesterday, when we arrived, was mostly filled with introductions. The de facto leader of the hanger, although she doesn't like to be called that, was Maya. She was almost as tall as I and had the firmest handshake I've ever experienced. Her chestnut brown hair matched her eye color almost exactly.

The thing I noticed most about Maya though, was how Esha lingered on her words more than others. How she laughed a little harder than the rest of us at her jokes, and once even purposely bumped a shoulder into Maya's arm after laughing especially hard.

In all my years, I don't think I've ever seen Esha show any sort of interest in another person like this. It is, quite frankly, adorable.

One thing we did not do yesterday was see whatever it is they're building here. They promised us several times we would get to it today, and I plan on holding them to that.

As I push myself carefully off my cot, it wakes Kian up.

"Hey, getting up already?" He asks.

"I really want to see what they're doing here. What they're building," I respond.

"Yeah, but at…" he pauses for a moment, wipes his eyes, and stares at his watch.

"6:47 in the morning?"

"I'm gonna make a little cup of coffee first. Want one?" I ask.

"Nah, I'm good. Wake me up when you're gonna go talk to Albie or Maya," Kian replies.

He turns back on his side, pulls the light blanket back over his shoulder, and falls back asleep almost immediately. My eyes linger on him for another 15 seconds. His messy hair covering up his face, his beautiful lips. I smile to myself.

As I begin to turn around, I see Mina in my doorway, which is really just an opening in a series of draped curtains forming makeshift rooms on the concrete floor of the hangar. I blush for a second before realizing I have no need to feel embarrassed or caught. I grab my backpack and start heading towards the water station to fill up my coffee pot.

"Trust me, I get it. With that jawline and those eyes? I absolutely get it," she says quietly to me, now following along as I walk.

"Mina, is this another partner I'm going to have to worry about with you?" I reply.

"Oh, no, Fin, I didn't mean anything by—" she replies before I cut her off and start laughing.

"Mina, I'm messing with you," I then say.

Her eyebrows raise and her mouth opens for a moment without saying anything.

"Wow. Wow, you got me GOOD," she finally spits out.

We reach the water station, and I ask her if she'd like some mushroom coffee. She looks around, narrowing her eyes, before getting close to me.

"Or, how about you make the coffee, but I provide some real, actual coffee grown on the ship for us to drink," she replies.

"I'm sorry, you have REAL coffee? Like from beans?" I ask, genuinely flabbergasted.

"Yeah, each person got a small amount of ground up beans, and I knew several people who never drank it and didn't want it, so they all gave it to me," she says.

"I've never actually drank real coffee. My dad used to talk about it sometimes, but I didn't even know it was possible to grow anymore," I say.

"They had a couple high humidity rooms on the ship so they could grow some tropical fruits and plants. I wouldn't linger too long on where the moisture came from, otherwise it'll ruin it for you," Mina replies, laughing.

"My life has been mostly gross for a few years now, I'm not worried about it at all," I respond.

We grab the water and head out to a private area to the side of the main hanger. The asphalt below us cracked and broken, I set up a small fire and place my pot on top.

As we wait for the water to boil, Mina explains how to drink it.

"We don't have any filters like they used to, so we'll pour it into the cup, wait a few minutes, and then just start drinking. Just drink slowly, and do not finish the last half inch or so of coffee. It'll be all the ground up beans and it's terrible. Trust me," Mina says.

Once the water boils, we each get our cups out, fill them, and put a scoop of grounds in. I'm overcome with excitement waiting to taste real, honest to goodness coffee for the first time in my life.

"You know, a long time ago, they used to have all sorts of fancy things to put in their coffee. Liquid caramel and vanilla, dairy products, all sorts of flavors and sugars. Imagine how good that must have been?" Mina says.

"How do you know all this?" I ask.

"My grandfather was a historian; he passed down all sorts of handwritten books to my dad and my aunt. So, when my parents passed away, they were one of the only things I had from them. Then when my aunt also passed, I had all these books that I buried myself in. Hence all the useless information I have," she replies.

"Sorry to hear about your parents. If you don't mind me asking, how old were you when they passed?" I ask.

For the first time since I met her, Mina closed in on herself. Her shoulders tightened; her facial expression changed.

"I was really young, but it's not something I like to talk about," she says.

"I understand. There's no pressure to talk at all," I say back.

It's silent for a moment as we wait for our coffee to brew.

"I lost my parents a couple years ago, just a short time apart. They didn't need to die. If all the doctors weren't getting ready to go on the ship they could have helped, but we were poor, and they decided my parents weren't worth helping," I say.

Mina raises her eyes to look at me, and a few tears fall down her cheek. She says nothing but instead nods at me. I understand entirely.

We sit for another few minutes before she wipes the tears off her cheek, clears her throat, and says,

"Ready?"

"I've never been more ready for anything in my life," I say back, only partly kidding.

I pick my cup up off the ground and cradle my hands around the bottom. It's still hot, and I breathe in the steam from the coffee. It smells a little earthy, and a little floral, which I was not expecting at all.

Mina raises her cup towards mine, and we touch them together as she says "Cheers."

I bring the cup to my lips and blow across the top. After I'm pretty sure it's cool enough to take a sip, I do so. It is not at all what I was expecting. It's a little bitter, and some of those floral notes come through. I like it, I think?

"Not what you were expecting?" Mina asks.

"Not at all, but I still like it," I say.

"Just wait until the caffeine kicks in, then you're really going to like it," she says, a smile crossing her face as she does.

We again sit in silence as we slowly sip our coffee. Looking out over the large, broken pavement, seeing the husks of old airplanes and other equipment. It's early, but it's already getting hot, and I enjoy the coffee as it cools. I pay close attention as I get towards the end of the cup so as not to drink the coffee grounds in the bottom, and when there is a half an inch left, I stand up, walk over to some dirt, and dump it out.

Mina follows me and does the same, and we rinse our cups out from our water bottles.

"Do me a favor, will ya?" she says.

"Yeah, of course," I reply.

"Don't tell anyone about this. I don't have much left and there's so many of us now." she answers.

"Of course. My lips are sealed," I respond.

"Alright. Wanna go figure out what the heck it is they're making here?" Mina then says.

"Abso-freaking-lutely I do," I say.

We walk back towards the rooms we were sleeping in last night, and I check my watch. It's 7:36, and time to wake everyone up. There's much more hustle and bustle in the hanger as we walk back in, and as we get to my room, Kian is sitting up on the side of the cot.

"Still up for making coffee?" he asks.

"Oh, uh…" I begin to say as Mina darts a look at me.

"Mina and I already made some mushroom coffee and drank it. Sorry,"

"It's all good. I can make my own in a little while," Kian replies.

He stands up, shirtless, and walks over to grab his top.

"Whew!" Mina whispers at me, smiles, and then walks in the direction of her room.

I walk over to Kian and give him a kiss, placing a hand on his abs.

"Good morning to you too, Fin," he says, grinning.

I turn around and now standing in my doorway is Esha and Garven, both smirking.

"Thought we should go find out what they're up to here," Garven says.

"Yeah, we should find Maya so she can show us around," says Esha, a little too eagerly.

I start to smile but stop myself. I want Esha to feel whatever feelings she has without feeling self-conscious. It's already taking everything I have not to say something.

Esha turns away first and walks a few feet away. Garven and I lock eyes, and we both begin to grin widely, and then we both have to try and contain a laugh. Kian and I walk towards the door, and quietly Garven whispers to me,

"Good for her."

I nod in agreement, and we head out to find Maya.

We quickly reach the end of the curtain made rooms, which they explained last night were to get people settled as they arrive. They're slowly building more accommodations in the upper part of the hangar, but they've had almost 20 people come in the last month, which is faster than they can build.

As we walk back onto the tarmac, Maya, Albie, and Elim are talking. Maya notices us and calls out,

"There you are! We were hoping you'd get here soon!"

The four of us, myself, Kian, Esha and Garven, hurry our pace up a bit. When we reach her, she says,

"Weren't there more of you yesterday?"

"Yeah, one of them is still sleeping though," Garven says.

"Well, they're gonna hate missing this I bet," Maya replies.

"Before we head over, I have a little bit of a favor to ask," she then says.

"Yeah, what's up?" I say.

"Well, these two here mentioned that you might have a special gift. I just so happened to slice my finger this morning and was wondering if you could maybe, I don't know, help me out?" Maya then asks.

It makes me uncomfortable, and I think Esha, Garven and Kian can tell.

"Seems a bit early to ask something like that," Garven says.

"It's okay, Garven. I'll try to pass her test," I say.

Maya smiles at hearing me figure it out so quickly.

"I've only done it once, so I don't really know what I'm doing yet, but I'll certainly try," I say.

"Appreciate it," Maya replies.

She steps closer to me and holds out her hand, unwrapping a small bandage as she does. I take a look at it and it's actually a decent gash, I wonder if it's a coincidence whether this happened this morning.

"Can we go somewhere a little more private?" I ask, as people I don't know are walking through the area.

"Sure, my office is right there," she says as she points just 30 feet away.

We walk to her office and Esha closes the door behind us. Maya moves two chairs so they're facing each other and sits down in one. I sit in the other and grab her hand.

I look down and stare at it for a moment, getting an especially good look at the wound. I don't know if that's helpful or not, but I don't know much of anything at this point so it's worth a shot.

I close my eyes tightly, and try to imagine the wound, her skin, and repairing it all, but nothing happens. I take a deep breath and close my eyes harder. I concentrate on the energy between my fingers and her hand and try to make a connection. After almost 10 seconds, I open my eyes.

"Sorry, I'm just not sure what I'm doing yet," I say sheepishly.

"You told me they're a healer, a Stonekeeper even. They don't look like a Stonekeeper," Maya says to Albie and Elim.

"I'm telling you; this guy was bleeding out from being hit by an arrow and Fin healed him from near death!" Albie says, pointing at Kian as she does.

"I was as good as dead," Kian says.

"We're telling the truth, Maya. Hell, look at them! You ever see that color green before in someone's eyes?" Elim chips in.

Maya sighs loudly and starts to stand up. I don't know if it's from not wanting to disappoint Albie and Elim, or maybe a fear of getting kicked out of the hanger, or some combination of things, but as she stands up, I grab onto her hand again and close my eyes.

I feel a connection between my fingertips and her wrist, almost like a small electric spark. Mentally I search for the wound and find it. I imagine the atoms themselves attaching to each other, slowly and surely closing the gap. I hear Maya say,

"Whoa," out loud, in an astonished voice.

I know I'm not done repairing her wound yet, but I'm getting tired, and I'm a little mad she made me do this to what, use me? Prove something to her? Whatever it is, I'm not thrilled about it, so I pull away, wound only half healed.

I open my eyes and immediately stare at her.

"I'll heal the rest after I see whatever it is you're doing here, if it's worth my time," I say.

She stares at me for a moment, checking to see if I'm being serious. Slowly, she begins to smile.

"I like you. You don't take crap from people, do you?" She says.

"Not anymore I don't," I reply back in a tone that surprises even myself.

She walks out of her office and motions for us to follow. We head single file out of the office, and walk further into the hanger. It has to be 35 or 40 feet tall, and the upper corners have significant rust on them. It's not the worst damage I've seen to a building, but I do wonder how many years this place has left standing.

We walk through a lot of mechanical parts strewn about the floor. Large spools with all types of different wires wrapped around it, metal pieces organized by shape and then size.

"Make sure to watch your step, all sorts of rusty things lying about," Maya says.

As we weave through the spare parts and scrap, we approach the side wall of the hangar. Maya swings the large doors open, and we enter a smaller hangar. I take a few steps before stopping dead in my tracks.

There they are: Two things I didn't think I'd ever see again in my life.

"Cessna 208 Grand Caravans, two of 'em," Maya says, no doubt noticing the four of our jaws nearly on the floor.

"Do… Do they work?" Esha asks.

"We've done a lot of very short, very low trips. Always flying away from the city so we're not spotted. But to answer your question, yes, they work," Maya replies.

Silence overtakes us again. I take a couple steps towards it before saying,

"But how do you power it? Didn't these things take gas?"

"They sure used to! We've replaced the top of the wings and body with solar panels, put some batteries and converters where the old engines were, and, hypothetically, can get 1500 or so miles on a charge plus flying during the day.

Flying at night is probably only 750 miles," she replies, beaming with pride while talking about it.

"Are you sure that's right? That seems far too far," Esha asks.

"We've put a lot of miles on these things, calculated the charge left, even accounted for battery drain and loss," Maya replies.

"That being said, it takes about two full days to get the batteries fully charged," she then says.

"This is amazing," Kian says as the understatement of the year.

"What's the plan? What are you going to use them for?" Garven asks.

It's a great question. Having transportation is great, but it seems like all the leaders in Toronto and Buffalo are compromised. Where is it even worth traveling to at this point?

"Well," Maya begins saying before pausing for a moment.

"For a while we had a bunch of different ideas. Some people wanted to fly around the Great Lakes to see if there were any other livable places. Some people wanted to fly farther north, towards the old Northern Canada, and settle up there hoping we can do larger scale farming. Lots of ideas." Maya says.

"And now?" I ask.

She looks at me intensely. Lowering her chin down slightly, not daring to blink.

"Now, I think you and your friends should take one of the planes and fly down to the last known location of the Saffire Stone," Maya says.

The conversation halts for a moment, and the four of us all look around at each other in disbelief. I have so many questions I need to ask, so many things I need to know.

"What?! How do you even know about the Sapphire stone? Why on Earth would I go? You want six of us to fly thousands of miles by ourselves? None of this makes any sense," I say, exasperated and nearly tripping over my words.

"That's insane, we can't just fly down to….to where? Where would we even be going? We don't even know if we're staying on Earth," Kian asks.

"First off," Maya begins, "The Stonekeeper has to stay on Earth if we want any chance of survival. Secondly, South America. The old capital of Columbia, Bogota, to be precise,"

Her voice so matter of fact that I feel like I'm losing my mind.

"Absolutely not, this is insane, all of this is insane," I say as I begin to walk away.

"I'll give you a few days to think about it. I have a feeling you'll be back with a different response," Maya says as I swing open the doors we just walked through.

This is completely nuts. Flying TOWARDS hotter weather? To a place to maybe find a stone? Has she lost her mind? We met her yesterday! I'm thinking to myself as I'm stomping away.

I'm walking quickly, with how upset I am, and I'm not paying any attention to where I'm going. I turn a corner and slam into someone hard. We both fall to the ground and the other person begins apologizing, even though this definitely wasn't their fault.

As the fog of anger lifts slightly, the woman I bumped into begins to speak again.

"Again, I'm so sorry, I didn't even see you there and I was rushing around, and…" she pauses for a moment.

Behind me, Kian, Garven and Esha catch up to where I am and begin to offer to help me up.

"Finley? Wait… KIAN!?" she says.

Kian and I both look up, and Kian speaks before I get the chance,

"Annora?"

CHAPTER 32: THREE MONTHS

Surprisingly, Maya ended up being right. In the three months since we first saw the plane, we did agree to fly down to South America and try to find the Sapphire Stone. It was a conversation with Maya and Annora that convinced me it was the right call.

"Throughout history, the great balance only stayed when there were five Stonekeepers. If there were only four, you would start to see chaos in the world. The fact that there has been so much pain and suffering in the world, so much destruction of the environment, means we cannot possibly have all the Stonekeepers," Maya had said.

I remained quiet during much of the conversation, before finally saying,

"You're right. There are only three of us, and there were only two for a long while before I got my powers. Not for nothing, the other two Stonekeepers are also old, and ready to… retire," I replied.

"How do you know that?" Annora asked.

"I can communicate with them. Anyone who is a Stonekeeper can communicate with other Stonekeepers," I say back.

"Okay, so we're right then," Maya says, unfazed that I was able to corroborate their theory.

"You need to head down there and lead the search for the next Sapphire Stonekeeper. It's the only way to truly build this world back," Annora then said.

"None of us know how to fly a plane, how to get there, nothing!" Auryn said.

"You don't have to go today. We're making some changes to the batteries and solar cells to try and boost them even more, especially while flying at night. There's a lot of test flights still to be had, and two of you will need to learn how to fly one of these things on longer and longer missions," Annora said.

"I'll fly it" both Esha and Kian said at the same time.

"Looks like we have our two volunteers," Maya responded.

"If we go," I reminded them.

"If we go," Kian said.

Going we are, and over the last few months, Esha and Kian have slowly learned all the controls, while Auryn, Mina and Garven have been helping with tweaking the batteries and solar panels.

For me, word spread fast that I was the Emerald Stonekeeper, and I've had many, many opportunities to learn how to heal people better. Elim was first, of course, and I was able to get his shoulder back into shape after three or four sessions. Then, people started coming to me with small cuts and bruises, and slowly I've learned to control my energy better. At first healing pretty much anything was exhausting, but over the past few weeks, I can heal a cut and barely notice.

Larger wounds still take it out of me though. One of the engineers, Joseph, fell from the wing of the plane and broke his arm in several places. I can't quite mend bone the way I can skin and ligaments, since it's so time consuming for a bone to heal on its own. I can speed the process up a bit, but I still haven't been able to get them fully healed.

It's been a strange three months for me, essentially waiting around for people to get hurt. Beyond that, I tend to their gardens behind the hangars. They've dedicated a ton of land to them, but they're only partially covered, and especially hot days can do real damage to crops.

I help with the system of pulling out extra blankets and stitched together cloths and hanging them over these tall clotheslines to create as much shade as possible on days where it's over a hundred degrees, which is often. It's tiring work, but for the first time in my life, I'm starting to see real, defined muscles in my arms, shoulders and neck.

Both Auryn and Kian have noticed, which, truth be told, feels good. I'm still splitting my evenings between them, with Auryn doing the same with Mina and myself. Kian is also spending a lot of time with Annora these days, which makes sense, but he's being a little more secretive than ever before.

I'm glad she's here though. She told us that after we left, it gave her the courage to pack up her things, and with a few friends, flee in the middle of the night. The road for her was long, but she didn't run into any difficulties.

We talked a little bit, as a group, about our more harrowing trip up, and what happened to us in Toronto.

"You all cannot catch a break, can you?" she asked, rhetorically.

Tonight, all these months after getting here, Garven invited us all to his room. He said he has something important to talk about, which feels weirdly ominous. Auryn, Mina, Kian, Esha and I are going to head over there around 8pm, a little past sunset. Until then, though, I'm going to be putting sheets up in the gardens until someone is injured and needs my help.

Today, Annora has decided to help.

"Honestly I need a break from working with engineers and mechanics, I could use some quiet," she says to me while we're heading out.

When we reach the first area, we begin unfolding some thin sheets from a large wooden chest left nearby.

"Fin… is it weird for you that I'm here?" she asks me out of the blue.

"What? Why would it be weird?" I reply.

"I mean. I'm Kian's first love's sister. I'm sure I remind him of her sometimes, and with you two being… whatever it is you are, I just hope it's not weird," she says.

"Whatever it is we are?" I ask, trying to keep my tone light.

"Yeah, you're dating, but not? It's not exclusive? I don't mean to judge, it just all feels a little weird to me," she says, with a tone I'm not exactly fond of.

"Have you talked to Kian about it?" I ask her.

"Kind of, yeah. One day, a month and a half ago I saw you and Auryn holding hands and then kissing as you walked into her room. My heart sank, I felt so bad for Kian, so I went to his room and told him, expecting him to blow up. Instead, he just told me it's not what I think, he knows, and everything is cool," she says.

"Everything doesn't feel cool to me, though, Fin," she then says.

I understand her. I really do. She reconnects with someone who probably feels like the closest thing to family she has left, and then it looks like his partner is cheating on him. I'm trying to find the patience to explain this to her without raising my voice, like hers has slowly started to do.

"If you want, I can explain it all to you, since he's apparently been too afraid to," I finally respond.

"Sure. I'd love to hear it," she says back, her tone flat.

I then tell her about Auryn and my relationship before the shuttle separated us, then meeting Kian and our journey together, and then Auryn coming back to Earth with Mina. About how weird it was for all of us for a while, and then about the conversation we all had together.

After several minutes straight of talking, I take a deep breath, exhale, and let silence fill the space between us.

"So, you're dating Kian and Auryn, and Auryn is dating you and Mina, but Kian is only dating you and Mina is only dating Auryn," she says, slowly connecting all the pieces together.

"Correct," I say.

"So, if they wanted to, could Kian date someone else? Or Mina, too?" she then asks.

It's certainly something I thought about often. Selfishly I kind of hope it never comes to that, but I would also have no right stopping him.

"Yeah, of course he could," I say after too long of a pause.

She looks at me with a continuing intensity that makes me uncomfortable.

"So, if I went over and asked Kian out right now, it wouldn't be weird?" She asks.

"Not between me and you, no," I respond, lying just a little bit.

"I'm not going to, of course, but I guess then that's fine," she says.

"Alright, so are we cool?" I ask.

"Yeah, we're cool. I guess I should also thank you for getting him here and safe, all in one piece. I heard about how you saved his life. I just… I really appreciate it," she says.

"Of course, Annora. I know how much he means to everyone, me included," I respond.

She gives me a halfhearted smile, and we go back to putting up the sun curtains for the gardens.

The day goes by slowly in the sweltering heat, and my mind wanders to what Garven wants to talk about later. I don't think he's ever called a group meeting. He's been a little different the past few weeks though, so I know something has been on his mind. He's been withdrawing into his work around the hangar, hanging out with all of us a little less, with the exception of Auryn.

I asked her a few days ago what was going on, and she told me that he's just been extra exhausted, which is understandable. We're all trying to pull our fair share, especially with the planes, since they're basically giving us one of them.

Annora and I each grab a plate and head over to a common table area. We're eating earlier than most, so it's pretty empty. We grab two seats across from each other at the end of a long rectangular table.

"So, Fin…" she says.

"Yeah, Annora?" I say back.

"I know it's not up to just you, but I also know it can't happen without you being onboard with it. So, I figured I'd ask you first," Annora says.

Whatever it is she has to say, it's making her fidgety. Her fingers alternate from tapping on the table, to intertwining themselves, to rubbing the sides of her upper arms.

"Whatever it is, just spit it out. We're cool, remember?" I finally say.

"Okay, sure. Yeah, that's true," she begins saying, tripping over her words a bit, "I'll just say it."

She takes a deep breath.

"I want to be on that plane with you. There are 10 total seats, there's only six of you. Maya is going to make you take one or two more people with you, people she trusts, and she trusts me."

"Oh," I say, genuinely surprised.

I don't think it's a bad idea, I guess I just thought it would be the six of us making the journey by ourselves. Plus, Annora has been learning to fly the plane occasionally as well, and it couldn't hurt to have someone else who can do that.

"I know it's a lot to think about, and you don't have to answer now, but—" she begins saying.

"Yeah," I interrupt her, "I think it's a good idea,"

"You… you do?" She responds, shocked at my quick answer.

"Yeah, I mean, you know us already, you've been learning to fly the plane, you're good at a bunch of different things. Sure, I think it's a good idea, but you know it's not just up to me, right?" I say.

"Yes, of course, absolutely. I totally understand. I'll ask the others, too," she replies.

Annora shovels the rest of her lunch into her mouth, barely chews, and finishes quickly. She then excuses herself, no doubt to run and find the others. I give her a little wave as she leaves, and she returns one, her face beaming with joy.

I have a nagging feeling, somewhere deep inside, that I've just made a mistake. I can't place why, but it's there.

Slowly my nervousness about it wanes, and I am now left alone at the table, eating what's left of my lunch, once again wondering what's going on with Garven. For a second time, my thoughts are interrupted by a question.

"Anyone sitting here?"

It's Maya, already starting to sit down in the same seat Annora was just in.

"I believe you are," I say while smiling politely.

We make small talk for a moment, her asking how I'm adjusting, if I'm getting nervous for the trip, how's the lunch today. I know she's trying to get to the point while still engaging in normal pleasantries.

"I wanted to talk to you a little more about your history, and mine," she finally says.

I look at her, intrigued.

"I know it probably feels insane that we're giving you and your friends a plane. It might feel even more crazy that we're asking you to fly to a different continent to, well, start saving the world. But my family has a long history alongside the stones, the keepers, all of it, and I know how important this is for the world," she says.

For the next 30 minutes, I listen to Maya talk, interrupting only to ask questions, or share some of my experiences. Her family is from Columbia, lived there even before the Spanish colonizers arrived in 1499. During this time period, the Sapphire Stonekeeper was well known to locals. Each time they passed, everyone quietly started the search for the next one, sometimes it was only months, and sometimes years went by.

That is until the early 1800s, when someone from a group of zealots that called themselves "The Blue Cloaks" became the Stonekeeper. It all changed at that point, according to Maya's family history.

Suddenly, if a dust storm came barreling through and you wanted to clean the air? Pay up. If the heat was unbearable and you wanted a breeze to help people and farm animals alike? Better make a donation to the Blue Cloaks.

So it went, for over a hundred years, until that Stonekeeper passed. Around that time, Maya's family fled. The Blue Cloaks were violent in their search for the next Stonekeeper, desperate to keep their hold on power. First her family fled to Costa Rica, then Mexico, and then, around 30 years ago, her parents came to Toronto, where they had Maya shortly after.

"I want you to know that I'm not trying to send you off on this dangerous adventure without giving it thought. I truly, from the bottom of my soul, believe that you're here to help save the world, and the only thing I can do to help is give you one of these planes," Maya says to me.

With that, she gets up, smiles, nods her head and says,

"See ya around, Fin."

As she walks away, I can't help but stare into the middle distance as my brain swirls with everything she just told me. Finally, I whisper to myself,

"No pressure then, Fin."

THE FOURTHEENTH DREAM

After Maya and I talked, I felt the urge to talk with Abdo. Over the past few months, I haven't spoken with him as much as usual. He's told me there's been increased unrest in his area. The Red Cloaks in the Sudan have been, according to him,

"Much more jumpy than normal."

I asked him if it had anything to do with me becoming the Emerald Stonekeeper, and he rightfully brought up that they'd have no way of knowing that it happened, since he's the only one there that knows.

When, in my trance, I call over to him, I mostly expect to go unanswered. When it picks up that he's in, I head over immediately.

When I get to the waiting room, the door opens right away, and I give it a gentle knock before entering.

"You know you don't have to knock, Fin. I've already gave the go ahead for you to come over," he says while chuckling.

"Earthly habits, I guess," I respond back, which he nods in agreement font with.

After I sit down, we talk for a long time. Abdo tells me that it's getting more dangerous for him, his friends, and his family in the area as the Red Cloaks exert more power and influence.

I talk about the recurring dream again and how much it worries me.

"I just can't see past a certain point, but I do know that it looks like it's happening from where I am now, at the airplane hangar," I say.

"Well, my guess is that it would happen soon then," he replies.

"That's not really helpful, Abdo," I say to him.

"I'm not always here to help, Fin," he says back.

I laugh at him saying it. How could something so cold sounding still sound as pleasant and warm as it does coming from Abdo?

"Just because I've been a Stonekeeper for a while, doesn't mean I have all the answers," he then says.

"I know, I know," I reply.

I then go on to tell him about Maya, and what she said about the Sapphire Stonekeepers, the Blue Cloaks, and her belief in me.

"So, you're still going to do it? Fly all that way? It seems so dangerous," Abdo says.

"I know, and I know you're worried that if something happens to me, that you and Sun-young will be left alone again, but I think this is the right thing to do. It's what my gut is telling me," I reply.

"It's hard to argue with the gut instinct of another Stonekeeper," he replies.

"Don't I know it," I say, laughing as I do.

We talk for several more hours. At least, I think it's several more hours, I still haven't gotten used to the way time feels in the trance. Abdo says that'll come eventually, and I sure hope he's right.

CHAPTER 33: VISITING MOM

"Is…is this some kind of messed up joke?" Auryn replies in a mix of shock and anger.

When we all arrived at Garven's room 15 minutes ago, no one could have known what was going to happen next. Well, no one except Garven, I guess.

"No. I mean it. I've thought about it so much over the last three months," Garven responds.

We all sit there in disbelief, unsure of what to say.

"I know this comes as a shock to you all, but I've made up my mind and I'm going to need your help to make it happen," Garven says, breaking the silence.

"But… why?" Esha asks.

Before Garven can answer, Auryn yells out,

"Yeah, Garven, why? Huh?"

I reach over and try to put a hand on Auryn's leg, to let her know I'm here to support her. She's so infuriated she doesn't notice.

Garven takes a long, deep breath.

"I can't get the image of mom, dad, and Forbin out of my head. The shuttle door opens, and out walks…neither of us? Can you imagine how devastated they will be?" He says.

"We can send word with someone on the ship! We can have them send a message when they're in range! It won't be a shock that neither of us are there!" Auryn pleads.

"That's not really the point, and I think you know that," Garven responds.

"Garven, please," Auryn pleads, tears beginning to stream down her face,

"I just got you back a few months ago, I can't lose you again."

"I know, Auryn. Truly I do, but you have people here who love and support you. When mom and dad pass, Forbin might have no one," Garven says.

Silence once again overtakes the room, except for a sniffle by Auryn as she wipes the tears away from her cheeks. She then stands up and says,

"I just, I can't be in the same room as you, as any of you, right now."

With that, she runs out the door. I stand up to go after here, but Garven grabs my arm and looks me dead in the eye while saying,

"She's going to need a little time, Fin."

I know he's right, but I still run after her. I just can't help it, seeing her in so much pain.

By the time I leave the room, she's down the long walkway and about to descend metal stairs with more steps than I care to count. I run down the walkway and make it to the top of the steps as she's descended 10 or so of them.

"PLEASE, Finley, I know you want to be here for me, but you NEED to LEAVE ME ALONE right now," she says, half yelling through the tears drenching her face, body shaking.

I carefully walk down a few steps. If she continues away from me, I'll turn around, but it just feels like she needs me, or a hug, or something.

She doesn't move, so I walk down the rest of the steps to meet her and wrap her in a big hug. She puts her arms around me and cries into my shoulder. Hard, heavy sobs mixed with gasping breaths, loud sniffles, and her quietly saying,

"No. Why?"

I say nothing. I want to tell her it'll be okay, but I don't know that. Maybe Garven will change his mind and want to stay, maybe he won't, I have no idea.

After another minute of her sobbing onto me, she lifts her head and takes a step back on the stairs.

"Thank you," she whispers quietly.

"I'm going to get some air, please don't follow me," she then says.

I stay where I am until she's down the stairs and heading out of the hangar, watching her the entire time. She doesn't look back once, and as she leaves my view, I turn around and walk back up towards Garven's room.

When I'm ten or so feet away from the still open door, I hear yelling.

"How could you make this decision without talking to any of us?" I hear Esha saying.

"I just needed to be sure, for myself," Garven says, doing the best to defend himself.

"Didn't you even think how this would affect me…us, how it would affect us?" Esha then says.

The room goes quiet as I walk into the doorway. Everyone looks at me, and Garven says,

"I'm sorry, everyone, but this is my decision and my decision alone. We can talk about it more tomorrow, but I've had a long day, and I'd like to head to bed."

Esha looks at him in stunned disbelief and angrily walks out of the room. Mina leaves, not saying anything at all. After her, Kian stands up, walks up to Garven, and whispers something I can't hear, then also walks out.

"I want you to know, I understand," I say to Garven, with just the two of us in the room together.

"I'm not going to say I'm not shocked, and sad, and a whole bunch of other feelings, but I get it," I then say.

He looks up at me, his face tired and defeated, and gives me a halfhearted smile.

"You have no idea how much I appreciate that, Fin," he says, before sitting on the edge of his bed, then rubbing his eyes with both of his hands.

I've rarely, if ever, seen him more exhausted than in this moment, the weight of a new world on his shoulders.

CHAPTER 34: GREAT CARINI

It's been almost three months since Garven told us he was leaving on the ship. Those first few days were rough, and as smooth as everything's been recently, there were many bumps along the way.

A half dozen nights Auryn fell asleep curled into my side, quietly crying. I'd pet her head and assure her that things were going to be okay. She would occasionally ask if we should also head back on the ship. Those were always the hardest conversations because I now have a real, honest purpose here on Earth.

"I'd never ask you to stay for me, Auryn, but I would love to spend our lives together. Whatever choice you make, I'll be okay," I would often tell her.

I'm not sure if I was telling the truth with me being okay, but I needed her to make the choice for herself.

Her having to choose between me or her family was causing her some sleepless nights. One thing that's helped is Mina wanting to stay on Earth, too. I think having both of us here is softening the blow of losing her brother, and maybe her family, forever.

As a group, the most difficult thing we've had to pull off in the past few months was getting a message to the ship's officers that Garven wanted a spot on it. We had to get both Garven and Mina into the city, secretly meet up with Harry to get apartment assignments for the crew, and get into their building without being spotted by any Green Cloaks. It was the first thing we've done in a while that went relatively smooth, but it was still stressful the entire time.

Rossi, the ship's captain, made a special exception to put Garven's name on the manifest under a different name, Carini. As a joke, we've all been calling him that ever since, which he hates with every fiber of his being.

When sneaking back out of the city from that mission, I couldn't tell if people were actually giving us strange looks, or if I was being paranoid. Once word had spread about the ship being back, there was a huge influx of people from Cleveland and Buffalo, so streets were busier, and sneaking around was more difficult.

Maya estimates that almost a hundred thousand people have come to Toronto since the ship landed six months ago, all trying to leave the Earth. Considering the ship only holds 80,000, I don't know how they're going to settle all that. Rumor has it people have been putting in their requests at the housing coordinators offices.

None of that concerns me much though. Five of us are not only staying but heading down to South America. Maya is convinced there will be people still in Bogotá. I asked her how she could be so sure, and she responded,

"Wherever each stone is, people survive, no matter the situation. It's been this way from the dawn of people, and it will continue until the planet goes dark."

I've never spoken so confidently about anything in my life, so I'm prone to believe her. That being said, we're making sure to take enough food to last us several months so if we get there and there's no people, we can return.

To make extra sure, I also checked in with Abdo and Sun-young. They both told me that when Ava was a young Emerald Stonekeeper, she had contact with the last Sapphire Stonekeeper, a member of the Blue Cloaks who apparently argued with the rest of the Stonekeepers and eventually stopped communicating with them. That Stonekeeper was still residing in Bogotá, and there hasn't been one since.

With the information from Abdo and Sun-young, along with Maya's family history, we can be reasonably certain the stone is still there, people are still there, and someone has the strength, or the power, or whatever it is that lets them touch the stone and become the next keeper.

It's all still a little fuzzy to me, how just one or two people can make such a difference for the entire planet.

"You see, Fin," Sun-young once said to me,

"We, the Stonekeepers, can help out locally, and even regionally, with our powers. As an individual, you help heal people and make a direct impact on that person. But also, the stones themselves cast their powers over the world as well, as long as there's someone to channel that energy. So, you might feel like you're helping just one person at a time, but your mere presence of being connected to the stone helps everything in the world *feel* a little better and *be* a little better."

"That sounds… impossible?" I said back to her.

"Didn't healing an arrow wound with nothing but your bare hands and concentration sound impossible just a few months ago?" She said back.

"That's… a fair point," I responded, laughing a little.

Here in the present though, things are starting to feel extra chaotic. Tomorrow, the ship leaves, so we'll have to say our goodbyes to Garven tonight. In another week, we begin our journey to Bogotá. The ship has already been packed up with hundreds of dried out meals, enough water to last a few weeks, and a ton of water filtration packs. Plus, hiking gear, extra clothes, all our personal items, and anything else we want to go on the trip. They had to test the weight of everything during flight to make sure the math still worked out with distances and charging.

If anything should happen to us on the ground during our trip, we'll have enough food and supplies to last us awhile.

We've also mapped out our journey. First, we're going to fly to Raleigh, which is around 550 miles. That's within the range we feel comfortable flying, especially for our first flight. They keep reassuring us that in absolutely ideal circumstances it could fly three times that. That's assuming we have a tail wind and full sun.

After stopping for two full days of charging, which we'll need to do every time, we'll fly to Birmingham (480 miles), then to San Antonio (750mi), Mexico City (690mi), Guatemala City (650mi), San José (530mi), and finally to Bogotá (780mi).

With stop and recharge days, flying days, and all, it should take us around two weeks if everything goes smoothly.

They also throw in duplicates of key parts of the plane in case we have repairs to make, things like batteries, solar panels, tires, and engine parts. They even threw in a few rolls of this old, super strong gray tape they've found. One of the engineers joked that if you can't fix it otherwise, use this tape on it and it'll be good to go.

Esha and Kian have been learning how to fly for the past six months as well. As more and more people have been traveling on foot along Lake Ontario's edge, they've had to fly directly north to avoid being seen. Annora has also been in the plane with them often, learning how to co-pilot.

All told, it'll be Auryn, Mina, Esha, Kian, Annora, myself, and Maya's cousin, Alejandra, who goes by Andy. Esha and Andy are both fluent in Spanish, and I've been trying to learn for years so I can muddle my way through a conversation. Mina, Kian, and Auryn have been trying to learn some recently as well.

Everything about taking the plane down to South America will have to wait though, because tonight we're throwing a small, private, going away party for Garven. Auryn has been a little iffy on going because of how overcome she'll be, but we've talked about how she'll regret it forever if she doesn't go.

For the occasion, Maya gave us a jug of wine some people at the hangar had made. They make about a dozen or so bottles a year, and hand them out for special occasions. It's a nice gesture.

I'll grab it from my side table and head over shortly.

Before then, I take out my notebook and write a little. None of it is especially good writing, but I like to keep track of things as they happen, and remembering Garven and all he's meant to us is as easy as flipping through this book.

Leading as many Raiders as he could away from Esha and I at the building along the Lake near Cleveland. Volunteering to head out for patrols in Buffalo. Helping rescue Kian and I from being kidnapped by the Green Cloaks. So many times, he's been selfless over the past several years.

He deserves happiness, and if that comes by getting on that ship and reuniting with the rest of his family, away from the struggle of survival, away from a dying planet, heck, away from a woman who's following us to try and kill us, then that's what he should do.

I'm going to miss him, but I'm happy I got to spend this time with him.

Later, at the party, I tell him all this to his face. We didn't plan it this way, but we all ended up talking to Garven alone, one by one, as the party wound down. Well after the wine was gone, I get my turn.

"I know, Fin. If it wasn't for you and Esha, I would have given up all the way back in Cleveland. You two were the reason I started to feel human again, and because of you, I got to see my sister again. So as much as you say I do for all of you, you did just as much for me," he tells me.

Maybe it was the wine talking, but there was so much sincerity, and thankfulness, in his voice, I instinctively get up off the side of the bed and hug him. We wrap our arms around each other for a long time, but it still feels like it's not enough.

When we let go, I give him a smile. A real, genuine smile, and tell him,

"If you ever get the itch to come back again, we'll find you. I don't know how, but we will."

"You know what?" He replies, "I actually believe you.

CHAPTER 35: NEW BEGINNINGS

I wake up with a pit in my stomach, and not just from the wine we drank last night. That dream happened again, and I can't help but worry that it has to do with our plane trip. I can't put my finger on why, since I'm seeing it happen from my point of view.

Is the plane on fire during a test run? In my dream the fireball is so fast, but I don't know if it has to happen exactly like that. When I felt the rain in the wildflowers in my dream way back around Buffalo, it ended up being sprinklers in a greenhouse. Things don't always have to happen exactly how I think they will.

I can't seem to shake it as I get up. I carefully try to get out of bed, but I had totally forgotten that last night, after we finished the bottle of wine, we decided bringing in a second bed to my tiny room was a good idea, so all four of us, not including Esha, are crammed onto these two beds.

What else don't I remember from last night? I think to myself as I try to step over Kian and walk towards my door. I slip out quietly and as I shut it behind me, I see Esha leaving her room as well. She has a sadness in her eyes that's unmistakable.

"I can't believe Garven is actually leaving today. I just, I didn't think he was going to go through with it," she says quietly.

"I know. I can't believe it's really happening either. I don't know what I'm even going to do without him around, honestly," I respond.

"Same. Really, really, the same," Esha replies.

We head down the walkway, and then down the stairs. As we get to the bottom, Andy sees us and waves us over.

"Hey, I know today's a rough day for you all. I asked Maya if we could watch the ship take off from the hangar roof, and she said yeah. So, if you five want to watch it by yourselves, I can take you up there in a little bit."

"I think I'd really appreciate that," I say.

"Yeah, I think that sounds nice," replies Esha.

"Perfect. I'll swing by your rooms in a few hours," she replies as she walks off.

We head over to the food station and grab some breakfast; they've also made some pots of mushroom coffee for the occasion. I look out through the hangar opening and see dozens of chairs lined up and facing in the direction of the city.

While grabbing some coffee, I overhear some people talking at a table right behind us.

"Good or bad, it's amazing they are able to still fly that ship. Imagine making another trip to B.52.C?" The first person says.

"That captain, I have got to give him credit, that's like what, four and a half years in space by the time he gets back? That's a crazy amount of time on that ship," the other person responds.

"Just a shame so many people are leaving. Makes it harder for us," the first person replies.

They're right. It's a technical marvel that it worked the first time, and the fact they could land, regroup, save more people, and take off again is truly impressive. It's also a big deal that they're taking another third of the population left in the Great Lakes, and probably North America, back with them.

It's good that if people want to go, they can, but we've been able to carve out an existence here so far, and I thought more people would want to be a part of that. Plus, ever since Garven said he was leaving, I haven't wanted to think much about how big of a day this was, or how impressive the technology is. I've just been thinking about Auryn losing her brother, and all of us losing a friend. Esha and I literally wouldn't be here without him, and I hope I got across to him last night how much he means to us, and how thankful we are.

We grab enough food for the two of us, and some to bring back to the rooms.

"So hey, did all of you end up dragging a bed into your room and like, sleeping together?" Esha asks.

"Yeah," I reply.

"So," she looks around for a second, "what happened with that?"

"Um, I think I just passed out and went to sleep? I was pretty tired by the time I laid down… I think," I say back, genuinely unsure of what happened.

"Sure, yeah… sure," she replies, and we grab our plates and cups and head back upstairs, arms full.

When we reach my room I knock, wait a few seconds, then enter. When I do I see Kian rubbing the grogginess out of his eyes. Auryn slowly turns over and then smiles at me. She then catches Kian in the corner of her eye and says,

"What the heck are you doing here?"

Immediately after, Mina rolls over and says,

"Why are you yelling, there is no need to yell."

From behind me, Esha busts out laughing, slips by me, and puts a plate full of breakfast on the small end table in the room, which we apparently shoved up against the wall last night to make room for the extra bed.

"Oh yeah, Superbed, ha!" Kian says, as if we're all supposed to know what that means.

"Remember? Last night I said we should all sleep in the same room, and then Mina said, 'on what, a super bed?'" Kian says, continuing,

"Then we all yelled 'SUPERBED!' and Auryn and I ran over to her room and grabbed her bed and dragged it in here?"

Mina starts laughing, hard.

"I remember Superbed! I'm so happy we made it!" She says quietly, no doubt nursing a bit of a headache.

Auryn and I lock eyes for a moment, smile, and then laugh. What a strange life I'm living right now.

After that was sorted, we let them know that we can watch the shuttle launch from the roof soon, so they should eat and get ready. I was worried Auryn wouldn't want to watch, but I told her how much I loved watching the shuttle leave when she left. That it was a memory I had cherished the entire time she was gone.

A few hours later, after lots of trying to figure out what happened last night, Andy knocks on my door. We had all eaten by then and returned to our rooms to get ready for the day.

"Ready to head up? Shuttle should be launching in a half hour or so, don't wanna miss it."

"Yeah, I'm all set. Our lives are all in the plane already so there's not much to get ready," I respond.

"Great, lets grab everyone and head up," she says.

She knocks on the rest of the doors, and everyone heads single file in line behind her. As we walk in the opposite direction of the stairs that take us to ground level, I look out over the hangar. People are still congregating around the food and coffee, at least 50 or 60 people in total. I see some walking towards the exits, where the chairs are on the pavement.

We reach the very end of the walkway and there's an emergency exit door. Andy pushes it open and leads us out onto another metal platform, this time with a ladder heading towards the roof. It must be 20 feet, at least, and we're already high off the ground. I tell myself not to look down and take one rung at a time. Slowly but surely, we make our way up. The last couple steps my arms might have been shaking a little from nervousness, but thankfully no one could see.

As I climb up and over the ledge, it hits me immediately.

It is hot on this roof. Oh boy, it's warm. The midday sun feels like its melting me as the heat radiates off the roof. I look over and see a half dozen chairs on the roof about 30 feet away, and underneath them I see a couple of blankets and sheets laid out.

"I knew I'd be hot up here, so I laid down the blankets and sheets an hour ago so the metal roof wouldn't keep cooking, and wouldn't reflect the sun at you all, hopefully. If it gets too hot, you can just come on back down the same way we came up."

With that, Andy dipped back over the edge and climbed her way back down.

As a group, we all headed towards are folding chairs. When we got there, it was significantly cooler than other parts of the roof, and I was really thankful for her thoughtfulness.

For the next half hour, we shared memories of Garven, and talked about how much his gruff personality had calmed down the past few years.

"I couldn't believe he was the same person, honestly. You two really softened him up!" Auryn said, elbowing my arm as we sat next to each other.

"You know, I really can't believe that in all the time I've known him, he hasn't punched me in the face once. I was really expecting that," Kian then says.

We laugh hard at that.

"I mean, I'll still do it for you if you feel left out," Auryn says, a smile across her face.

As I'm laughing, I feel a strange tingle in my body. It's brief, but as I try to focus my eyes, it happens. Suddenly I am in.

THE FIFTEENTH DREAM

A fireball shoots across the daylight sky, brighter than the sun. Blinding to the point of needing to shield my eyes, I lose track of it for a brief second. I look up again just as Auryn begins to say,

"What the f—"

She's cut off by the sound of it, getting shriller by the second.

It came from west of the city and is streaking towards downtown. It's the fastest thing I've ever seen in my life. Slowly rising into the air. I look in the direction it's heading and see smoke filling the downtown corridor already.

The ship.

In a matter of seconds, with the ship rising from the smoke of downtown Toronto, it's visible a few hundred feet above the ground. The missile, on a collision course with it, screaming through the air.

"NO!" Auryn begins to yell as it makes contact with the ship.

I can see the explosion half a second before I hear the thunderous sound from it. Everything slows down. The fire shooting out the bottom of the reusable rockets sputters and then stops completely. The ship loses momentum quickly and starts a slow but sudden freefall onto the shoreline of the lake.

CHAPTER 36: THE DECENT

I am snapped out of my trance by the sound of the screaming missile. Mina was shaking my shoulder as I came to, which is new, but stops as she sees the missile flying across the horizon.

It happens too quickly in real life, and there's nothing I can do in the next few seconds to stop it.

"What the f—" Auryn begins to say.

My dream, instantly repeating itself: Downtown Toronto already filled with smoke from the rockets on the spaceship. The ship itself leaving the smoke behind as it heads on its journey. The missile making impact. The muffled sound of the explosion, of twisting metal, of the screaming people watching from the ground below us, deafening sounds barely registering above a whisper.

The horrific silence of the shuttle seemingly floating in air for a few seconds, before its trajectory changes, slows, and heads crashing back towards the earth.

The screams from Auryn and Esha, Mina and Kian. I am dazed by what is happening, hoping it's yet another dream, that this time I can warn everyone about. Everything plays like an old movie, like the projector my dad set up and was able to use just once, before the bulb blew.

No sound, just movement, but everything in slow motion.

"I can't get the timing of it right, it's supposed to play at a normal speed," he said, five or so minutes before it became unusable forever, sitting in the room collecting dust, left behind when Esha, Garven and I started our journey.

On it, a random family's old home movies from a century or more ago. A small child running through the yard, splashing in a shallow plastic pool. A mother smiling and waving directly at the camera. A daughter covering her face with her hand and running up the stairs.

Everything slow, rhythmic even, happening in a time before the world ended.

My head turns slowly, and I see Auryn's mouth open and screaming, but I hear nothing.

Kian darting up from his chair with such a force that it topples over behind him.

Esha, turning to face me. In slow motion I can see her mouth forming my name as she yells.

I wish more than anything in the world that this is just another dream, but I am faced with the fact that this is the real world, and the real world will not allow me a single moment of peace.

PLANET B.52.C

Arthur had promised Alia that he would slow down and enjoy retirement, but when the opportunity arose to keep watch on the skies above, he couldn't pass it up.

Sure, it would be another year or two, at least, before the ship would be back from Earth with Garven, Auryn, and Fin, but to sit back, watch the skies, and help the colony for a few hours a day? How could he resist?

Which made this day in particular even more strange. Checking the instruments, it looked like a ship was approaching, but this would be nearly impossible. He clicked on the intercom system to the other observation tower and before he could even begin to speak, the woman on the other end said:

"You seeing this?"

"I was just about to ask you the same thing," Arthur responded.

As he continued to watch his instruments, he decided to look through the high-powered telescope, hoping to maybe catch a glimpse. Then, the alarms in the tower started blaring.

Expectedly, the intercom clicked through to him. It was the Colony Council, all five members, on screen.

"What's going on up there? We just received word there's a ship on the way? Is it close? Is it ours?" They asked.

"Looking through the long-range scope now, please stand by," Arthur said in his most professional voice.

As he scanned the skies, searching for any sign of movement, something caught his eye. He locked onto it with the automated tracking system, and adjusted focus. Arthur could hear the repeated questions in the background but was so taken back by what he was seeing he couldn't even answer.

He looks away from the telescope for a second, shuts his eyes hard, and opens them again. He bends down to look through the scope again and confirms what he had seen before.

Arthur then stands up tall, brushes some crumbs off his work suit from the snack he had an hour ago, and walks over to the screen where five council members are angrily staring at him. They did not appreciate being ignored for the last 20 seconds.

"Council, there is indeed a ship on its way here, and it's close," he pauses for a second, "very close."

"Is it ours? Did they have issues and turn around? Should we ready the landing pad early?"

As Arthur is about to respond, an all-colony transmission comes over the loudspeaker. The word is repeated over and over again, with increasing urgency.

Everyone on the colony became dead silent, and finally Arther and the Council could hear it:

"助"

Arthur checks his computer screen to see a singular word, translated, along with the transmission:

"Help."

Molly, the best cat ever, with author RJ Zielonka.